This book is dedicated to Brantly.

Thank you for laughing at all my dumb jokes.

<u>**Praise for Minerva Spencer & S.M. LaViolette's**</u>

"Spencer creates characters worth rooting for. Readers will be eager to see Phoebe's sisters find their own matches next."

-Publishers Weekly on **PHOEBE**

<u>**THE BOXING BARONESS**</u>

"Swooningly romantic, sizzling sensual...superbly realized."

–Booklist **STARRED REVIEW**

A *Library Journal* **Best Book of 2022**

A Publishers Marketplace Buzz Books Romance Selection

"Fans of historical romances with strong female characters in non-traditional roles and the men who aren't afraid to love them won't be disappointed by this series starter."

–Library Journal **STARRED REVIEW**

"Spencer (*Notorious*) launches her Wicked Women of Whitechapel Regency series with an outstanding romance based in part on a real historical figure. . . This is sure to wow!"

-Publishers Weekly **STARRED REVIEW**

<u>**THE DUELING DUCHESS:**</u>

"Another carefully calibrated mix of steamy passion, delectably dry humor, and daringly original characters."

—*Booklist* STARRED REVIEW

VERDICT: Readers who enjoyed *The Boxing Baroness* won't want to miss Spencer's sequel.

–*Library Journal* STARRED REVIEW

A *Library Journal* Best Book of 2023

"[A] pitch perfect Regency …. Readers will be hooked. " (***THE MUSIC OF LOVE)***

★*Publishers Weekly STARRED REVIEW*

"Lovers of historical romance will be hooked on this twisty story of revenge, redemption, and reversal of fortunes."

Publishers Weekly, STARRED review of THE FOOTMAN.

"Fans will be delighted."

Publishers Weekly on THE POSTILION

NOTORIOUS

"Brilliantly crafted…an irresistible cocktail of smart characterization, sophisticated sensuality, and sharp wit."
★*Booklist STARRED REVIEW*

"Sparkling…impossible not to love."—Popsugar

"Realistically transforming the Regency equivalent of a mean girl into a relatable, all-too-human heroine is no easy feat, but Spencer (Outrageous, 2021) succeeds on every level. Lightly dusted with wintery holiday charm, graced with an absolutely endearing, beetle-obsessed hero and a fully rendered cast of supporting characters and spiked with smoldering sensuality and wry wit, the latest in Spencer's Rebels of the Ton series is sublimely satisfying."

—Booklist STARRED review of INFAMOUS

"Perfect for fans of Bridgerton, *Infamous* is also a charming story for Christmas. In fact, I enjoyed Infamous so much that when I was halfway through it, I ordered the author's first novel, Dangerous. I look forward to reading much more of Minerva Spencer's work."

—THE HISTORICAL NOVEL SOCIETY on INFAMOUS

"LaViolette keeps the tension high, delivering dark eroticism and emotional depth in equal measure. Readers will be hooked."

-PUBLISHERS WEEKLY on HIS HARLOT

"LaViolette's clever, inventive plot makes room for some kinky erotic scenes as her well-shaded characters explore their sexualities. Fans of erotic romance will find much to love."

-PUBLISHERS WEEKLY on HIS VALET

"[SCANDALOUS is] A standout...Spencer's brilliant and original tale of the high seas bursts with wonderfully real protagonists, plenty of action, and passionate romance."

Her Villain

S.M. LAVIOLETTE

Author's Note

Das Rheingold was performed as a single opera only one time. That performance took place in Munich in 1869, not in London. The London performance is a product of my imagination.

Chapter 1

London

Late October 1871

Calliope Fowler stared at Robert Brook in shock, just like the other thirteen women who were crowded into the brothel owner's study along with her.

"But… what will happen to us?" Callie asked, putting into words what all of them were wondering.

Brook bowed his head and rubbed the back of his neck. It was a gesture they had all seen too many times. It meant that he was giving up and admitting defeat. Usually, that was something he did when a customer got too rough with one of them and they asked Brook for help.

He would start off aggressive and strong, but when faced with one of their wealthy clients he would drop his head, rub the back of his neck, and back away like a dog cowering to a bigger, more powerful, dog.

The room was so quiet that the only sound was the chilly November wind that rattled the poorly glazed windows.

Finally, Brook looked up. "You will all have to vacate the building by Friday."

The room erupted in protests that ranged from disbelieving to angry to terrified.

Brook held up his hands, palm out. "There's no use coming the ugly with me. The building has been sold, and that is all there is to it."

"You mean it's been lost at a card table," Deborah snarled. She was the oldest of the whores and did not flinch beneath Brook's glare.

And why should she roll over and show her belly to the useless, gambling, lying turd of a man? Callie thought. What could Brook do to any of them that was any worse than kicking them out of the only home they all knew?

"We need more time!" somebody shouted.

And then everyone began talking and yelling and sobbing all at once.

Callie slipped out of the room rather than join the futile argument. Already her mind was racing. Where could she go? What could she do? Being a whore was hardly her dream come true but working for Brook—as loathsome as he was—had been safer than any other choices available to her after her father's death almost a year before.

For months after the funeral Callie had tried to find a position as a governess, but without a letter of recommendation, there had been no chance of securing a respectable post. It was more than a little ironic that Callie's name among the punters who came to Brook's was *the Governess* for her ladylike manners and the proper way she spoke.

She sighed as she trudged up flight after flight of stairs. There was no use thinking about *what ifs* or what might have been or the life she'd had before. When Callie succumbed to the inevitable nine months ago and took the job at Brook's she had known that she was closing the door on any sort of decent life by choosing to sell her body rather than starve in the street.

Up in the tiny garret room she shared with a woman named Flora, Callie sat on her bed and stared blankly at the wall across from her.

She was still sitting there thirty minutes later when Flora stomped into the room and flung herself onto her bed. "Brook ran out of the 'ouse when it looked like the girls might kick his arse from 'ere to next Sunday. I doubt we'll see 'im again afore we leave." Flora snorted. "It's just as well 'e's gone. One of the others might 'ave murdered 'im an' then we'd all be in the soup."

Callie smiled wanly at that improbable prediction. Men like Brook never got what they deserved; they just destroyed lives and then moved on, leaving wreckage in their wake.

Flora was in her late twenties and while not the oldest woman working at Brook's—which was Deb, who at thirty-two was finding it difficult to still generate business—Flora had been whoring since she was thirteen. It would not be easy for either Deb or Flora to find new places to work, at least any place that was decent.

"What are you going to do?" Callie asked.

Flora shrugged. "I dunno. Prolly go over to Carlton's and see if 'ee'l 'ave me."

Callie didn't point out what they both already knew: John Carlton was a cruel, brutal man who preferred the easy money to be had from selling virgins and gave most of his whores the sack when they turned twenty-one.

Flora eyed Callie. "Carlton likes you. You'll be all set," she added grudgingly.

"I am not going to work for that man," Callie said, her gorge rising at the thought of ever touching—or being touched—by John Carlton again.

Flora rolled her eyes. "Yer too picky by 'alf. Carlton is 'ansome and plump in the pocket. So what if 'ee likes a bit o' the rough?"

A bit o' the rough had left Callie bloody and scarred and unable to walk for three days. Why Carlton went to other brothels when he owned one himself was a mystery. As usual, Brook had been too terrified to do much but babble a weak chastisement when Carlton had beaten Callie. And even that tepid protestation had dried up when Carlton had peeled off a few banknotes from the fat roll he kept in his pocket and flung them at Brook.

"Where will ye go if not to Carlton?" Flora persisted.

"I don't know. I will find something."

Callie didn't want to admit that she was determined to find a job other than whoring, even if she had to lie and scheme. It had never been her intention to sell her body until she was old and worn out like Deb. At the most, she had hoped it would take a year of suffering through the job to save up enough to buy passage on a ship and leave England far behind her. Callie wanted to go somewhere far from Brook's brothel and Pigeon Alley—and the hell that her life was now—and start fresh.

Thus far, Callie had saved enough money for a decent shared berth on a ship—she'd heard too many nightmare stories about steerage to even consider that option—and she had a little extra set aside for when she reached the end of her journey.

Unfortunately, it was a thin cushion and not enough to set her mind at ease. The last thing she wanted was to run out of money in New York City or Boston and be forced to sell herself. Nine months of working as a whore had already destroyed a good part of her soul. If she fell into the life again, she would not be able to climb out a second time.

Callie knew she could go to France for a whole lot less than passage to America—and she spoke fluent French—but she had already serviced too many customers from Paris to want to go to that city, either.

No, only an ocean would put enough distance between this life and the next.

And Callie needed more money before she could break free of this nightmare.

She just needed one more well-paid job.

Chapter 2

London

A week later...

David Remington rarely found things humorous—he had not been born with an easy ability to laugh—but it did strike him as amusing that Sir Andrew Morton had arranged their meeting for nine o'clock at night. Apparently the man believed that a clandestine, nocturnal meeting was somehow less likely to attract attention than one held during regular business hours, when the massive building was crawling with hundreds of people and David could have gone unnoticed.

While all the civil servants had gone home by nine o'clock, the army of janitors who serviced the vast complex that made up Whitehall were still hard at work and roaming the corridors. Already three or four had passed David, who was sitting in a chair outside Sir Andrew's office, as inconspicuous as a horsefly in a bowl of custard.

Evidently, Sir Andrew believed that custodial staff were too stupid to find the situation suspicious. Or, far more likely, Sir Andrew—like so many other men of his class—gave no thought at all to servants.

It was now twenty-seven minutes after nine o'clock. As one of Her Majesty's finest, Sir Andrew Morton had no qualms about keeping a nobody like David waiting.

David didn't care how long he kicked his heels.

In truth, he didn't care much about anything.

Some people would say that was a problem, and maybe it was, but it also meant that he was perfectly suited for his job.

He had no pride or reputation to protect. And he had the patience and persistence of a spider lurking in a web. David could sit and wait for days. In fact, he had done so countless times, often in rain or snow or sweltering heat.

Sitting in an uncomfortable wooden chair outside a room in Whitehall presented no hardship.

With nothing to do but wait, he allowed his mind to wander back to his other job—the legal, legitimate one—at the London Stock Exchange, or just the Exchange, as men like David and his ilk called it.

His ability to pay close attention had made investing in the Exchange not only lucrative, but as close to enjoyable as anything David had ever done. At first glance, the stocks that were bought and sold on the Exchange seemed like a vast confusion. But if a person paid attention and watched *very* closely then patterns began to emerge from the interplay between the flow of money and investments and the political and social life of the nation. Occurrences that seemed random or inconsequential—like the size of women's bustles—could drive market forces. A man who invested in the components that comprised a bustle could, at the right moment in time, parlay that information into a fortune.

The one thing David did best was pay attention. As a result, he was an extremely wealthy man. He wasn't sitting outside Sir Andrew's office because he needed money. His reason for being there at nine o'clock—now nine-thirty-six—at night was not money, but vengeance.

The door to Sir Andrew's office opened and the man himself stood on the threshold. He glanced up and down the corridor, as if to make sure nobody was watching, and then said, "Come inside," not wasting a greeting on a man like David.

He led David through a small anteroom, where his secretary must usually sit, and into a far grander office.

"Sit," he ordered, gesturing to the chairs in front of a large mahogany desk while he shut the door and locked it.

David sat.

"I trust nobody noticed you out there?" Sir Andrew barked the question at David.

For a man desperately climbing the slippery rungs of the diplomat ladder he was doing a terrible job of hiding his loathing for David. Shouldn't a diplomat be a little more…diplomatic?

"Several janitors saw me," David said.

Sir Andrew startled slightly, as if he'd expected David's voice and accent to be rougher and match David's illegal trade. The man really needed to do a better job of guarding his expression.

"Servants hardly matter," Sir Andrew said, waving a dismissive hand and then lacing his fingers and leaning on his desk, which was clear of anything other than a leather portfolio. "The job I have for you is sensitive."

David waited.

A look of annoyance flickered over Sir Andrew's face, as if he had expected some other response from David. As if anyone in their right mind would go through all this idiotic cloak-and-dagger secrecy for an *in*sensitive job.

Sir Andrew turned to the portfolio and flicked it open. "I have read your military record. Not the official one, of course," he added with a smirk, glancing from whatever he had on the desk to David. "In addition to your many other, erm, skills, I see you've effectively handled, er, the termination of high-ranking foreign officials and dignitaries in the past."

David had no intention of acknowledging such a statement aloud, regardless of how true it was. Or, rather, *because* of its veracity.

"This one is a bit different," Sir Andrew went on. "This one needs to be done on British soil."

David didn't bother correcting the other man's mistaken assumption that he had never carried out the will of the government *inside* the national boundaries. He was weary of Sir Andrew's prevarications and didn't want to drag the conversation out any longer than necessary.

Sir Andrew scowled when David remained silent. "Not especially talkative, are you?"

"People don't pay me to talk."

Sir Andrew's lips clamped together and his jaw worked, as if he wanted to say something. After a moment, he appeared to conquer his urge and, instead, returned to his portfolio. He flipped through the sheets in front of him and extracted something, offering it to David. "This is your target."

When David reached for it, Sir Andrew held it back. "This is in the deepest confidence. If you were to say anything about what we are discussing, you would find yourself facing—"

"Termination?" David guessed.

Sir Andrew smiled sourly. "I am glad we understand one another."

David doubted that, but kept his opinion to himself, instead leaning forward to examine the document, which was a photograph of a very famous person.

He looked up to find Sir Andrew waiting, his expression excited and avid, as if he expected David to be shocked.

"How much are you paying?" he asked, sliding the photograph back toward Sir Andrew.

Sir Andrew's lips parted, but no words came out.

Irritation, an emotion David experienced more often than most others, flickered through him. What had the man thought? That David would shy away from such a job? Why was he wasting both their time with theatrics?

"How much?" he repeated, allowing his annoyance to show in his voice.

"We will pay twice your usual rate."

"Three times."

Sir Andrew made a sputtering noise and opened his mouth. "But that's—"

"My fee is nonnegotiable," David said before the other man could speak. "And I want half deposited in advance."

"*What*? You usually only ask for a quarter!"

"As you said yourself, this is not a *usual* job, is it? When do you need it done?"

Sir Andrew was clearly struggling with the desire to tell David to go to hell. But the knowledge that he didn't have anyone else to do the job—at least if Sir Andrew wanted it done right—triumphed over anger.

"It *must* be done on December twentieth—no sooner—and no later because he leaves for his country estate on the twenty-first. And it absolutely *must* look like an accident."

"Fine."

"There is one more thing—the reason we are approaching you so early." He paused and chewed his lower lip, glancing down at the documents in his portfolio yet again.

"What?" David asked when Sir Andrew seemed to have frozen.

The diplomat cleared his throat and then looked up. "You need to arrange for several shipments to reach their destination before December twentieth. You will receive word of when they arrive and where they need to go. You do not need to know what they are. Understood."

"Yes."

Sir Andrew blinked at that, yet again expecting more. More talking, more questions, more objections, or more demands for more money, whatever it was that people typically quibbled about.

"Is that all?" David asked.

"Well… yes."

David stood and Sir Andrew flinched back in his chair, as if David might attack him. What a fool.

Still, the fear rolling off the other man was more than a little appealing. And arousing.

David savored the sharp aroma of Sir Andrew's apprehension a moment longer and then took a card out of the inside pocket of his coat and tossed it onto the desk. "That is my banking information. I don't begin working until the money is in the account." He turned to go, but Sir Andrew's voice stopped him.

"You don't have any questions or—"

"On the twentieth and must look like an accident. Shepherd four shipments to their destination. I will receive word when and where. Does that sum it up correctly?"

Sir Andrew glared at him but nodded.

"Then I will let myself out."

***

Sir Andrew Morton released an explosive sigh, took out his handkerchief, and mopped his brow when the door closed behind the man who had gone by many names but now used the sobriquet, David Remington.

The door in the paneling behind Andrew—invisible except for a faint line along one side—opened soundlessly and a man who called himself *Wilson*, although that wasn't his real name, stepped into Andrew's office.

"You heard all that?" Andrew asked.

"I heard it."

"Will you pay it?"

Wilson—a man almost as dangerous as the one who had just left—chuckled, the laugh hollow and dry, reminding Andrew of the sound that dirt made when it dropped on a coffin. *His* coffin if what had just transpired in this office ever became known.

"The men who are backing this would have paid double what Remington is asking," Wilson said. "Evidently Remington is not as smart as he thinks he is if he does not know how highly his services are valued. Have the deposit made immediately."

"I don't trust him."

"Why not?"

"There is something not right with him."

Wilson laughed. "He kills people, sows political mayhem, and unseats governments for a living, Morton. You aren't meant to *like* him; you are meant to *fear* him." He gave an exaggerated sniff and then sneered at Andrew. "And I can smell the fear oozing out of you like sweat, which means that *he* smelled it, too."

"I don't care if he did," Andrew retorted, which wasn't true at all, but he would be damned if he allowed Wilson to gloat any more than he already was. "I have never seen anyone with such a dead look in his eyes." Although Wilson came a close second.

"You don't have to like him—he is not marrying your daughter and we are not asking him to join our club—he just needs to do the job. And Remington has been Her Majesty's most efficient killer for almost two decades." Wilson smirked. "And now he is *ours*."

Andrew irritably balled up everything from the portfolio and threw it into the fireplace. Even with the flames blazing the room was chilly and he went to stand in front of the fire, warming his hands before turning back to the other man. "How can you be sure Remington won't betray us and sell this information to the highest bidder?"

"You read his file. He has no interest in helping the government after the way he was so callously and wrongfully discharged."

"But even so—"

"You worry too much. There will be somebody keeping an eye on Mr. Remington."

"What about after he's done the job? Surely it can't be safe to have him running about with such information?"

Wilson smiled and it made Andrew shiver and feel as if he would never be warm again. "Rest assured that Mr. Remington will never get to enjoy the money he will earn from this assignment."

***

A few miles away...

Callie glared at Brook through angry tears. "That money was all I had in the world. I know one of your *ruffians* must have come across it when they were stripping our rooms of anything saleable. I *demand* that you question them and get it back!"

Brook sighed and rubbed the back of his neck and Callie knew all was lost before the slimy worm even opened his mouth.

Something inside her—something that had been simmering for the last seven days as she had walked what felt like every street in London scrounging for even the meagerest employment with no luck—boiled over and she flung herself at Brook.

Even though he was larger than her by six inches and at least three stone, she had the advantage of surprise and knocked him to the foyer floor.

Callie promptly crawled up onto his chest, straddling him, and grabbed his lapels and shook him, rattling his head against the floor. "That is my *entire* life's savings, Brook! You need to—"

Brook recovered quickly from his shock and flipped her over, pinning her arms with his knees before slapping her face so hard that Callie actually saw stars.

"Listen to me, you mad bitch! I don't have your bloody money and even if I did, I wouldn't give it back to you. It was stupid of you to hide it in your room and you have only yourself to blame. If you want to earn more bread and honey then you need to get that gold-plated cunt of yours over to John Carlton's place. The man has offered an outrageous sum to fuck you so you'd be wise to accept him before he just takes what he wants without your permission. Now, get your—"

"Are you open for business?"

Both Brook and Callie jolted at the sound of the voice.

Brook twisted around. "Who the fuck are you?" he bellowed at a figure standing in the shadows beside the door. "And what the fuck are you doing in here?"

"The door was open. My name hardly matters. As for why I am here, your establishment was recommended to me as one that regularly tests employees for disease." The man stepped into the light and glanced around the foyer, evidently uninterested in the fact that two people were scuffling around on the floor at his feet. He finally looked down at them. "Are you not open tonight?"

"Does it fucking *look* like we're open, mate?" Brook bellowed, gesturing irately to the empty foyer.

The man gave Brooks a blank stare before his eyes slid to Callie. He blinked slowly, reminding Callie of a snake, and then said, "Do you work here?"

Callie gawked and found herself nodding.

He reached into his coat and his hand came out with a silver notecase. "I'd like to engage your services."

Brooks gave an outraged squawk and scrambled off Callie, grinding her arms into the floor in the process. He ignored her pained cry and strode over to the other man, towering over him. "Do you really think you can come into my place of business and just poach—"

His words were abruptly cut off by a blood-curdling scream—his—before he fell to his knees, rolled onto his side, and curled into a fetal position, whimpering pitifully.

The punter, meanwhile, was still standing exactly where he had been, not a hair out of place.

"What did you do to him?" Callie asked. "I did not even see you move."

"Are you interested in the work?" the stranger repeated, the flat tone of his voice oddly jarring given that Brook was sobbing at his feet.

Callie swallowed as she studied him. He was above average height and solidly built, nowhere near as bulky as Brook, nor as handsome. His hair and eyes were both brown and his face was pale and clean shaven. His features were neither hideous nor especially attractive, just… average.

He was, in almost every way, nondescript. Indeed, if somebody asked her to describe him an hour from now, Callie suspected she would be hard-pressed.

He slipped his notecase back into his coat and turned on his heel.

"Wait!" Callie called, scrambling to her feet. "Yes, I want the work," she added when he just kept walking.

He stopped and turned. "How much?"

"For how long?"

He paused, considering her question, and then said, "The rest of the night. I do not wish to watch a clock."

"Where would we go?" she asked.

"Don't you have a room here?"

She laughed bitterly and gestured toward the two pitiful bags on the steps. "Those are my things. I no longer have a place to live."

Another man might have expressed sympathy at her situation. This one merely said, "A hotel, then."

"Ten shillings for the entire night," she said before she could lose her courage.

One of his eyebrows rose. "That seems expensive."

It was *very* expensive considering she had no crib in which to entertain him. "For two nights, then," she amended. "And I will come to wherever you live, so you will not need to spend money on a hotel." That would also give her somewhere to stay.

Callie squirmed under his impassive stare and was about to drop her price when he nodded. "Done. I will hail a hansom." He turned away, leaving her to carry her luggage.

Five minutes later Callie, the stranger, and all her earthly possessions were in a cab headed toward a street she had never heard of.

She smoothed her skirts, biting her lip in chagrin when she saw the torn flounce. It must have happened during the scuffle. It was her best day dress—something she had managed to keep from *before*. That was how she thought of her life, as being divided into *before* and *after* her downward slide into shame and poverty.

Although maybe, after today, she should find another word for this new phase of her life, whatever it was.

She slid her gaze to the man beside her, but he was staring straight ahead, sitting with a stillness that was… odd.

He was odd.

And Callie had just sold herself to him for two entire days.

She cleared her throat. When he didn't move, she said, "Erm, sir?"

He turned to her.

For a moment, Callie was struck dumb by the expression in his eyes. Or the lack of expression. A lack of anything, for that matter. She had been forced to look into the eyes of far too many men over the past nine months, but never had she seen a pair of orbs as lifeless and flat as this man's.

She shivered and his gaze briefly dropped to her torso before lifting back up. Still he did not speak.

"My name is Callie Fowler," she said. He didn't acknowledge her name by so much as the flicker of an eyelid. "It is short for Calliope, which means *beautiful voice*. I don't have one—a beautiful voice—if that is what you were wondering." She gave a nervous laugh. It was an introductory quip she had used times beyond counting. It usually elicited a smile or even, on occasion, a chuckle. But never just… *nothing.*

A faint furrow appeared between his eyebrows. "I am beginning to wonder if there might be some misunderstanding. I have engaged you for sexual intercourse—not for conversation. Or singing," he added after a pause.

Callie gave a startled laugh. "There is no misunderstanding. I assumed that was why you came to a brothel. But I would still like to know your name."

"You may call me David." And then he turned his face forward.

Callie studied him for a few moments before saying, "Are you saying that I should *not* talk?"

"Talk as much as you like," he said, not turning to her. "Just don't expect me to acknowledge or answer everything you say."

Well.

Plenty of men didn't like listening to whores talk, but most of them had enjoyed talking about themselves. *Ad nauseum.*

Not this man.

Still, he hadn't said anything about not *looking*, so she allowed herself a leisurely inspection of the man she would soon be bedding.

His clothing was well-tailored but subdued, all gray, black, and white with no color in his necktie or waistcoat.

Although his hair was neatly barbered, the cut was functional rather than fashionable, the thick brown curls closely cropped. His dark brown eyes were deep-set, the brows well-marked. His nose neither too long nor too short, just… average. His upper lip was thin but the lower one was fuller, although not so lush as to attract notice.

Indeed, the impression of averageness she had noticed earlier was borne out after a closer inspection.

The only things about him that were out of the ordinary were his inflectionless tone and dead gaze.

He hadn't raised his voice or reacted violently even when Brook had attacked him.

Callie had no evidence that he was dangerous—although he had certainly sent Brook flying across the room without any visible effort—but this man was deadly. She felt it in her bones.

And Callie had just sold herself to him for two entire days.

***

The hansom dropped them off in a part of town that must have been built in the last few years. All the buildings looked so similar it was a bit disorienting. Callie followed behind David, carrying her own bags as he evidently didn't believe that sporting women deserved such a courtesy.

He led her to a black door that looked just like the dozens of other black doors on the long curving street. There was a jingle of keys and then he opened the door.

Callie stepped into the foyer and turned in a circle. It was even emptier than the one at the brothel.

Still hatted and coated, he led her up the stairs. The walls were bare, there were no knick-knacks, not even a carpet runner.

He stopped on the third floor, turned right, and opened the second door before standing back and gesturing her into a room that was bare except for a bed and two nightstands.

"You may put your things in the dressing room," he said, and then pointed to a closed door. "There is a commode and shower bath through there." He gestured to the mantle over the dormant fireplace. The only ornament was a rather ugly clock. "It is half-past ten right now. I will return in an hour. I want you to bathe and wash off any cosmetics or perfumes. I do not care for either. Once you have cleaned yourself get onto the bed naked and wait for me." He turned and left.

Callie dropped her bags and hurried to the door just in time to see him disappear into a room on the other side of the stairs, his boots echoing on the bare wooden floor.

Callie stood there and stared, still a bit stunned by his abrupt order and departure. When she decided that he wasn't coming back she closed the door and then sagged against it.

What in the world had she got herself in for?

Chapter 3

Three quarters of an hour later Callie was lying between deliciously soft, clean sheets, her hair still a little damp even though she had dried it as well as she could in front of the fireplace. The fire hadn't been burning when she'd entered the room, but there was ample coal to build a delightful blaze—unlike at the brothel, where she had always been cold—and the room was, if not warm, at least no longer freezing.

Her eyelids were heavy and she was drifting toward sleep, the combination of the hot, steamy shower bath and cozy bed conspiring against her.

She glanced at the clock and saw she still had five minutes to wait. Something told her that her new employer would arrive not a second before or after the appointed time.

Callie tried to make herself care that he was an intensely disturbing man, but the shower, the clean bedding, and the impeccably tidy—if disturbingly empty—house was lulling her into a false sense of security. As if a man who liked to be clean and orderly could not possibly be a murderer or woman beater.

But then he didn't look as if he had enough emotion to get angry and beat anyone. Although he had certainly done something to Brook to hurt him badly.

She smiled at the memory of the vile brothel owner whining in pain.

But thinking about the despicable whoremonger reminded her that all the money she had earned on her back—every single penny except for the few shillings she'd had in her reticule—had been stolen.

Oh God.

Anger and fear and hopelessness struck her with the force of a locomotive. What in the world was she going to do? She had spent the six days before today answering every single job announcement she could find.

It had been demeaning and disheartening, but always—at the back of her mind—was the knowledge that she had enough money saved up to keep her going until she could find something.

But now…

Something hot spilled onto her chest and she realized, with horror, that she was crying.

Tears were the last thing a punter wanted from his whore.

She lightly dabbed her eyes with the sheet and had just readjusted the blankets when the door opened.

David stood in the doorway for a moment, his form limned by the lights in the corridor behind him. She had turned off the gaslight before climbing into bed, but he turned it back on again, not stopping until the room blazed with light.

Callie swallowed as she looked at his face. Although why she expected to see some sign of… anything, she didn't know.

His eyes slid from her face down her covered body and then back up. He took a step into the room and shut the door behind him before his hands went to his trouser placket.

"Get on your hands and knees, bottom facing me," he ordered in his low, toneless voice.

Callie gawked, but then quickly, and rather ungracefully, did as he bade her.

His feet came to a halt somewhere behind her and she felt the movement of air across her exposed skin.

"Spread your legs."

She slid her knees apart.

"Wider. Yes, that is good. When was the last time you fucked?"

Callie jolted at the blunt question. "Er, last Sunday."

He made a noncommittal noise and then she felt his hands on her hips. They were warm and slightly roughened, which she had not expected as he dressed like a clerk or somebody who sat at a desk all day long.

One of his hands slid from her bottom up her back. When he reached her shoulders, he pressed and Callie obligingly lowered to her elbows.

"All the way down," he murmured, sounding distracted—which was more emotion than she had heard from him thus far.

Callie complied, intensely aware of what he would be seeing. Although she had given herself to hundreds of men, only rarely had any of them wanted to look at her—at least not unless they were putting themselves inside her.

He separated her buttocks and her anus clenched in response.

He lightly glided a finger over the taboo pucker. "Have you taken a man here?"

"That costs more," she blurted.

His finger stilled. "How much more?"

"A shilling."

A long pause, and then. "And your mouth—how much for that?"

Callie swore she heard humor in his voice this time and took a risk, "Another shilling."

He made a low, considering humming sound and then said, "Agreed."

It was an *outrageous* amount of money, but Callie hated being taken in the arse and suspected that she would earn every single penny of it.

Oh dear God. What have I just agreed to?

She squeezed her eyes shut and readied her body for the painful ripping and tearing invasion that would leave her bloody and aching for days.

But there was no searing pain. No pain at all, in fact.

Instead…

Callie's eyes sprang open when she felt something wet and hot and so deliciously soft that for a moment, she simply could not believe it.

But then David did it again. He *licked* her there.

Callie hissed, her mind reeling. His mouth felt divine. Not just because of the arousing sensation, but the mere thought of such a filthy activity was wildly erotic.

He was not at all tentative or shy about what he was doing, either, stroking her hole with the flat of his tongue, keeping her cheeks spread wide and working her with firm, rhythmic licks until she was all but thrusting her bottom at him, silently, shamelessly begging for more.

One of his hands slid from her buttock to her sex and nobody could have been more astonished than Callie when his fingers encountered copious moisture.

She *never* got aroused with her patrons, quite the reverse, actually. Most nights she had to oil herself in advance because some men became offended when she did not get wet.

But Callie was aroused right now, almost unbearably so.

David circled a finger around her clitoris, his erotic caressing sure and confident and every bit as skilled as her own hand.

Even in the midst of her sensual daze Callie could not help wondering how such a cold unemotional man had learned his way around a woman's body.

He maintained his stroking and resumed his assault on her arse, using his lips, tongue, and even his teeth on her sensitive pucker, the sound of his sucking, grunting, and licking lewd and arousing in the otherwise silent house.

The orgasm, when it came, shocked her with its intensity.

Callie had never climaxed with a man before, only by herself, and rarely had she come so hard, unable to bite back her loud cries as one powerful contraction after another wrung her out.

Just as the waves of pleasure began to ebb Callie felt something hot and hard press not against her arse, as she had feared, but against her sex, which was slick and swollen from her climax.

He was thick and long and entered her slowly, not stopping until his still clothed groin pressed her sensitive skin, his shaft throbbing inside her. Keeping her filled, he rocked his hips, the thrusts so slight that they scarcely merited the name. And yet he was inside her so deeply that Callie swore she could feel him rooting around in her belly.

The sensation veered between pleasure and pain and she found herself pushing back to take more, even though it was not comfortable. She had never felt anything quite like it and her body was desperate for more.

Just when Callie thought she might climax a second time, David withdrew almost all the way, until only his thick crown still breached her. The sudden emptiness inside her was too much to bear and she pushed back against him, frustrated to be so close to an orgasm and have it jerked out of reach.

"Stay still," he ordered, reminding Callie who was paying whom.

He used her body's moisture to wet his thumb and then stroke her tight pucker. Unlike every other time that Callie had been taken back there, the gentle probing of his slick finger was arousing rather than painful.

His free hand slid between her thighs and he quickly located her engorged bundle of nerves, his touch teasing and maddeningly light.

And if those tantalizing sensations weren't torturous enough, he began to pulse his hips, fucking her with shallow thrusts and scattering what little remained of her wits.

The pleasure built inexorably, until Callie shook with need and her mind began to unravel under the overwhelming sensual assault.

And then he suddenly stopped, his fingers and cock disappearing from her body and leaving her on the edge of release.

Again.

Callie ground her teeth to keep from begging—or shouting and demanding.

She was so, so close! What possible enjoyment could he derive from such teasing? And what was he doing *now*? Had he stepped away?

She began to twist around when he spoke.

"Do not move," he said, spreading her buttocks with both hands, once again exposing her.

And then he *spat* on her hole.

Callie gasped and every muscle stiffened in shock at his coarse, demeaning action.

He spat on me.

She should have curled in upon herself and died.

Instead, the vulgar act propelled her already over-stimulated body toward her second orgasm of the night.

Chapter 4

Very little in life astounded David. In fact, he recalled the last time with crystal clarity. It had been the night he'd had his hands around the Prussian ambassador's neck and was choking the life out of him when the door opened and the man's wife entered.

What had just happened when he'd spat on the woman's hole—and she had climaxed again—was a surprise of a far more pleasant sort than the Prussian debacle.

The whore was beautiful, like a painting of an angel he had once seen. Her long blond curls and doll-like blue eyes were an attractive coda to a lush, curvy body.

But her appearance wasn't why David had offered her work. She had simply been the first woman to hand. He had not even noticed what she looked like when he had entered the foyer of the whorehouse. She could have been as ugly as a mud fence and he would have still offered her work. All he had been thinking about at the time was that he was horny and wanted to fuck.

Wanting to fuck was almost as rare a feeling these days as experiencing surprise. The last time David had sunk his prick into a female had been two years, eight months, and three weeks ago. He had ejaculated since then of course—sometimes several times a night—but into his own fist, the activity perfunctory and all but joyless.

But then suddenly, tonight, he had been as hard as a poker upon leaving Sir Andrew's office earlier.

It had been the fear he'd smelled on the man, of course. It had been so intense that David had almost come in his trousers.

The only thing that made him harder than fear was violence.

He was fully aware of how wrong that was, but he didn't care.

The woman's reaction to his spitting had been his second surprise today, and it had gone straight to his balls.

David could hardly wait to take her arse, but he forced himself to be patient for just a bit longer. The reward would, he knew, be worth the minor delay of gratification.

He slid a finger inside her cunt, slowly fucking her tight, silky sheath until her contractions diminished. Only then did he position his cock at her tight pink furl and pull back his foreskin, rubbing the spit into her hole with his sensitive crown, milking his shaft until more droplets oozed from the tiny slit, adding even more lubrication.

"Relax your body," he ordered when he began to press against her pucker and she tensed.

Her muscles eased a little, but if he entered her now it would be painful. While David did not particularly care about her pleasure, he knew his own enjoyment would be diminished if he had to listen to her cry, so he reached below her again and teased her engorged nub until she began to pant and flex her hips.

He penetrated her slowly, never pausing his fingering. She stiffened beneath him, whimpering when his fat crown stretched the outer ring of muscle, but she relaxed a little once he sank deeper into her tight passage.

Her cunt had felt glorious, but this… well, while not nearly as wet and soft as a pussy, there was something about taking a woman's arse that appealed to David's primitive side. And the fact that the woman found it demeaning and clearly did not care for it only made him like it more.

He didn't stop his invasion until his pelvis pressed against her soft cheeks. Once he was hilted, he flexed his hips and filled her a little bit more.

She was breathing fast, her body shaking, perspiration sheening her creamy white skin.

He let her adjust to the fullness inside her while he stroked the wet, swollen folds of her cunt, using her arousal to slick his shaft as he slowly withdrew.

David gave a low, animal grunt of pleasure at the sight of his prick stretching her tiny hole. Watching his hard shaft disappear inside her was almost as satisfying as the feeling itself. The woman—Calliope, she called herself—was small, slender, and yet softly curvy. David was not a big man, but his hands looked huge on her tiny waist and his ruddy shaft looked thick enough to split her heart-shaped arse in two.

He wanted to fuck her all night long, but by the tenth stroke it was becoming difficult to pace himself; his hips jerked and his balls were so full and tight they hurt. She shuddered beneath him each time he drove deep, but she pressed back for it, trying to take even more of him.

He smiled to himself at her silent, eager submission. Even though it hurt—or maybe *because* it hurt—she wanted more, harder, deeper.

And so David gave her exactly that, hilting himself with each thrust, until her pale skin was red and sweat slicked, her breaths ending in ragged little cries each time he bottomed out, the sound of his balls slapping against her wet cunt filling the room.

When he knew his time was near, he positioned the pad of his finger at the base of her swollen bud and massaged the source of her pleasure with tight circles, his thrusts becoming jerky and uncontrolled.

"*Come*," he growled as his balls began to empty their load.

He felt her finger join his just as he lost control of his faculties, his hips jerking and his shaft spasming as he emptied into her tight, convulsing body.

***

Callie stared at the ceiling, intensely aware of the soft, even breathing coming from beside her.

What an amazing revelation tonight had been. She had the vaguely shocking thought that *she* should have paid *him* for all the climaxes he had given her. Who knew it was possible to experience such pleasure with a man? And a patron, at that.

However, as grateful as she was, she had never expected him to *sleep* with her. Didn't he have his own room? Certainly this room could not be his as there were no personal items in the bathroom and the dressing room was empty.

Callie's irritation dissipated as her thoughts went back to the events of the last few hours. She had fallen asleep after the fourth—fifth?—orgasm, even before he had removed his cock from her arse.

It had hurt when he'd entered her—a lot—but the pain had been different than the other times. Instead of tearing and bleeding, this had started off as a torturous stretch, and then an almost unbearable fullness.

Until it became bearable.

And then it became pleasurable.

Callie never would have believed that was even remotely possible.

She lifted her head and squinted at the clock above the still glowing fireplace. It was past two. Was he going to take her again tonight? He *had* paid for two days.

She flexed her bottom and winced. She was sore, but the cold sticky spend leaking out of her was almost worse than the ache in her arse. Would he notice if she got up to use the toilet?

Moving as slowly as she could, she turned just enough to steal a look at him.

He was staring at her.

Callie gasped. "Oh! I thought you were asleep."

"No."

"I need to use the necessary."

"So, use it."

She rolled away from him and slid from the high bed, quickly making her way to the other room. Once inside it, she shut the door and then turned up the light only a little. Her reflection in the mirror startled her. Her hair was a wild blond bush and her eyes looked almost black in the low light.

But the most shocking thing was her slack, satiated expression. How could she be happy about this?

She scowled at her reflection, but it refused to stay.

Evidently having multiple orgasms put a stupid look on her face and turned a woman's brain to mush.

She found a washcloth and wet it under the tap, marveling at the wonder of hot water without having to heat it.

Once she'd cleaned herself thoroughly, she glanced at the cloth and then thought about the man in the other room. Didn't four, possibly five, orgasms deserve a bit of extra consideration from her?

Sighing, Callie rinsed out the cloth before returning to her temporary employer.

***

David glanced at the bathroom door. Was the woman planning to stay in there all night?

He reached down and gave his tumescent cock a stroke. Whatever was wrong with him was still wrong. Although David often came twice in one night, the episodes were usually separated by several hours. Tonight, he had ejaculated more than he had ever come in his life, and yet he was hard again.

It was fortunate that he had engaged the woman for two days. At this rate, he would wear her out.

The door opened and she approached the bed and stared down at him. "Oh!" she blurted when she saw his erection. "That was fast."

It *was* fast. David was on the other side of forty, so he could appreciate just how fast. Even when he'd been younger, he had never managed this many erections so close together.

He wasn't interested in why it was suddenly happening now. He just wanted to enjoy it while it lasted.

"I brought a cloth," she said. "I thought—"

He patted the bed beside him. "Sit here and clean me."

David clasped his hands behind his head and closed his eyes.

Her hand was firm and confident, almost businesslike, and he knew she must have bathed a goodly number of cocks, even though she couldn't be older than twenty-one or perhaps twenty-two. Many whores were already worn out by her age, but perhaps she had entered the sporting life later.

He blinked at his thoughts. It was unlike him to be curious about others—at least not unless it was part of an assignment. But then none of his behavior today had been typical.

He waited until she had carefully and thoroughly cleaned his loose balls before his hand shot out and closed around one of her wrists.

She gave a startled squeak and he used his other hand to remove the cloth and toss it aside.

"I want to fuck your mouth," he said, spreading his thighs to indicate where he wanted her.

He heard a soft sound that might have been a laugh, but she moved without comment to kneel between his knees.

David closed his eyes again.

And then the hot wet heaven engulfed him.

If she had been the sort of whore who tried to make him ejaculate as quickly as possible so her job would be over, he would have set her straight immediately.

But—yet again—the woman pleasantly surprised him.

She teased and licked and kissed his shaft, all the while working the loose skin of his sac with her hand in a way that was soothing rather than annoying. She sucked the fat, sensitive crown like it was an especially tasty sweetie. And when it was almost too much, she lowered her mouth and took him deep, until David felt the back of her throat.

Again and again she sucked him to the edge of bliss, teasing and working him into a frenzy of need.

When he could take her taunting touches no longer, he grabbed a thick handful of her hair and wrapped it around his fist.

"I am going to fuck your throat. And I will be rough."

She shuddered and his lips curved faintly at yet another sign that the woman reveled in crude use and a certain degree of pain, which was just as well given how much David liked to administer it. Choosing her had been serendipitous indeed.

David held her hair tightly and forced her head down. Her lips closed around him and she swallowed him deeply, until her nose was buried in his pubic curls.

He held her still, keeping her full until he felt her body begin to panic for air. Only then did he release her, impressed that she didn't gasp and snort, but merely filled her aching lungs.

Again and again, he throated her, keeping her full longer each time, her body pliant in his hands, her mouth worshipping him without words.

When he could control himself no longer, he drove deep and lifted his hips from the bed, his cock spasming as he shot down her throat.

It was too soon after his last orgasm and it hurt to come, but he welcomed the pain, vaguely aware that he had released her hair and was slumped on the bed, truly sated.

He felt her rise above him, her silky hair tickling the head of his cock before she rolled over onto her side.

David took only a few seconds to come back to himself before he pushed up off the bed and stood. He tucked his now limp prick back inside his drawers and buttoned his fly. A moment later he was across the room, his hand on the doorknob, when she spoke.

"Good night, David."

He opened the door and closed it behind him without saying a word.

Chapter 5

Callie woke to sunlight streaming through the curtains, which made her realize there were no drapes, only rather thin curtains.

She squinted at the clock, saw it was just after seven, and slumped back onto the bed.

Staring up at the ceiling made her remember last night—and the shock she'd felt upon waking to discover that David was lying on the bed still fully dressed, except for his cock.

That had been a first.

Why didn't he take off his clothes? Was he shy? Disfigured in some way?

A sharp knock on the door made her yelp and she clutched the sheet to her chest just as the door opened and David stood on the threshold.

"There is breakfast downstairs. It will soon be cold." He closed the door.

Callie snorted. What an odd, odd man.

Her stomach grumbled and she winced at the soreness in her arse as she rolled from the bed.

She had no time to dress, so she pulled on her nicest dressing gown and gave her tangled hair a few dozen strokes with the brush. Once the worst of the knots had been tamed, she stood back and studied the result in the mirror.

Her Villain

I look like a woman who spent all night being fucked six ways to Sunday.

Callie laughed at the vulgar phrase, which Flora had taught her. Thinking about Flora made her wonder how her friend was doing at Carlton's brothel. It had flabbergasted her that John Carlton had hired Flora as he was notorious for only engaging young women. Callie hoped that for Flora's sake she managed to avoid the abusive brothel owner's attention.

She pushed the unpleasant thoughts from her head and ventured downstairs, easily locating the dining room by following the smell of ham and coffee.

David was already seated with a heaping plate and a newspaper spread out beside it.

He didn't even glance up when she came in, but shoveled food as coolly and efficiently as he appeared to do everything else.

Callie poured a cup of coffee, took a gulp, and then sighed blissfully. It was strong and expensive, judging by the delicious taste.

She stared, dumbfounded, at the three full chafing dishes. Who in the world would eat all this food?

Well, that was scarcely Callie's concern. So, she shrugged the thought aside and filled a plate with eggs, ham, and toast before taking the only other place that was set.

After a moment she looked from the neat stack of newspapers to David. "May I read one of those?"

He slid the pile toward her without looking up or pausing his chewing.

The next hour was one of the strangest, and yet most relaxed, of the last year. They worked their way silently through the papers, trading them without a word once they'd finished reading them.

Not since Callie had lived with her father had she had access to so many newspapers, all of them quality publications and not gossip rags, which was largely what there had been at Brook's.

David ate a second heaping plate of eggs, ham, and potatoes, answering her earlier question about who would eat all the food. For a man who was muscular—Callie had not felt any fat on his hard body—he certainly put away a lot of food.

Once he had eaten the last crumb, he wiped his mouth, tossed the napkin onto the empty plate, and then carefully refolded the newspaper and set it aside before turning to her.

"The woman who cooked this only comes in the morning. I generally eat my midday meal elsewhere. For the evening meal I send a boy out to fetch food. There are several decent pubs not far away." He stood. "Do what you want with the day. But I will want you again at nine o'clock tonight."

"Bathed, naked, and on the bed?" Callie said with probably more sarcasm than was wise.

He blinked at her. "Yes," he said. And with that, he turned and left.

Callie was getting accustomed to his abrupt departures so she merely topped up her coffee and went to look out the window.

A moment later he emerged from the house, hatted, coated, and gloved, and hailed a hansom.

Just as the cab pulled to a stop, a pair of street curs trotted up to him. To Callie's amazement, the two dogs immediately sat and gazed up at David, their pitiful, ragged tails thumping the icy ground. He turned to them and she saw his lips move. The dogs both rolled onto their backs and he bent low enough to give each of the filthy beasts a quick scratch on the belly before turning back to the waiting cab.

And then he climbed inside it and was gone.

The dogs stood and watched until the cab disappeared and then trotted down the street.

Callie realized her mouth was hanging open and shut it. Truly, the man was simply too strange to comprehend.

She exhaled heavily and then turned away from the window, glancing around the room. Like all the others Callie had seen, the walls were bare of ornamentation and there were no carpets on the wood floor. The furnishings were minimal, nothing but the buffet, table, and chairs.

The door opened and a woman who was probably in her mid-fifties entered. And then stopped in her tracks when she saw Callie.

"Hello. I'm Callie," she said when the servant only stared.

"I'm Mrs. Jenkins," the other woman said, her gaze sliding to David's empty plate, which she picked up before lifting the coffee pot.

"It is empty," Callie said, and then smiled ingratiatingly. "So is my cup," she added hopefully.

"You'll be wanting more?" Mrs. Jenkins said, sounding less than eager.

"I don't want to be a bother. Could I come down to the kitchen? I know how to make coffee."

Mrs. Jenkins grumbled. "Aye. Come down."

Thirty minutes later the older woman had lost most of her hostility and was entertaining Callie with tales of her husband, eleven children, and multitude of grandchildren. She had warmed up considerably when Callie had offered to wash the dishes.

By the time Mrs. Jenkins was ready to leave, she had unbent to the point that she offered several of her cookery books when Callie expressed an interest in cooking dinner.

"It would do Mr. Remington good to eat less of that rubbish from the pub."

Remington. So that was his name.

Mrs. Jenkins eyed Callie. "You really know *how* to cook, I hope?" She cast a protective glance at the modern cookstove, which was clearly her pride and joy.

"Oh yes, I cooked for my father for years." Of course, the stove in her childhood home had been ancient. But how difficult could it be to learn how to use this one?

Mrs. Jenkins grunted and shuffled toward the back door. "You leave the mess for me to clean up in the morning." Never had a woman meant her words less.

"I wouldn't dream of it," Callie said, earning the first genuine smile of their acquaintance.

Once she had locked the door behind the housekeeper, she made herself a fresh pot of coffee, and then sat down to plan a menu before nipping out to do her shopping.

It would take some of her precious reserve of money to buy the ingredients for a meal, but Callie needed to do something to convince David Remington that he should keep her around for longer than just a few days.

Her father had always claimed that food was the way to a man's heart. Callie hoped it was also the way into his home.

***

David paused on the threshold and sniffed. At first, he thought the scent might be a phantom smell—he had experienced that in the past, although usually the odors were foul—but this smell was delicious and—

"Oh! I did not hear you come in."

The voice came from the top of the staircase and David looked up, his eyes widening slightly to take in more of the sight.

"I was not sure if you meant nine o'clock was when you wanted to eat or—" The whore caught her full lower lip with her teeth, as if to hide a smile. "Or if it was when you wanted to do the *other*." She descended the staircase, holding the skirts of her blue gown in one hand. "So, I planned dinner for seven rather than any later."

David might be defective or deficient in just about every way that mattered to other human beings, but even he could recognize beauty.

She had been pretty the night before when she'd been scuffed and flustered and messy from her fight with the brothel owner. But this was a whole new woman. In fact, David wasn't sure he would have recognized her if he had not been expecting her.

Her gown was elegant and simple, the dark blue somehow serving to make her eyes look even more like a summer sky.

David blinked at the bizarre thought.

She stopped in front of him and craned her neck to meet his gaze, the action making David realize just how tiny she was.

"I made dinner," she said, just in case he had not understood her the first time.

"Did you?" he said, snapping out of his strange daze and removing his hat. There was only one item of furniture in the foyer and it was a coat stand that had been in the house when he had leased it. He hung up his hat and then pulled off his gloves and put them in his coat pocket before hanging his coat, too.

When he turned around, she was still there. "What is it?"

She blinked. "I'm sorry?"

"The food. What did you cook?"

"Roast beef, rosemary potatoes, and I will put in the Yorkshire puddings now that you are here. Oh, and there is an apple pie for dessert. I, er, found a basket of apples in your cold cellar."

"I have a cold cellar?"

She laughed and the sound was shocking. Perhaps because this house was always so silent. "You do. I fear the apples were a bit old and tough—almost dried—but they will plump up nicely in a pie." She hesitated. "Would you like a drink before dinner?"

"Why are you doing this?" As soon as he asked the question her face fell, the sparkle disappearing from her large blue eyes. He supposed that a different man would feel… something at crushing her spirit.

He felt nothing other than mild interest at how clearly and openly she broadcast her emotions for all to see.

"I just—well, I thought maybe you might keep me for longer if I was useful."

The words came out so fast that it took him a moment to untangle them.

David stared, waiting for more, curious as to where she was headed.

Her pale cheeks kept darkening and she shifted from foot to foot. "Did I make you happy last night?"

Happy?

David gave the question some consideration. Had he been happy? He'd certainly been physically satiated. Last night he had slept for all of four hours, about two more than usual.

"Never mind," she said, and then spun on her heel and darted for the stairs.

She was fast, but David was far faster. He caught her elbow and firmly pulled her back.

"What?" she demanded, turning her face away from him.

He took her chin and forced her to look at him. She was crying. The force of the emotions swirling in her eyes— obvious even to somebody like him—set him back on his heels.

For a second, he could almost *feel* what she was experiencing, like an elusive scent that teased at his memory.

But it was gone in a blink.

"You want me to keep you?" he asked.

She swallowed convulsively. "I just thought that you would—"

"Do you want me to keep you?" he repeated. David wasn't interested in listening to her babble about what she thought he thought. Because she would never know what he thought. Ever. All he wanted was a nice, simple answer to his question.

"Well… yes, just for a while."

"How long?"

She shook her head, confusion stopping the flow of tears. "I don't know. Is—is this your home? It seems so empty."

"For the time being it is."

"Are you staying long?"

"As long as I need to."

She gave him a look heavy with one of the few emotions he *was* familiar with: frustration. "It is just…"

"What?" he asked, beginning to feel frustrated himself, something that was common whenever he talked to other people. Which is why he avoided it.

"I don't have anywhere to live and some men stole my money and I can't find a job—at least not one that isn't wh-whoring," she stumbled on that word.

David thought she was finished, but she was only drawing a breath before continuing.

"And this house is large and there are more rooms than one person could possibly use and I could even sleep on the top floor which must be servant rooms although it is lo—"

David's arm shot out before he even thought it, which was disturbing because he almost never did anything without thinking first.

His hand landed around the woman's delicate throat and he forced his fingers to relax.

She let out a squeaky breath but didn't try to get away. Smart girl.

"You are never to go into the room on the top floor," he said.

"I didn't! I give you my word. It was locked." Her hands closed over his forearm and he glanced down. Her fingers were delicate and pale and something about the way they looked on his black sleeve caught his attention for a moment.

When he finally looked up, he saw her eyes were filled with terror. She swallowed and he felt the delicate structure of her throat flex beneath his palm.

"I'm sorry," she said, a tear sliding down her cheek.

David released her and she stepped back and quickly dashed the tear away with the back of her hand.

"The top floor is not for you," he repeated.

She nodded and swallowed, lightly touching her throat.

"I left no marks," he assured her.

Again, she nodded and dropped her hand. She began to turn.

"Where are you going?"

"I was going to finish cooking. I can bring you your meal wherever you like."

"I will eat it in the dining room."

"Very well."

"You will join me."

Her forehead furrowed slightly, but she nodded. "It will be about half an hour."

David watched her go and then took his hat and coat from the hooks and carried them up to his chambers.

He removed the gloves from the pockets and put them in their usual place before hanging up his coat and hat. Then he stripped off his clothing and turned on the shower bath. He shaved in the steamy room after bathing and by the time he had dressed in fresh clothing not quite twenty-five minutes had passed.

He had just entered the dining room when he heard footsteps behind him and turned to find her laboring under a heavy tray.

He closed the distance between them in a few steps and reached for the tray.

"You don't have to do—Oh, thank you," she said, when he removed it from her hands.

He set it down on the table which he saw had been set with fancy dishes he had never seen before.

"I hope you don't mind me using these," she said, following his glance. "I found them in the butler's pantry.

David didn't know what a butler's pantry was, or that he had one. He lifted the lid off the huge tray and saw several smaller dishes beneath.

"I found some wine in the cellar—not far from the apples. Would you like—"

"I don't drink wine." He saw that she was holding a bottle and opener. "But help yourself."

While she turned back to the bottle he lifted the covers.

The meal was simple but looked cooked to perfection. He'd not had Yorkshire pudding since he'd been a very young boy.

A lifetime ago.

Chapter 6

Callie fiddled with the bottle so clumsily that David wordlessly took it from her and opened it using a few efficient moves.

"Thank you," she said.

He poured her a glass and they both sat.

She was so confused by what had happened between them in the foyer that she wanted to go up to bed, crawl into it, and pull the covers over her head.

But instead, she had to get through this meal and make this man so happy he could not bear to part with her. Not that Callie was sure he knew *how* to be happy.

Once, long ago, her pride would have rebelled against abasing herself like this. But pride was a luxury when it meant sleeping on the street or working in John Carlton's whorehouse, warming his bed, and enduring his abuse.

There was nothing but the sound of clinking cutlery for a few moments while they each picked a dish and put portions on plates. Callie opened her mouth to protest when David placed a huge, bloody slab of roast beef on her plate, but decided it wasn't worth it.

She took a big gulp of wine and then forced herself to eat at least a few pieces of the meal she had cooked, even though she'd never had less of an appetite in her life.

"This is good."

Her head whipped up and she met his flat stare. He pointed at the Yorkshire pudding on his plate, or what was left of it, and said, "I haven't had one of these in thirty years."

Callie blinked at this unprecedented deluge of information.

Fortunately, he didn't seem to require a response and went back to decimating the contents of his plate. He wasn't a rude or disgusting eater, he just ate as if he were getting paid to do so, as if it were his job.

Which made her wonder what it was that he did to afford such a huge obviously expensive house. "Do you go to a job in the City?"

He froze and his head lifted slowly, until she was once again staring into eyes that were both a bottomless pit and yet a brick wall at the same time. "Why?"

"I was just making conversation."

He resumed chewing and turned to his plate.

Callie breathed a shaky sigh of relief and made a mental note not to ask any more questions about what he did for a living. Her gaze dropped to his hands as he wielded his fork and knife with the dexterity and precision of a surgeon. He had nice hands, long-fingered and elegant, but strong, too. Capable hands.

The sort that can grab you by the throat before you even see him move, a voice reminded her.

Callie didn't want to remember that terrifying interlude. He hadn't hurt her—he was right: there were no marks, not even faint ones, because she had checked in a mirror—but he had scared her almost as much as Carlton had that night when he'd tied her to the bed and brought out that whip.

Callie hastily shoved that nightmare back into the box where she usually kept it locked.

"What is it?"

She looked up. "I beg your pardon?"

"You looked frightened just then. Why?"

"No, I wasn't scared."

"Now you are lying."

Her jaw sagged.

"Never lie to me," he said.

Callie stared, hypnotized by his gaze.

"What were you thinking about?" he repeated.

The words came out in a hasty rush. "About a customer who tied me up and whipped me."

He stared at her as he chewed his food, waiting until he'd swallowed before saying, "It scared you?"

She nodded.

"Because you don't like being tied up and whipped? Or was it the man, himself?"

Callie was both nonplussed and intrigued by his distinction, one she would not have made herself. "It was him. And—and he hit me hard. Until I bled."

He nodded, as if he were filing away her answer. He didn't look outraged or startled or anything else. He just went back to his food.

Callie sighed, relieved to be out from under his dark, unnerving stare.

She drank her wine and poured another glass, surreptitiously watching David as he systematically cleared his plate. There was something satisfying about watching a person eat the meal you'd cooked, even when that person put the food away as if they were pitching hay into a barn.

When he finished, he looked up and reached for the cover on the roast. He paused and glanced at her mostly untouched plate. "You aren't hungry?"

"Not really."

He pushed his plate aside and then reached out and slid hers across the table.

And then he proceeded to demolish her plate, too.

***

David finished eating his second serving of apple pie, pondered the wisdom of having a third helping, decided against it, and pulled out his watch. Dinner had taken less than forty-five minutes.

He looked across the table at her.

She smiled uncertainly but did not speak.

He did not like to go off his schedule. It made his skin itch and he got irritable. When he got irritable, he… broke things.

But it was only six minutes until eight, which meant there was another sixty-six minutes to get through until David could take her upstairs and fuck her.

"There is a nice drawing room," she offered, her voice tentative.

He stared. Was she suggesting they fuck in the drawing room?

"I saw a card table and—"

"I don't like cards."

"Oh. Well, there were some other games. I believe I saw draughts and chess—"

"Chess?"

"Yes. There is a box with fine ivory pieces."

"You play?" he asked, yet again surprised by this woman.

"I do."

David stared at her, wondering if it would be better to just break his schedule and take her upstairs now. Because if there was one thing that annoyed him more than going off his schedule it was playing chess against an idiot.

She cocked her head. "If you would rather, we could just go upst—"

He stood. "Let us play a game of chess."

***

David looked up from the chessboard. "You let me win."

Callie opened her mouth to deny it, but then noticed his tight lips and the vein throbbing in his temple and suddenly

66

remembered what he had said earlier about lying. She swallowed and said, "I did."

"Why?"

"Er, because most men don't like to lose."

"Purposely losing is like lying."

"Ah."

"I hate lying."

He had not raised his voice, but that just made him sound more menacing. "I'm sorry," she said, the pulse in her throat suddenly pounding.

"We will play another game. This time you will play to win."

Ten minutes later David was staring at the chessboard. He had replaced all the pieces he'd lost and then played out the moves. Callie was impressed by his mental recall.

Once he had played it out, he looked at her.

For the first time since she had met him twenty-four hours earlier, there was a spark of life in his normally flat gaze.

"Again," he said.

It took her about ten minutes longer the second time—he had begun to move his pieces more cautiously—but she beat him again.

After he replayed their moves, she swore that his lips twitched when he looked up. Almost as if he was about to smile. But he didn't.

Instead, he asked, "How did you learn to play like this?"

"My father taught me. He was a professor of mathematics and loved the game."

Rather than ask the question which her few friends had asked at this point—how had Callie gone from being a professor's daughter to whoring—he said, "How many moves do you play ahead?"

"Usually seven or eight, but on occasion as many as twelve or fifteen."

His expression was easy to read: it was admiration. "That is masterful."

The words were, strangely, even more moving when spoken in his flat tone and her face heated at his praise.

He stared at her for a long, uncomfortable moment. And then the clock chimed.

***

It was nine o'clock and David's cock was rock hard. Astonishingly, he couldn't decide whether to fuck her or play another game of chess.

She stared at him, her huge blue eyes windows to every single thought racing through her beautiful head: anxiety, fear, indecision, and more emotions that he could not identify. David simply could not imagine containing so many emotions inside his head. How did she not go mad? He experienced a few emotions, of course, but never any that were as tempestuous or powerful as hers obviously were.

What must it feel like to be so susceptible to one's own feelings?

Her Villain

Although he could not identify many of the emotions that flickered over her face her thoughts were not difficult to read. Right now, for example, she was wondering if he would keep her. No doubt she was worrying that she would be out on the street tomorrow morning.

Until approximately thirty-three minutes ago—which was when she had won the first chess game—David had decided to spend the night fucking every one of her holes and then leave enough money for a hansom cab on her nightstand and tell her to be gone in the morning.

He had decided to send her away because even the thought of her tight cunt milking him dry two or three times a night wasn't enough to overcome the thought of her running loose in this house, prying into his business on the third floor, and asking increasingly inconvenient questions about him and what he did.

But now…

How could he just toss her out onto the street given the way she could play chess? When had he last enjoyed games so much? It had been years. Not since he had been on a mission with a man he'd only known as Jackson, a sniper who had been the best David had ever seen. Jackson had been the one to teach him the game and the two of them had played chess for hours every night in between fulfilling their various tasks. Jackson had beaten him every single time. Except for the last game.

David stared at her hard, trying to decide whether she would allow him to do more things to her if she was desperate and boiling with insecurities about her future, or if she would be a better fuck if she felt grateful to him for keeping her?

He knew that such a cold, manipulative thought made him a bad man. But that realization was nothing new.

After a few moments he decided that the tension currently rolling off her had a certain appeal. It was very close to fear, an emotion he had never experienced himself, but one that he recognized and enjoyed.

Yes. He would wait to tell her his decision. It was more interesting.

"Go upstairs and get on the bed, as you did last night. I will be up in a half hour." It meant deviating from his schedule, but he suspected she would be so anxious after waiting another half hour that he would discover just how much she was willing to do to convince him to allow her to stay.

Chapter 7

Callie stripped off her clothing and—thinking about how David had used his mouth on her body last night—took a quick but very thorough shower bath. She had only had access to the wonderous device for two days and already she didn't want to think about living without the luxury. At the brothel they had used a tub down in the kitchen. If you were lucky, you were the first one to get the water. If you were *not* lucky…

It was not a good memory.

She had wrapped her hair in a towel to keep it dry while she showered so she unpinned it and then brushed it until it was a froth of glossy curls.

Callie stared at the clock after she had positioned herself on the bed, draping herself as attractively as she knew how. The fact that she had less than twelve hours to convince him to let her stay pounded in her head like a war drum. What could she do to change his mind?

David Remington was, hands down, the strangest and most awkward man she had ever met. But he was clean, generous in the bedchamber, and he seemed to be financially secure. Other than the whole throat-grabbing episode, he did not appear to be violent.

The house was in a very nice neighborhood and even though she'd not looked around much today, there were several streets on either side that had enough shops to offer excellent employment opportunities.

If she could stay here and not need to pay any rent—at least not with coin—then she could save all the money she earned. She would opt for steerage and take her chances, anything to get out of England.

If only—

The door opened and, just like the night before, he turned up the light until the room was blazing.

Unlike the night before, however, he held something in his hands.

Callie's breathing stuttered when she recognized a riding crop.

She pushed up, her hands shaky as she drew her knees up to her chest and wrapped her arms around them.

"What's that for?" she asked in a hoarse whisper.

He ran his cold eyes over her, his gaze as unreadable as ever. "How much would it cost to tie you up and use my crop on you?"

She knew she was breathing, but she couldn't seem to get enough air. "You—you—I told you that story in—in—"

"In what?" he asked, coming closer, until she could see the other items that dangled from his fingers—straps of leather, belts it looked like.

"I cannot believe that you would use what I told you against me like this," she said, her voice breathy and feeble sounding.

"Why not?" When she didn't answer, he said, "You can say *no*."

But she couldn't say *no*. Because if she did, he would never allow her to stay.

He reached out with the crop and lightly dragged the keeper up her thigh. "How much to tie you face down on the bed and let me raise a few welts with my crop? I won't whip you hard enough to make you bleed."

Callie felt woozy, and her mouth—which had just been flooding with bile—was suddenly dry. She had to swallow repeatedly and moisten her lips.

"Forget it." He lowered the crop and began to turn.

"No! Wait! I will—I will do it if you allow me to stay," she blurted.

He held her gaze. "No."

Callie had never hated anyone so fiercely in her life—not even Carlton. At least with him, you knew what you had. But this man had the appearance of something else. But he was a swine, just like—

"I have already decided that you can stay," he said.

She gawked up at him, positive she must have misheard. "W-what?"

"I said that I have already decided that you may stay."

"When?"

"When what?"

"When did you decide that?"

"After the second game of chess—the second *real* game."

She pushed up onto her knees. "Why didn't you say something?"

"I just did."

"I mean, why did you wait until now to tell me? You must have known how it was tearing me up inside worrying about tomorrow?"

"Yes, I knew."

She shook her head, unable to wrap her mind around what he'd done. "Why?"

"I wanted to see how much you would do to convince me to allow you to stay." He tossed the whip and belts onto the floor and reached for his placket. "Now I know."

Something snapped inside her. "You *swine!*" She lurched forward and shoved him hard in the chest with both hands. Or at least that's what she tried to do, but he moved so fast his hands were a blur, catching both her wrists and holding her with an ease that brought her to her senses. She steeled herself for a slap or some other violent retaliation.

But he just held her immobile.

Even though Callie knew it was futile she thrashed and squirmed and tried to alternately pull him down and then push him over. He was far stronger than she would have ever believed, his body absorbing her assault the way a tree's branches swayed in the wind, but the trunk never budged.

In the end, it was Callie who was gasping and tired.

"Are you finished?" he asked, not in a taunting way, but as if he just wanted to know.

What a freak.

Callie nodded.

He released her and then ran a hand through his hair, pushing back the thick brown locks that had fallen forward in the scuffle. His erection, hard, long, and wet, thrust out of the gap in his unbuttoned placket.

"You're hard," she accused. "It aroused you to do that—to be cruel to me."

"Yes." His gaze moved speculatively over her body and then settled on her breasts.

"What is wrong with you?" she demanded, tears of anger and frustration gathering in her eyes. "You are *sick* to get enjoyment that way."

"Get on your back and spread your legs."

"Are you even listening to me?"

He raised his eyes from her breasts. "Are you listening to *me*?"

Her breathing, which had been ragged and fast, suddenly froze in her chest. Callie looked into eyes that held nothing of the admiration she had fleetingly seen in the drawing room, and none of the satisfaction she'd glimpsed while he had eaten her food.

All she saw was the full face of the predator that lurked just below the bland surface.

She swallowed jerkily and quickly laid on her back and spread her legs.

The moment she did, his hand dropped to his cock and he began stroking, his eyes roaming her body. "Spread your pussy and show me how wet you are."

Callie hadn't thought it possible to hate him even more, but when she lowered her hands to her sex, she felt how swollen she was. And when she parted her folds, she was so wet that her fingers slipped. How could she have become wet from his cruelty?

Because I liked it. Because there is something wrong with me.

His eyes lifted to hers and he nodded, as if something had just been confirmed.

Callie was afraid she knew exactly what it was.

He stared at her sex for a long time while he almost absently pleasured himself, his gaze brooding.

Callie's eyes slid to the whip and belts on the floor, her body tightening at the sight of them. Was he going to use them? She had told him he could. Was it too late to negotiate a price for—

He released himself, slid his arms beneath her bent knees and pulled her toward the edge of the bed. Her fingers were still spreading her lips and he knocked her hands away and then stroked the swollen folds apart with his long fingers, his flat gaze suddenly as sharp as a surgeon's scalpel as he opened her until there was nothing left to hide.

It was beyond humiliating to be examined like a—a *thing*. But it was even more humiliating that her body appeared to like his treatment, so much so that she was drenched, evidence of her arousal trickling from her slit down the crack of her arse.

He traced the liquid with the pad of one finger to her back hole, slicking her with her own moisture and then probing her.

Callie winced, still sore from last night. But if he noticed or cared, he gave no sign. Instead, he kept pushing until he was inside her to the top knuckle. With his other hand, he caressed and rubbed her clitoris with almost clinical efficiency, demonstrating that her body was his to command regardless of how angry she was at him, and bringing her quickly to a powerful orgasm.

It was difficult to hold on to her anger when he smashed her defenses with weapons like pleasure.

***

David waited a few seconds after Calliope's contractions had ebbed before once again lowering his mouth over her sex.

Her eyes flew open and she yelped. "No! Please—"

David grabbed her hips when she tried to scramble away from him. "Hold still," he ordered sharply.

She immediately stopped squirming.

He should have tied her to the bed—at least her legs—and then he would not have needed to waste his hands keeping her spread open.

"Please, please, please," she begged, the words barely recognizable. "I cannot—it is too much! I just… cannot."

"You can and you will," he said coolly, and then tongued the stiff little bundle of nerves. David was fascinated by her tiny erection and he was curious to find out just how many orgasms he could force from her body. Last night, when he had come twice in fairly rapid succession, his balls had hurt, but the experience had been extraordinary.

He suspected that the discomfort she was feeling right now was similar and it made him harder than ever to know that he could make her come again and again and she would do nothing to stop him.

He could use the belts and whip on her and she would not protest.

David briefly considered doing exactly that, but decided he was enjoying himself too much to bother with binding her just now.

Perhaps later—after he had tired of forcing orgasms from her—he would see how far he could push her.

She was right; he *was* sick. Her pain and fear were as delicious to him as the meal she had cooked. And just like the meal, he wanted to come back for seconds and thirds, until he was sated.

She whimpered and began to squirm—but not enough to annoy him—when he sucked her tiny organ into his mouth.

It did not take long before she was no longer trying to get away. After only a few moments of insistent tonguing she thrust her fingers into his hair and held his head down while pumping her hips and grinding her sex against his mouth.

Almost immediately she began to shake, crying out as she came.

Once again, David did not allow her to enjoy her orgasm.

Instead, he resumed his sucking, forcing yet another climax immediately on top of the last one, until she was sobbing, begging, and babbling gibberish even as her cunt soaked his face.

As much as he wanted to keep forcing pleasure on her, his balls were aching and so he gave her one last suck and then hopped up onto the bed, lined his cock up with her slick pink hole, and slammed himself balls-deep.

She gasped, her back arching in a sinuous curve that thrust her full breasts up. They jiggled enticingly and he decided that he would fuck them, too.

Later.

He hooked his elbows beneath her knees and held still inside her, able to feel the echoes of her last orgasm. Her body jerked weakly as each contraction passed, her sheath exquisitely hot and tight.

David watched closely as he withdrew from her, his cock glistening with her juices. She mumbled something beneath her breath as he pulsed only his crown inside her, the loud squelching sound of penetration crudely erotic.

She began to lift her hips and make small, frustrated noises and it entertained him to realize that she was trying to take him deeper.

The greedy little bitch! So much for claiming that she could not take another orgasm.

He was tempted to deny her what she wanted, just to see those tantalizing emotions that flooded her eyes. But he needed to come, so he began to work her with deep, increasingly savage strokes, fucking her so hard that the bed skittered on the wooden floor.

David took his release when it came—not delaying it as he had done the night before. The need to pump her full of spunk was too strong, the primitive claiming suddenly critical.

He drove himself deep and then stiffened as he erupted. His cock spasmed over and over and the orgasm seemed to last twice as long as usual.

His eyelids were heavy as he withdrew, feeling yet another of those primitive pulses deep in his groin as his slick shaft slid from her tight passage, his ruddy prick liberally coated in both their juices. Her opening clenched around nothing after he left her body, as if trying to beckon him back. David pushed two fingers into her and stroked her while thumbing her little nub.

It took scarcely a minute before her back was again arching, her hips lifting off the bed, her lithe body taut as she came.

He waited until she sagged back down before withdrawing his fingers and holding them in front of her flushed, sweaty face. "Suck," he ordered, his softening cock giving a throb of interest at the flicker of self-loathing in her gaze when she opened her mouth and did as he told her—and more—sucking hard enough that her cheeks hollowed, tonguing between his fingers until there was nothing left.

David gave her one last look before he pushed off the bed, his gaze lingering on her splayed thighs and wide-spread sex, which was flushed dark pink and glistening with his spend.

He dropped to his haunches so he could examine her more closely.

She shifted on the bed, trying to pull her thighs together, her hand sliding down to cover her sex when she realized where he was. "David? What are—"

"Keep your legs spread," he barked, slapping away her hand and then parting her pussy lips so he could see her opening.

His cock, which had begun to soften, hardened so fast at the erotic sight of his spend oozing from her cunt that he felt dizzy. "Fuck," he muttered.

"What is it?" she asked.

He ignored her. Instead, he took her beneath her knees again and pulled her toward the edge of the bed, until he could hook her legs over his shoulders.

"David?"

"Hush," he muttered, reaching over her thighs to open her again, and then sinking his tongue into her pussy.

***

Callie moaned as David commenced fucking her with his tongue.

No, he wasn't just fucking her, he was *feasting* on not only her, but his own seed. He was not bothering to be quiet about it, either, and loud, obscene slurps and grunts filled the otherwise quiet room.

It was so *filthy*. And yet powerful bolts of arousal shot from her sex to her womb, over and over and over again.

Once he finished inside her, he licked and sucked her swollen folds, methodically cleaning every trace of his orgasm from her sex. It was so carnal and crude and erotic that—amazingly—another climax began to build. Callie had believed that he had sucked her clitoris raw and she would need days to recover before she could have another orgasm.

Evidently, she had been dead wrong.

His mouth, when it finally engulfed her throbbing bud, was gentle and hot and so deliciously soft. Rather than force the pleasure from her as he had been doing all night, he tenderly licked and sucked her toward bliss.

Callie was still shaking from the strangely powerful orgasm when he stood and looked down at her, his gaze hooded and his cock jutting out of his placket, long, hard, and leaking.

Oh God. He is not finished.

He climbed up onto the bed, straddling her chest.

"Push your tits together."

Her hands moved before she really understood what he was doing.

His hips lowered over her chest and he held his prick in one hand, guiding it between her breasts.

And then he began to flex his hips.

Callie knew this sort of thing happened, but no punter had ever wanted to do it to her.

He was already slick from being inside her, not to mention he produced more pre-ejaculate than any man she had ever been with, so his cock slid between her breasts easily.

She risked a glance up at him and met his gaze. Something about the fact that he was completely clothed and she was naked made the moment feel even more depraved. Callie wanted to look away but his eyes held her riveted.

His lips parted slightly, his breathing faster and faster.

As she watched, a subtle shudder passed through his body and his eyelids fluttered, every muscle in his face going taut.

And then suddenly he pulled out and jerked himself with his fist, jet after jet of spunk crisscrossing her breasts and her fingers, which were still pressing them tight.

He aimed higher and a hot ribbon laced her chin and lower lip.

On impulse, Callie stuck out her tongue and licked up the salty, bitter liquid, earning a harsh growl of approval and a hot, hungry stare for her effort.

His hand slowed and then stopped, until nothing more came out.

Again, she acted on impulse and pushed up onto her elbows just high enough to lick his crown.

His jaw flexed and his nostrils flared—the equivalent of a scream from any other man—and he pushed forward enough that her mouth filled with cock.

Callie gently licked him clean, until he pulled away, obviously too sensitive.

He held her gaze while he tucked his prick back into his trousers and buttoned himself up.

With a graceful move he slid from the bed and his eyes moved over her body, slowly consuming her, lingering longest on her sex before he finally turned to leave.

"David," she said before he reached the door.

He stopped but didn't turn.

"Thank you for letting me stay."

Just as he'd done the night before, he opened the door and left without a word.

Chapter 8

Callie woke up early the next morning and arrived in the dining room just as David did.

"Good morning," she said brightly, taking the seat she'd had the day before and pouring herself a cup of coffee.

He didn't answer. Instead, he turned to the breakfront and heaped his plate with food.

"If you don't want me during the days, I was going to find a job," she said, savoring the rich coffee.

His broad shoulders stiffened and he pivoted slowly toward her. "What sort of job?" he asked, the dangerous glitter in his eyes so shocking that her throat closed up until only a little air could get through. Had she thought his flat, blank look was intimidating? She would never regret the expression again after seeing this new one.

She swallowed convulsively and licked her lips.

He lowered his crushing gaze to her mouth and she instantly felt relieved to be out from under the weight of his stare.

Callie inhaled shakily and said, "Not the sort of work you are thinking."

"What am I thinking?" he asked.

"I'm not looking for work whoring." She had almost said *more work whoring* but caught it at the last second.

It had been the right thing to say. The danger that had invaded the room like a miasmic funk dissipated instantly and he grunted and turned back to the buffet, evidently satisfied.

When he sat down and reached for a newspaper, she quickly said, "What do you expect of me? I need to know so I do not run afoul of your wishes."

He forked a chunk of ham and some eggs into his mouth and chewed, his attention on the front page of the newspaper.

Callie had given up on him answering when he looked up and said, "I want you in the drawing room at eight o'clock ready to play chess. And I want you freshly bathed, naked, and waiting on the bed at nine o'clock, ready to be fucked."

That was… direct.

Callie waited for more, but instead of speaking he began to reach for the newspaper again.

"That is all?" she asked.

Irritation briefly registered on his normally inscrutable face as he looked up at her.

That was twice in one morning that she had identified one of his expressions. Perhaps she was learning to read him?

"What else is there?" he asked.

"Cooking meals? Taking care of the house? Cleaning? Other errands?"

"You can cook if you want, but I don't expect it. I can order food. You don't need to clean. The housekeeper brings in maids three days a week. And I don't have other errands."

This time when he reached for the paper, she didn't interrupt him.

****

As Callie trudged home several evenings later her spirits were as low as they had ever been.

She had spent the last few days—every hour from seven to six—on a fruitless job hunt. After almost eleven hours of it, she had decided there was only one thing to do: she would need to forge letters of recommendation for herself tonight and use them tomorrow.

Callie had written her own letters when she had first looked for work and they had worked a charm. She had quickly received an offer of employment. But then, three weeks into her job as a companion for a querulous old woman, the employment agency had somehow discovered that she'd manufactured her work history. They notified her employer and she'd been sacked from her job and was fortunate that she had not ended up in gaol.

Lying definitely held dangers, but without the money she had saved, her choices were limited. She could either falsify documents or get a job working for Carlton.

So that meant she really had only one choice.

She walked down the narrow alley that led to the servant's entrance. But when she tried to open the door to the kitchen, she discovered it was locked.

"Blast," she muttered, marching back toward the front door.

That was locked, as well. She banged the knocker and waited without much hope. It was only a little after five. Yesterday David had not returned until close to seven.

Callie was gnawing on the inside of her cheek and considering what she could do for the next few hours while she waited when the door suddenly swung open.

David stood on the threshold, wearing only trousers that hugged his well-muscled thighs, a close-fitting waistcoat, and a shirt with the sleeves rolled up to expose forearms ropy with muscles, prominent veins, and lightly dusted with dark hair.

It was the most skin he had exposed thus far.

"Hello. Did I disturb you?" she asked when he stared at her as if he'd never seen her before. "I'm sorry about knocking, but I need a key so I can come and go."

His gaze, even more distant than usual, sharpened slightly, and then he turned and jogged back up the stairs without uttering a word.

Callie stared at his receding back until he disappeared.

"It is nice to see you again, Calliope," Callie mimicked in a low, flat voice, the words echoing in the empty foyer.

She sighed and made her way to the drawing room, where she had found some paper and a quill in the secretaire desk while she'd been snooping yesterday.

An hour later she had three different letters of recommendation ready. She had decided to set her sights lower than the last time—no companion or governess positions—and write letters from fictional tea shops and bakeries in Bristol, Liskeard, and Leeds. If any of her prospective employers wondered why she had lived in such an odd, far-flung assortment of places she would say that her father had been a teacher who had moved a great deal.

She had just folded up the letters when the door opened.

"I am ordering food," David said, not bothering with a salutation. "What do you want?"

"Whatever you are getting is fine."

"It usually comes within half an hour." He turned to go.

"Shall I set places in the dining room?" she called after him.

"Fine," he said, shutting the door behind him.

"You are a strange man," she muttered to herself as she folded each of the letters multiple times to make it appear they'd been well-studied.

Once that was done, she went up to her room and took off her walking costume. She debated going without a shower bath, but there wouldn't be much time between chess and fucking, as David had so charmingly termed it.

Thirty-five minutes later she was bathed, brushed, and garbed in a gown that would have been too simple for most dinners, but she doubted her host even noticed her clothing. In fact, she wondered if he would recognize her if they passed on the street.

Still smirking about that, Callie collected cutlery and linen from the butler's pantry and went to set the table.

"Oh." She said stupidly when she found David already seated at the table, staring straight ahead at the blank wall. "Is the food here?"

"No."

She opened her mouth to ask what he was doing sitting in an empty room, staring at nothing, but then closed it and went about her business.

"If you want wine, you should fetch a bottle," he said, his voice startling her. "I only ordered ale with the meal."

"Ale is fine."

He took out his watch, frowned, and had just replaced it when there was a rap on the front door.

He left the room and a few moments later he returned with a large hamper and set out the few dishes.

They each helped themselves to portions of stew and fresh, hot bread.

"Oh!" she said, springing up from her chair. "There is still some apple pie from last night." She had baked a second pie yesterday, as he had eaten the first one over the prior two nights. "I will go and fetch—"

"I ate it."

She stopped and turned back to him. "I'm sorry?"

"I ate the pie when I returned home."

"All of it?"

Slowly, like the faintest hint of the sun rising over the horizon, his pale cheeks pinkened. "Yes. All of it."

Callie bit back a smile. Who would have guessed the man had enough blood pumping through his veins to cause a blush?

She took her seat and they ate in silence. That was fine because her thoughts were on tomorrow and what jobs she would apply for. Callie could save money if she only took a hansom to the farthest point and then walked back toward the house. Then it would not matter if—

"I am partial to sweets."

She looked up. "I'm sorry?"

"Sweets," he repeated. "I like them."

"Who doesn't?" she asked, genuinely confused as to what he was on about. Really. The man had scarcely spoken a word in days and now he decided to whitter on about—

"It was rude of me to eat the entire pie." He gave her a hard look, as if he wasn't quite sure if she was teasing him.

"I made it for you. I am glad you enjoyed it. There are more apples; I will make another tomorrow."

He stared for a moment, and then went back to his meal.

Callie could only shake her head, struck afresh by what a bizarre man he was.

"What do you do all day?" she asked before she could stop herself.

He looked up slowly, still chewing.

Her face heated. "I'm sorry. I know you don't like me to pry. I just—"

"I work at the Exchange."

Her eyebrows shot up.

Something like humor flickered across his face. "You look amazed."

"I guess I am."

"What did you think I did?"

She opened her mouth to blurt *something more dangerous*, but caught herself in time, instead saying, "I don't know."

"You're lying."

She dropped her spoon with a clatter, suddenly annoyed. "Sometimes lying is polite."

"I don't like lying."

He had lowered his voice and the hairs on the back of her neck stood up.

She swallowed down her unease and said, "I thought you did something less, er, mundane."

"Like what?"

"I don't know," she insisted. "Just maybe something…dangerous. Lion taming perhaps," she said, hoping to inject a bit of levity into what had become a tense conversation.

He quirked one eyebrow at that and went back to eating.

Lord.

***

"Checkmate in two."

David looked from Calliope—was that boredom he saw on her face?—back to the board. He still held her queen in his hand. He had been sure that she'd erred and had felt the closest thing to joy he had experienced in years when he had taken her queen with a mere pawn.

But now that he looked at the board it took him only a few seconds to see what she meant. It *was* checkmate in two.

Bloody. Hell. He shook his head, amazed by the audacity of her move and how brutally effective it had been. White queen to black king's pawn, which had put him in check. The move had amazed him, mainly because it had appeared to be a monumental—and fatal—misstep.

David had jumped on her queen without hesitation, too excited by what appeared to be a rare blunder on her part to notice the bishop lurking in wait.

He slowly turned his king on its side. His skin prickled and his entire body flushed. The room was cold, so the heat wave made no sense. Why did he feel feverish? Was he getting ill? He plucked at his starched collar to cool his skin. It was a stupid action as that would hardly help the rest of the shirt, which was plastered to his back like a second skin.

What was wrong with him?

He looked up. She wasn't paying attention to him but pushing back the cuticle on her thumb.

He felt a pain in his hand and opened his fist to find he was still clenching her queen so tightly there were indentations in the flesh of his palm.

He dropped the piece into the wooden box with a clatter and she looked up at the sound. "So, do you want another ga—"

David stood and she gaped up at him. "Is something wrong?"

His hands went to his placket. "Bend over the settee and lift your skirts. *Now*," he barked when she just stared.

She scrambled ungracefully to her feet and hurried to comply.

David's cock was as hard as a pump handle and leaking just as freely as a tap as he approached her. He scowled when he saw she was wearing drawers.

He shoved his fingers into the split and tore the flimsy garment in half.

She squeaked and started to turn, but he set his palm on her upper back and held her down. "Stay," he ordered.

"Those were silk."

"I will pay you for them."

He kicked her feet apart and she mumbled something else but he didn't hear her. Her grumbling turned into a moan when he cupped her sex, pleased to discover that she was just as aroused as he was. Was that because she had beaten him *soundly* twice tonight? Did she enjoy it as much as he did?

David shook the thought away and spread her arse cheeks, amused when she stiffened. She didn't like backdoor fucking.

Too bad.

He wet his thumb on his cock and smeared the moisture over her tight pucker.

"Are you going to take me there?" she asked, her voice strained as the back of the settee pressed against her midriff.

"Yes."

"We didn't discuss that as a regular part of the—"

"How much?" he asked, breaching her with his thumb.

"A shilling!" she yelped.

It was an outrageous sum. David could have half-a-dozen whores offering him every hole for that amount.

"One shilling as often as I want it," he said.

"Three for—" she gasped when he pushed his cock into her tight cunt. "Three," she repeated in a firm if high-pitched voice.

"That's highway robbery," he said, lazily stroking in and out of her.

"You wouldn't say that if it was your arse we were discussing."

Her words were so shocking that he froze.

"I'm sorry, I didn't mean—"

David threw his head back and laughed.

***

David was laughing. The inhuman machine of a man was laughing and Callie was bent over and could not see what a laugh looked like on his face.

It was over as quickly and as abruptly as it started. "You are too right about that," he muttered, still working her arse with his thumb while he continued to stroke her with his cock. "Three shillings it is. I will take your cunt, first." He punctuated the words with a savage thrust of his hips that made the wooden back of the settee bite into her painfully.

Fortunately, the thought of three shillings made the pain more than bearable.

So did the two orgasms he forced from her in rapid succession.

Callie was still dazed and breathing heavily a short time later when he gave her buttock a stinging slap and said, "Reach back and spread your cheeks."

Callie bit down the retort that sprang to her lips and obeyed. This time, she was expecting it when he spat on her hole, but that didn't stop her face from scalding.

He dipped his fingers inside her cunt and added her shocking wetness to his spit, the gesture so matter-of-fact it only added to her shame and made her even wetter.

He made a low humming sound that reminded her of a cat's growl, his skilled, relentless fingers working her arse with an almost detached deliberateness, pumping into her with one finger and adding more lubrication before easing in a second.

Even though he took his time, it hurt. But her body responded far differently to his use than it had to any other man. Not only was she producing a mortifying amount of moisture, but her body became pliant and receptive and every part of her thrilled with anticipation.

How had this happened to her? And why?

"Keep yourself spread," he barked when her hands loosened.

Callie opened herself wider, clenching her jaws when he pressed the hot, blunt head of his prick against her back hole and slowly entered her, not stopping until his private hair was pressed against her skin. She had to bite her cheek to keep from whimpering.

He slowly withdrew and Callie felt more spit hit her hole. His thrusts were shallow, working the moisture into her and easing the burn.

After a few moments he pushed her hands away, replacing them with his own, spreading her cheeks to the point of discomfort.

Callie dropped her hands to the settee cushions and pushed herself up enough that the back didn't cut into her midriff.

He worked her at a leisurely pace, pausing from time to time to slap her arse, alternating buttocks until her bottom was on fire, both inside and out.

Callie closed her eyes and concentrated on not clenching, which would only make him feel bigger, keeping her muscles as relaxed as she was able.

"Good," he muttered, the single word of praise the equivalent of garrulous gushing from any other man. His fingers dug cruelly into the flesh of her hips and she knew there would be new bruises to join the host of others. He liked marking her. Well, as much as he appeared to like anything, that was.

His thrusts became harder and faster and she felt the moment when he lost control, pounding into her with a ferocity that was probably leaving bruises inside her body, as well.

He did not make a sound when he bottomed out inside her, only the thickening of his shaft presaging his ejaculation. He filled her with jet after jet of heat, his body rigid as he came.

Once the last spasm had passed, he withdrew from her without lingering. He never lingered.

Callie pushed up off the settee with a groan and rubbed at her stomach and ribs while shimmying her hips to lower her skirts. The movement of air around her nether region reminded her that he'd torn off her best drawers.

When she turned, he had already righted himself, only the faintest flush indicating he'd just engaged in a carnal act.

Callie located her torn clothing and picked it up, frowning when she saw there was no way of repairing them.

"It is eight-forty-one," he said.

She looked up to see him examining his watch.

"We have deviated from the schedule so I will come to you at a quarter after nine. You will be waiting for me—"

"Bathed and naked and on the bed," she finished for him.

He blinked at her interruption, but nodded, replaced his watch, and then left the room.

Callie could only stare at the wooden door that closed behind him, which told her about as much as his face did.

***

Callie woke up later than she wanted the following morning, largely because David had been insatiable the night before.

She had mistakenly believed that their session in the drawing room would have dulled the edge of his desire. But he had shown up on the dot of a quarter after nine, freshly shaved and bathed and as stiff as a poker.

He had turned on the light as brightly as ever, strode to the bed, took a pillow, and threw it onto the floor before proceeding to open his trousers.

"On your knees." Remarkably, those were the *only* words he said before leaving her bed three hours later. That was it, three words.

Amazing.

He had taken her mouth, her cunt, and her arse—*again*—evidently determined to get his three shillings worth—before buttoning up and leaving her exhausted.

Callie felt him in every part of her body as she went through her morning routine.

By the time she reached the dining room, he had already left the house for wherever it was he went—the Exchange, apparently. The food on the buffet had cooled and she ate only a piece of ham and toast before gulping down two cups of coffee.

Five hours later she had blisters on one heel and a new position at a tea shop that was only a ten-minute walk away.

Her uniform—which consisted of a white pinafore, white mobcap, and a hideous blue and white striped gown—ate up almost all her remaining money, but she would get it back when she turned the uniform in.

It wasn't a wonderful job, but it was a job. With the money she earned from the tea shop and the shillings she would earn selling her cunt and arse and other bits to David—although he had not yet paid her—she *might* be able to afford a decent ticket and have a little money for when she arrived in America.

Callie needed to find out just how long David would be keeping her. A month would not suffice, but *two* months…she might be able to manage that.

The house was empty when she returned, but David had left a key on her nightstand, so she let herself in and made a cup of tea, putting her feet up while she enjoyed it, wincing from the working over David had given her body last night.

Callie knew that he would do the same tonight if the urge seized him. He was not a gentle lover and he had absolutely no interest in intimacy of any kind. There was nothing about himself he wanted to share—except his cock, mouth, and fingers—and he didn't want to know anything about her, either.

He was the most inscrutable, unknowable man she had ever met.

And he was also an extremely generous one, not just with his money, but also with his body. Callie had experienced more orgasms in the past few nights with him than she had in the last year.

For the first time ever, she looked forward to sex. Even his obsession with her arse was not enough to dissuade her.

Sometimes, it was hard to remember that he was paying *her* for bed sport, rather than the other way around.

Her Villain

You had better remember it, my girl, because that is all he wants from you: pleasure.

Chapter 9

David could not pinpoint exactly when he had begun to look forward to going home. Nor could he recall when he had begun to think of the mostly empty house as *home*.

He was not sure he liked either feeling.

Homes were not for men like him. He had never had one and never expected to.

What he had now was a whore who played chess with him and allowed him to fuck her, for a price. That was not a home, was it?

Or maybe it was? What the hell did he know?

David scowled at the unproductive thoughts as he inserted his key and unlocked the door. When he opened it, a delicious scent slapped him in the face.

He paused on the threshold, inhaling until his lungs threatened to burst.

David absently shut the door behind him and took a step toward the stairs, his body operating on instinct.

But at the very last minute, he pivoted to the right—striding toward the kitchen—instead of going up to his room as he always did.

The door to the kitchen had been propped open and heat and delicious smells wafted through the opening.

He paused on the threshold and stared.

Her Villain

Calliope was dressed in a worn frock David had not seen before, the gown like something a maid would wear, with only a petticoat and no crinoline beneath it. Her abundant blonde hair was tucked under an ugly mobcap and she wore a long apron. She had not heard him because her attention was focused on the large wooden worktable she was bent over, her lush bottom swaying from side to side as she hummed something tuneless.

The delectable smell that had beckoned him into the kitchen had to be lamb, and he could also smell buttery pastry and apples.

David crossed his arms and leaned against the doorway, content to inhale deeply and watch.

When she moved to the side, he saw that she was making tarts.

She stood with a sigh, massaged her lower back, and slowly turned. And then shrieked when she saw him. "David!"

"What are you making?" he asked, strolling toward the worktable.

"How long have you been standing there watching me?" she demanded, fists on hips.

He shrugged.

"You are the man who plans his day to the minute. How long?"

"Seven and a half minutes. What are these?" he pointed to the pastries.

"What do they look like?" she retorted.

"Apple tarts," he admitted, turning toward the stove and sniffing.

She grabbed his upper arm and turned him back around, but only because David allowed her to do so.

"Are you *smiling*?" she asked in open disbelief.

"No."

She laughed. "Yes, you are."

He ignored her teasing. "Is that lamb I smell?"

She nodded and moved to the stove, stirring the contents of one pot and then lifting the lids on two others and generally bustling about. She glanced over her shoulder. "Do you want some tea?"

His gaze slid to the tarts.

She laughed again. "You won't have to wait long, the batch in the oven is almost ready."

He took a seat at the small wooden table. The kitchen was warm—far warmer than anywhere else in the draughty house— and it smelled good.

"I will have my tea and tart here," he declared.

She just smiled and put the kettle on the hob.

David sat and watched her bustle, for once, not checking the time.

***

Callie shook her head as David pulled a third tart toward him.

"What?" he asked, pausing before putting it into his mouth.

"If you eat that you will not have room for dinner."

"I will have room," he assured her, and then took a bite that consumed half the pastry.

Callie topped up his tea—which he took black, despite his obvious love of sweets—and poured a little more into her own cup.

She leaned on her elbows and watched him enjoy his food. "I got a job today."

He grunted and swallowed, his gaze straying to the remaining pastries. Instead of reaching for one, however, he took a gulp of tea.

"A job? Why, congratulations, Calliope! Where will you be working?" she asked, pitching her voice low and making it as emotionless as possible.

He looked up, his eyebrow lifting at her imitation, which Callie personally thought was astoundingly accurate.

"How nice of you to ask, David," she chirped in a perky voice. "I will be a waitress in a tea shop."

"What shop is that, Calliope?" she mimicked.

"It is called *The Duke's Crumpet*, David. There is even a picture of Harriet Wilson on the sign."

"Who is Harriet Wilson?" David asked.

Callie's eyebrows rose. "You have never heard of her?"

"Would I ask if I had?"

No, that was a good point. He might be generous with his money, but he was parsimonious when it came to words.

"She was a whore who had many powerful and wealthy men as clients, one of them the Duke of Wellington. She published a memoir that was less than flattering when referring to the Iron Duke's bed skills. The tea shop is a play on words—instead of the duke's strumpet, his crumpet."

He stared. Evidently, the wordplay was lost on him.

"Er, where did you go to school?" she asked.

His eyes, which she had already believed shuttered, shuttered even more and he stood and took out his watch, glanced at it, and then turned and strode from the room.

Callie watched him leave, waiting until he disappeared before saying, once again in his voice, "Thank you for the tarts, Calliope. They were exceptionally delicious. How amusing that a tart can make such delicious tarts."

Callie laughed again, this time at herself for expecting something different from him. She had known him less than a week but he was the most predictable, if least comprehensible, person she had ever met.

You always did expect too much from people, her father's shade commented.

That was true. *But I've certainly lowered my expectations in the year since your death, Papa.*

But her father did not reply.

Callie sighed and stood, removing the rest of the tarts from the oven before they burned.

Chapter 10

A week later...

Y ou were not paying attention, Calliope."

Callie looked up at David's accusatory tone.

"What?" she asked.

He gestured to the chessboard. She glanced at it and saw that she had wandered into check without realizing it.

"Oh."

He scowled.

"What?" she asked. "Aren't I allowed to lose on occasion? I promise you that I did *not* lose on purpose."

"No. You lost because your mind was elsewhere."

She shrugged.

"What is distracting you?"

"Why do you care?" she retorted. And then bit her lip when she saw his face darken. But then her reaction—cowering like a dog—suddenly annoyed her. "What?" she taunted. "Talking was not something you wanted. Or don't you recall saying that? Except now you have decided that you want me to talk. Make up your mind, David—am I to talk, or keep my mouth shut? Which is it?"

"If something is interfering with the time between eight o'clock in the evening and five o'clock in the morning, then it concerns me."

"*Hmph.*"

"What is distracting you?" he repeated.

"I spoke to somebody I used to work with today—a woman from Brook's." A woman she heartily disliked, but Callie kept that fact to herself.

"And?" he prodded.

"We met by accident and it was…well, it was extremely unpleasant."

"What happened?"

She gave an exasperated huff but could see that he wasn't going to let this go. In the future she'd need to remember to be upset between the hours of five-oh-one in the morning and seven-fifty-nine in the evening.

"The night you and I met I had just learned that all my money had been stolen."

"I remember."

That surprised her, but she didn't comment. "I thought it was the men who had come to haul off the furniture who'd stolen it, but this woman said—" Callie stopped, not wanting to verbalize what she had learned, simply heartsick.

"Said what?" he asked. "What did she say?" he demanded impatiently when she did not immediately answer.

"She said that Flora took the money!" Callie shouted, angry that he was forcing her to speak the words.

He recoiled slightly at her raised voice. "Who is Flora?"

"I shared a room with Flora at Brook's. I *thought* she was my friend. She was—she was the person who took me in hand when I first started working there and didn't know anything." She had also kept Callie from slitting her wrists, but—again—she kept that to herself.

David grunted—his default response when he couldn't be bothered to speak.

"That is all you have to offer me?" Callie demanded, and then mimicked his grunt.

He turned back to the board and began setting up the pieces again.

Callie had given up on him answering when he spoke.

"You are stupefied that somebody you thought was a friend betrayed your trust and stole from you?" he asked, not looking up from the board.

"Yes."

"It upsets you?"

She snorted. "Well… *yes*."

He replaced the last pawn, turned the board until white was facing him, and then looked up. "People will always betray your trust. The sooner you accept that, the sooner you will stop being a victim."

Her jaw dropped. "That is not true."

"It is."

"No, it is not."

"Name somebody who has not betrayed your trust."

"My father," she said without hesitation.

"Why are you a whore?"

She flinched as if he'd slapped her. "How dare you!"

He looked genuinely taken aback. "What? Is that not what you are? I met you in a brothel."

"It is a job and what I was forced to *do*. But it is *not* the sum of who I am."

He sighed and said, "Why did you turn to whoring?"

"Because my father died and—" she broke off and stared at him.

"And he did not leave you enough money to secure your future?" he guessed. "He neglected to ensure that his *daughter* had adequate means to survive without turning to prostitution? He was an intelligent man and yet not smart enough to know how hard life is for a *woman* without a provider and protector?" The way he emphasized the words *daughter* and *woman* drove his words home harder than a mallet would have done.

Callie just stared.

David turned back to the board and moved his king's pawn. When he looked up, there was nothing on his face to indicate that he had just attacked Callie's love for her father.

No, David merely took him off the pedestal where you placed him. And he is right to do so.

Callie shook her head, as if to dislodge the unwelcome, unpleasant thought.

"Your move," he said.

Fury flared in her at his cool words. David thought he could just *assault* her with words and then play chess?

Well, she would show him.

For the next ten minutes she concentrated harder than she could ever recall doing, choosing her moves with a brutal detachment that would have made a great military commander like Wellington proud.

"Check in three," she said, looking up for the first time.

His eyes moved over the board as he played out the remaining moves.

Rather than look irked at such a sound thrashing, he smiled. Or at least he tried to, but the expression was like a suit that didn't quite fit. "Congratulations, Calliope. That is what happens when you concentrate."

Callie ignored his patronizing comment, shoved back her chair with a screech that made David wince, and stormed from the room, slamming the door without a word.

There, let him have a bit of his own medicine for a change.

***

It was true that David had little ability to recognize common social cues. But even he knew that Calliope had left the drawing room in a temper.

When he reached for her door handle at nine o'clock, part of him wondered if he would find it locked against him.

David wondered what he would do if it was.

As it transpired, the door handle turned with no resistance and the sight that greeted him was mostly a rewarding one. Yes, she was naked. But she was under the sheet and blanket tonight. A small rebellion, he supposed.

He turned the gas up all the way and stepped into the room before closing the door behind him. He was already hard—he had been since she'd thrashed him in that second game—and his hand went to his placket and he quickly released his erection.

"Did you know my father?"

David stopped mid-stroke. Why would she ask such a bizarre question.? "No, of course I did not."

"Then how can you know he betrayed me?"

Oh. It was back to that. He had hoped that subject was finished. Evidently not. He sighed and stood where he was, dropping his hands to his sides and staring briefly down at his bobbing prick before looking up again.

"I have already said what I have to say on the subject, Calliope. I don't wish to discuss it again." He gestured demonstratively at his cockstand. "Not now, especially."

"For your information, my father fell ill unexpectedly—an influenza that settled in his chest and killed him in less than a sennight. He was only four-and-forty."

David registered, with mild interest, that her father had been only two years older than David was now. Or at least two years older than David *thought* he was.

As to the rest of what she said, he had neither the desire nor inclination to respond.

It turned out she didn't need a response.

"My father had no reason to believe he wouldn't be there for me for years to come. He did *not* betray me."

"If that is what you believe then why do you care what I think?"

The question confused her and her jaw worked for a moment before she said, "I don't care what you think. I just want you to understand."

"I understand what you've said." That was certainly true. David reached for his dick, which was only half-hard now.

"You *understand* my words, but you still think I'm wrong."

Irritation spiked inside him. "I am finished talking about this."

She pushed up higher on her knees, the movement causing the muscles in her thighs and belly to flex and make her lush tits jiggle enticingly. But what came out of her mouth was *not* arousing in the least.

"That is too bad, because I am not," she said, crossing her arms and hiding her breasts from him, forcing him to look up and meet her angry, accusatory gaze. "Sometimes a person must do things they don't want to do."

"How much?" he asked.

She blinked. "How much what?"

"How much will it cost for you to leave this subject behind?"

Her lips parted, her expression one of profound shock. "A pound!" she retorted, fire sparking in her eyes.

"Done." He resumed stroking his cock, vaguely amused at the look of shock that replaced her fury. She had not expected him to accept her outrageous demand. He probably wouldn't have if he wasn't so bloody aroused from the thrashing she'd just administered across the chessboard. He needed to be balls deep inside her *now*.

"You will pay me a pound to stop talking about my father?" she repeated in disbelief.

"I will pay you a pound for no talking at all," he amended, his head beginning to ache from the uncustomary amount of conversation he had already been forced to endure.

He studied her face, which seemed to be making the shift from astounded to… something else, he was not sure what. It was exhausting just watching her get buffeted by a storm of emotions. David could not even imagine—nor did he want to— just how tiring it must be for *her*.

There had been times in his life when David had regretted his emotional deficiencies. But at moments like this he could not help thinking that *he* was the fortunate one.

"For how long?" she asked.

David considered her question. Did he want her to stop talking until the twentieth of December, when she left?

It was… tempting.

She flung up her hands. "I cannot believe you."

"What?" he asked, confused yet again.

"Do you have to think that hard about it? Would you really rather I not talk at *all*?"

He considered her question. "I like to discuss chess strategy," he eventually admitted.

"And that is all?"

He paused, and then nodded. "For the most part."

Her nostrils flared and she smiled tightly, displaying two rows of even white teeth. "Well then, there you have it. I will not speak for the duration of our arrangement unless it is about chess. How long am I allowed to live here, by the way—I had better ask that now, before it is forbidden."

David blinked. Her suggestion sounded both logical and agreeable. And she wasn't shouting or crying. But there was… something in her tone that made him suspect he was not understanding the full scope of what she was saying.

Christ. Trying to understand this woman's motivations made his head hurt. What did he care what she was feeling or thinking?

I don't care, he assured himself.

There. That was settled.

David looked up from his uncharacteristic inner turmoil to find her glaring at him. "What?" he asked.

"How long may I stay?"

"You may stay until the twentieth of December."

Her eyebrows knitted. "That sounds very specific. What happens then?"

"Something that is none of your concern." David wondered if he should give himself a few extra days without her. Because he suspected he would have a difficult time concentrating with her in the house, even if she wasn't talking. But he disliked going back on himself once he had spoken, so he let the offer stand.

She stared at him, as if expecting more. When he remained silent, she nodded. "So. Five weeks," she said, staring at the wall behind him, saying the words more to herself than to him.

"Five weeks and five days," he corrected.

Her gaze snapped back to his. "Right. Five weeks *and* five days. How many hours?"

David glanced at the clock on the mantle, doing a rapid mental calculation before turning back to her. "Seven. Or eight at most."

"Thank you," she said, her voice sweet. But the smile that curved her mouth was not the usual one. It looked…odd.

Before David could ponder the matter more closely, she was talking. Again.

"When do I get the quid for not talking?"

He gave her question the consideration it deserved. How did one pay for such a thing?

"And all the other money, too," she added.

"I will pay you for the rest tomorrow. And I will advance you a quarter of the pound."

Rather than look pleased, her eyes slitted. "Half in advance."

"But what happens if you speak?"

Her jaw sagged. "Are you saying you want money back if I do?"

"That only seems fair."

Her breathing became labored. "Would you like to put values on every word and use that to assess the fine? Or maybe it would be better to charge by the subject matter?"

Something about the set of her jaw set off warning bells. David ignored them and said, "That seems time-consuming and unfeasible. There are a great many words in the English language," he added when she merely stared. "But your question has merit. You will likely have lapses. I cannot expect perfection, so—"

"Because only you are perfect."

David frowned. After a moment, he decided to ignore the interruption. "Five lapses without any charge. After that, a penny each time."

She opened her mouth, closed it, snorted, and then said. "Fine." Without another word she laid herself out on the bed, her legs spread wide, her body open for his use.

Just the way he liked her.

David experienced a sudden, and rare, surge of contentment at having negotiated a complex social situation that was fraught with many pitfalls—most of them invisible to him—with such success.

Perhaps he was not, as he had always believed, destined to wander clueless when it came to communication.

***

Callie had never met a more clueless individual in her life.

Nor had she ever been so furious. There hadn't been a word invented yet to describe how angry she felt.

David wanted silence, did he?

She would give him silence. He would be fortunate to get so much as ten words out of her before December twentieth came around.

And just what in the world was that strange date about?

Oh, why did she even care? She would probably be ready to *run* from the house—and the infuriating, maddening, frustrating man—before even half that time had elapsed.

David threw a cushion onto the floor. "I have decided I want your mouth," he said, slowly stroking his cock, which had deflated during their argument so that it was more flaccid than she had ever seen it. Yet more proof, if she had needed any, of how much he hated talking. Talking to *her*, at least.

Callie knelt in front of him, hating how slick her own thighs were. Her body's enjoyment of degradation enraged her almost as much as David did. How could her mind want one thing and her greedy, duplicitous cunt, another?

"Suck me," he ordered in his dead, flat voice.

Callie eyed his cock—outraged by the clenching in her sex at his cold command and the way her mouth flooded with moisture at the thought of taking him—and clamped her jaw tight, pursing her lips.

What is wrong with me? Why would I lust after a man who just told me he doesn't want to hear me talk? A man who is willing to pay me a ridiculous amount not to talk. A man who views me as three convenient holes to fuck.

Oh, and a chess partner.

David's hand paused its stroking, his cock hard and leaking.

Callie swallowed before she drowned.

He slid a finger beneath her chin. After a second of struggle, she allowed him to tilt her face until she was forced to meet his gaze.

"Is there a problem?" he asked, looking genuinely perplexed.

Don't allow him to see how badly he has hurt and insulted you. And—whatever you do—don't let him see how aroused his obnoxious behavior has made you!

The sharp voice penetrated the haze of anger clouding her brain. David was still waiting for an answer, his eyebrows descending as time stretched.

Callie shook her head—she wouldn't waste the word *no* on him.

He stared at her for a long moment before removing his finger from her chin.

Callie lowered her eyes to his slick pink shaft, experiencing the same odd relief that flooded her every time he released her from one of his intense stares. Why did his lifeless unreadable gaze affect her so?

David nudged her lips with his wet crown. "Suck."

He sounded almost annoyed. The temptation to delay even more was strong. But her desire for him was even stronger.

Callie opened her jaw wide and he slid the fat head of his cock into her mouth.

Her sex clenched so hard at the heat, weight, and taste of his thick shaft that for one horrifying moment she thought she might orgasm then and there.

Oh, God. He would never allow her to forget if she did.

"Eyes on me," he barked.

She jolted slightly at his command and lifted her gaze to meet his.

His eyes were dark and unknowable, his features without expression.

Why on earth did she find that combination so unbearably erotic?

Because you really are a whore, aren't you? a disgusted voice in her head taunted.

She certainly was a greedy whore where David was concerned, there was no denying it.

He stared intently as she tongued and sucked his fat, salty head, swallowing his copious pre-ejaculate as if it were a fine wine. She had never met a man as wet as David and it was— along with everything else about the annoying man— excruciatingly arousing and made her body respond in kind, until she could feel her arousal sliding down her thighs.

He pulsed shallowly into her mouth.

Suddenly, it became very, very important that Callie make him feel *something*—some emotion that was too strong to be contained by his walls and barricades and shutters.

She had sucked more cocks than she cared to count, but never before had she wanted to utterly destroy a man with her mouth.

Callie wasn't going to just suck him.

She was going to make love to him.

****

David did not believe that the eyes were the windows to the soul—he didn't even believe people *had* souls—but eyes were the window to more than a few human emotions. And the way Calliope's pupils swallowed up her sky-blue irises told him that sucking his cock aroused her.

David knew that her arousal didn't just displease her, it infuriated her. And a great deal, too, judging by the whorl of emotions that flickered across her face. She hated how her body responded to pain and humiliation—like a well-trained hound to its master's voice—and that dichotomy was without a doubt one of the most arousing combinations David had ever encountered.

It was obvious to David that Calliope had been raised to be a good girl, to be virtuous and modest and preserve her maidenhead for some handsome, kind, caring husband who would fuck her once a week with the lights off, so as not to outrage her delicate sensibilities. A respectable man who would fill her belly with one child after another, constantly breeding her with the same assiduity he employed when it came to keeping his mares in foal or his hunting bitches producing litters. He would likely keep a mistress for his more interesting amorous pursuits and Calliope would have never been the wiser when it came to vulgar eroticism. Or how much it aroused her.

One single misfortune—her father's premature death—had smashed the future she had been born to live to flinders, utterly changing the trajectory of her life.

She would have loathed the coarse physicality she had been forced to endure at the brothel and would have begun planning her escape from Brook's from the moment she'd started working there, saving her pennies for the day when she could afford to leave her life of shame far behind her.

David might not have a clue about a great many things, but he knew most men didn't give a tinker's fuck about pleasuring a woman—especially not a whore. The sheer wonder on Calliope's face the first time he had given her an orgasm had been proof of how rarely she had experienced them. At least with a punter.

In the past, David had carefully chosen his whores, making sure they could endure his vigorous demands.

But Calliope had been a random choice.

David had been in a rare state when he had arrived at Brook's that night. Indeed, he could not recall ever engaging in a sexual transaction with so little forethought.

Staring down into her hot gaze right now he had to admit there just might be some truth to the concept of *luck*, something he had never given much credence to in the past.

Not only did she appear to appreciate his fierce sexual appetite, but they also shared an appreciation for pain and humiliation.

And then there was their mutual interest in chess, as well.

Yes, it was almost enough to make a person believe in luck.

David had believed that the no-talking transaction might have angered her. But based on the way she was working his knob—with more skill than any five whores combined—he assumed that he had misread her expression.

Her full lips were stretched around the rock-hard head of his cock like she was sucking on an especially juicy plum, her tongue flicking his slit, her hand stroking his shaft.

David swallowed as her other hand slid between his thighs and she cupped his ballocks over his trousers and drawers, making him wish that he was naked and could feel the skin of her hand on his sac.

He slid his feet apart to give her hand more room to fondle his heavy balls, his breathing turning ragged when her mouth began to sink down his shaft, her eyes becoming hooded when she took him all the way to his root.

David slid a hand around the back of her head and kept her there, his nostrils flaring when her body tensed and her eyes flew open as he blocked her throat. He held her full of cock until a single tear slid down one cheek.

Her body sagged with relief when he released her. David dropped his hand, allowing her to pull away if she wanted.

Instead, she throated him again, this time keeping herself full until he felt her gag reflex.

Again and again, she took him all the way, her hands massaging his full balls with exactly the right amount of pressure, her tongue cradling and stroking his shaft. Her lips sucking his slit as if his cock was some mythical fountain of youth and—

"Fuck!" he groaned, his orgasm ambushing him and startling the word out of him.

***

Callie didn't bother to hide her smirk as she finished licking the last of his spend from his half-hard cock. She could now add *euphoric* to the short list of emotions she had seen on David Remington's face. She had to admit the expression looked very good on his normally controlled features.

Of course it had not lasted long. Callie had barely milked the last drop of spunk from his balls when he withdrew from her mouth, his bland, emotionless mask firmly in place.

Or maybe it wasn't a mask. Now, there was a thought. A terrifying one. What if he was really as dead as he looked?

His gaze held hers for a moment, his breathing still faster than normal as he stared at her. "On your back, legs spread wide."

His crude, cold command sent the usual shameful spasm of pleasure from her swollen cunt to her womb and breasts.

Once she was positioned the way he wanted, Callie turned to stare at the wall while he stood between her spread thighs and parted her lower lips with his fingers.

"Did you come while you sucked me?" he asked.

She shook her head.

He lightly strummed her wet, swollen flesh. "You were close, weren't you?"

She swallowed, thought about ignoring him, but then jerked a nod.

He gave a satisfied grunt—when had she learned to translate his various grunts?—and then released her and laid down on the bed beside her. "Get up on your hands and knees. I want you to fuck my face."

Callie turned to him, her lips parted in shock. How could she still be confounded by the things this man said?

He cocked an eyebrow at her, as if to say, *what are you waiting for?*

She clumsily rolled over, her entire body blushing as she positioned herself over him.

"Higher—you need to have your cunt in my mouth, not on my neck."

Was that amusement she heard? Callie inched up a little.

He gave an exasperated huff and then grabbed her hips with both hands and positioned her the way he wanted her.

"Spread your thighs wider. Yes, just like that," he murmured, pulling her lower, until her sex rested against his mouth. He closed his lips around her engorged bud and sucked.

Callie whimpered and her hips jerked.

He gave an approving growl and released her pulsing clitoris with a wet, lewd *pop*. "Good. Now, fuck me." He spoke the words directly against her sex—which made them sound more like, "Funnfeee." The vibrations against her sensitive flesh were delicious and her hips jerked again.

"Oh, God," she whispered, as he thrust his tongue as deeply inside her as it would go, his nose, lips, and chin buried in her sensitive folds, his hot, wet, soft mouth unlike anything she had ever felt.

She rolled her hips and pressed down against him, earning an encouraging growl.

The next time, she pressed harder and his fingers dug into the flesh of her arse to hold her against him.

Her body moved without any instructions from her brain, her spine turning to jelly as she undulated, grinding her sex against his eager mouth, her mind on nothing but the pursuit of her own pleasure.

Callie forgot that the most private part of her body was in a man's mouth. She forgot that a tongue was thrusting into her body. She forgot about everything except how divine she felt.

How divine *David* made her feel.

Unfortunately, it felt too exquisite to last for long and she climaxed far too quickly, lowering all her weight onto his face and *grinding* into his hot, willing mouth as her body shook and her mind fractured into a thousand tiny pieces.

Somewhere beneath all the pleasure that had filled her to near bursting was the thought that David had managed to wreck her far more efficiently than she had him.

If Callie wanted to elicit a genuinely shattering show of emotion from this man, she would have to be far, far more creative when it came to the erotic arts.

Chapter 11

A week later David was beginning to question the wisdom of the No-Talking Bargain, as he thought of their agreement in the privacy of his mind.

At first it had seemed perfect. They ate their meals without any bothersome conversations. Calliope willingly and patiently answered his questions when they played chess. She greeted him every evening in her bed, naked and appropriately obedient and submissive. Indeed, the sex was superlative and he was certain she looked forward to their evenings as much as he did. Certainly, she derived far more orgasms than David was able to force from his own body, although he, too, had never ejaculated so often or so powerfully in his entire life. Indeed, David felt as if he'd been saving himself all these years just for *this* time with her.

All in all, their arrangement was both rewarding and required very little effort on his part.

After a few days of silence David began to realize just how much she had chattered through dinner and chess and even during sex.

Now the house was once again like a tomb.

Just the way he liked it.

She no longer came to breakfast, which meant he could enjoy his newspapers and meal in peace, not that she had been much of a bother in the morning as she, too, appeared to prefer quiet reading to yammering early in the day.

In any event, David discovered the reason for her absence in the morning was because she needed to be at her new job far earlier than Mrs. Jenkins prepared his breakfast.

After three mornings of breaking his fast alone, something extremely unusual happened to David. He became curious about where Calliope worked. Yes. David became curious about another human being—and not one he needed to kill or maim or capture to satisfy his government masters.

His curiosity, a behavioral anomaly, was cause for some introspection.

After contemplating the matter for another two days, David decided there was nothing for it but to satisfy his curiosity about her new job and see where it led.

And so here he sat across the street—in a competing tea shop, which had no famous whore on the sign and was boringly named Quality Teas and Cakes.

He had arrived first thing that morning when the tea shop opened and had commandeered the table in the shop's one bow window because it offered an excellent view of Calliope's place of work.

David had been watching her for seven hours and his curiosity was still not satisfied.

It was clear from the way Calliope's section in the shop filled up first that she was popular with her clientele, almost all of whom were male.

She smiled as she worked and appeared genuinely happy, not that David was a good judge of such things.

From what he could see from his vantage point, she was accomplished at her job—efficient and friendly—and made the tea shop a far more inviting environment than the one David was currently sitting in.

At two o'clock his entertainment was over and the sign in the window of the Duke's Crumpet turned to *closed*.

David stared at the now-dark shop and considered his afternoon, which had absolutely flown past, and what he had learned.

Something about seeing her chattering with all her customers had made him feel… disgruntled. He could not say why that was, but it—

A throat cleared behind him and David's waiter, a skinny man with an unfortunate propensity to sweat, smiled nervously at him when he looked up from his thoughts.

"I'm afraid we are closing now, sir." He glanced at the untouched tea and pastry in front of David, the fifth batch he'd ordered to justify monopolizing a prime table. "Was it not to your liking?" he worked up the nerve to ask—after *five* unconsumed orders, which told David that the man didn't really care about his answer. He just hadn't asked after the first uneaten pastry and undrunk tea because he had not wanted to jeopardize future sales.

So why had the man asked *now*—right when the shop was closing?

David felt a stab of annoyance. It was one of those pointless social interactions that left him irritable.

He decided the man's question was one of those not meant to be answered so he threw ample money onto the table, got his feet, and walked home following the same route that Calliope must walk, his thoughts on his afternoon and why he had sat there all day.

David still had no answers to his questions the following morning and was tempted to go back to the same tea shop and watch Calliope again. Perhaps if he watched her long enough, he would know what was bothering him.

But he forced himself to resist the urge and, instead, ate the meal Mrs. Jenkins had laid out for him.

Mrs. Jenkins, with whom David unfortunately did not have a No-Talking Bargain, cornered him in the breakfast room and commenced upbraiding him for not eating *yesterday's* breakfast.

"If ye don't want me food, then why am I makin' it?" she demanded, hands on her hips.

"Because I pay you to do so," David coolly responded.

She started speaking again, but he stopped listening. Instead, he continued eating while she stood there haranguing him, his thoughts sliding back to yesterday.

Last night, at dinner, he had considered asking Calliope about her job. But then he'd recalled the No-Talking Bargain and, because he hated to go back on his word, he had kept his mouth shut.

And he had not wanted to ask her during their chess hour because that was only for chess.

He definitely had not wanted to speak of it later, when he'd gone to her room.

Quite frankly, he wasn't sure when—

"—so, may I, sir?"

He looked up, not realizing that the woman was still in the room. "May you what?"

Mrs. Jenkins's lips pursed tightly, reminding him of a frog's mouth. "May I bake Miss Fowler a birthday cake, *sir*." She spoke to him slowly and loudly, as if his hearing or mental faculties were defective.

Why would David care what she baked? Suddenly, one of the words she'd used caught his attention. "Birthday?"

Mrs. Jenkins heaved a put-upon sigh. "It is Miss Fowler's birthday next week. Or didn't you just hear me just tell you all that? Do I need to repeat it again? Like I was sayin'—"

He ignored her questions, along with all the other unwanted pieces of information that flowed out of her mouth and pondered the interesting tidbit about Calliope's birthday. Birthdays were a subject he knew nothing about, other than that people seemed to like celebrating them.

David tried to imagine how such a subject might have come up between Calliope and the surly yet garrulous housekeeper and failed. Evidently, they had formed some sort of acquaintance in the short time Calliope had lived here. People were like that, he'd noticed.

"—and so then there was the—"

"Fine," he said, interrupting her blathering.

She blinked at him. "Fine, what?"

"You can make her a cake." He paused and then added, "I also want you to make dinner that night."

Now where had *that* come from?

"What night?" Mrs. Jenkins asked.

"On. Her. Birthday," David said, taking perverse enjoyment in using the same tone on her she had just used on him. Judging by the ugly flush that spread up her neck and across her cheeks, she did not like being spoken to as if she were an imbecile.

"But I don't work in the evenings," she whined.

"I will pay you to do so on that day."

"How late? Mr. Jenkins don't much care to have me out galivantin' about at night."

"Just make the meal and then leave," he said, already beginning to regret his impulse.

She chewed on that for a moment before giving a grudging nod. "Who will serve it?"

"She will."

"You want 'er to serve 'er own birthday dinner?" Mrs. Jenkins screeched, looking so scandalized that one would have thought David had asked her to strip off her clothing, climb naked onto the breakfast buffet, and get on all fours.

"*Fine. I* will do it," he all but snarled, desperately wishing he had never started the conversation.

The woman continued to stare at him.

"*What?*" he said, making the word as ominous as he knew how.

"I don't s'pose you got 'er a gift?"

"Gift?" he repeated stupidly.

She turned her face toward the ceiling and her lips moved, almost as if she were praying. When she looked down again, her expression was a long-suffering one. "Aye, a gift. Something that she would like but can't or won't get for 'erself. Something special that nobody else would get 'er."

David digested that and drew an utter and complete blank.

"Do ye want any sug—"

"No," he said firmly. "I do *not* want suggestions. I will think of something."

She grunted at that. "What shall I make for the dinner?"

"Whatever she likes," he said, turning back to the portfolio that was open beside his rapidly cooling breakfast, hoping that would indicate the conversation was over.

She lingered a moment longer, until David thought he was going to have to sack her to get rid of her.

Finally, after a few heavy sighs, she turned and shuffled from the room.

David straightened the documents and closed the portfolio once she'd gone.

A gift?

Christ. How had this gotten so complicated so fast?

He put the matter of the gift out of his mind for the moment. There was something else about the conversation he'd just had that bothered him, but he could not put his finger on it.

His inability to recognize what was bothering him was, in itself, disturbing. His mind was normally a spare, orderly place, but lately it felt like an attic that was jumbled with unwanted bits and bats.

David pondered the matter on his way to the Exchange. And he was still thinking about it several hours later, when he was supposed to be examining a prospectus for a steam shovel investment.

Now that he had been impulsive enough to organize a birthday meal, he wondered—yet again—about the No-Talking Bargain. Even David could see it would be strange to arrange a celebratory meal at which the guest of honor was not allowed to speak. Perhaps he should propose a moratorium for that evening?

The more he thought about it, the more he liked the idea. Yes. He would give her a night without the ban.

Would that satisfy the need for a gift? After all, only David could lift the no-talking restriction.

No, he concluded after considering the idea from several angles, he would have to think of something else for a gift.

"Here he is!"

The grating voice came from beside him and David looked up to find Gideon Banks, a man he had met several months earlier while trading, grinning down at him for some reason.

Beside Banks was a dark-haired man with a faintly exotic cast to his features. Although he was smiling, David instantly knew the man for what he was: dangerous.

David stood, not taking his eyes off the stranger.

Banks smirked at his companion. "Smith, this is David Remington, the man I told you about." He turned to David and clapped a hand on his shoulder. "Remington, this is Smith. Don't bother asking him his first name, he doesn't have one." Banks laughed, as if he had said something humorous.

David gritted his teeth against the unwanted physical contact, barely suppressing an urge to break the other man's hand. Instead, he shifted away from Banks until the hand dropped from his shoulder, and then inclined his head at Mr. Smith. "Pleasure to meet you," he murmured.

"Gideon told me that you expressed some interest in the South American copper venture I'm forming," Smith said.

David perked up. "Yes."

Smith kept looking at him, as if he were expecting more.

Banks laughed. "I told you he was a man of few words, Smith."

"I am sure you make up for that, Gideon."

David barked a laugh.

Banks's eyes widened in exaggerated shock. "Good Lord! It laughs!"

Smith ignored him and said to David, "I'm going to hold a dinner at my house soon and will invite the members of my syndicate as well as several others who are interested in the copper investment. It will be just an informal gathering." Smith took out a card and handed it to him.

David studied the plain rectangle of paper which indeed had only the name *Smith* on it, with an address that was, if not in Mayfair itself, close enough. It occurred to him as he stared at the card that this was the first dinner invitation he had ever received.

No doubt it would be an evening fraught with obstacles, the social equivalent of a journey through a dangerous foreign land without any guide.

"Some of the men will bring spouses or companions," Smith said. "So you can bring somebody if—"

"I say, how did things work out on your visit to Brook's?" Banks asked, interrupting Smith, who just sighed and gave the younger man a long-suffering look.

"It is no longer in business," David said.

"Brooks's is closed?" Smith asked, obviously surprised.

Banks snorted. "Not *that* Brooks's, Smith. I'm talking about the whorehouse—the one owned by Walter Brook." His deceptively angelic features took on a lascivious cast. "Brook has a whore who can do the most amazing thing with a cricket ball."

Smith gave his friend a sardonic look. "If you project from your diaphragm, you might get a bit more volume, Gideon." He gestured to a group of businessmen nearby, all of whom were gawking at Banks, eyes wide with shock. "There still might be somebody in the far back corner of the room who did not hear you."

Unoffended, Banks just laughed. "So, no luck at Brook's. Well, you could always try Tosca's or—"

"Thank you," David said. "I am not in need of a new establishment."

"Ah." Banks gave him a knowing look and nudged him in the ribs. "Set up a mistress, did you."

David ignored the question and moved out of range of Banks's elbow before turning to Smith, handing the other man one of his own cards. "I would like to come to dinner. And I will bring a companion." *A social guide*, he might have said.

"Excellent. I will send an invitation once the date is firm."

Smith dragged Banks off soon afterward and David suddenly had a burning urge to see Calliope and get his conversation about the No-Talking Bargain over with as soon as possible.

It was one o'clock, so he wouldn't have much time before the tea shop closed, but he decided that it would be best to have the discussion there as she was unlikely to want to argue at her place of work.

***

"Another one in your section, Callie," Fran, one of the other waitresses said with a scowl, glaring at Callie, as if it was her fault that people liked her service.

"Thank you, Fran," she said, forcing herself to smile at the sour woman who was not happy with Callie's popularity. Fran herself was given to snarling at the patrons and offered slow, surly service, so her section was always the last of the three to fill up.

Callie loaded her tray with her order and went back into the dining area. She glanced at her section and then almost flung the tray of pastries and scalding tea over the table she was supposed to be serving when she saw who her new *customer* was.

The three men she'd almost covered in food and boiling water laughed at her unusual clumsiness. "Careful, luv!" one of them said.

They were regulars—three young sons of wealthy bankers and merchants who were trying very hard to behave as if they were the dissipated offspring of aristocrats.

Callie disliked them, but they always left her a little something extra, which many customers did not do.

Unfortunately, one of them also liked to do a bit of groping.

"Not your usual graceful self—although just as lovely. Had a late evening, sweetheart?" the groper teased, reaching around to squeeze her bottom.

Callie smiled tightly and shifted away. "Who had the lemon tart?" she asked, even though she knew exactly who'd ordered it.

"That's Highgate," the groper said, leering up at her. "I prefer a different sort of tart, myself."

All three laughed and Callie was beginning to wish she *had* covered them in scalding tea and pastries.

Once she had extricated herself from them and nodded at another table's request for more tea, she presented herself in front of David. "What are you doing here?" she hissed. "And that question was *not* one of the five *lapses*," she added quickly.

David pulled his flat gaze from the trio of boisterous young men and looked up at her. "I have decided I no longer want the no-talking bargain to hold."

Callie goggled for a second and then said, "I'm not giving that money back."

His lips twitched, but it was too slight to call it a smile. "You can keep the money I've advanced and I will pay you the rest."

Callie had no such restraint about smiling and couldn't help the smirk that twisted her lips. "Maybe I *like* our bargain and don't want to talk?"

He sighed. "How much will it cost for you to talk?"

She laughed at his pained look. After all, any expression was cause for celebration. "Don't worry, Mr. Remington. I won't charge you for talking. So, was that all you had to tell me? Or is there another reason you've deigned to visit my place of employment?"

"Are the apple tarts here as good as the ones you make?"

She smiled, and this time it was genuine. "No. But they're better than the ones across the street. And, yes," she said, although his expression never flickered, "I saw you over there yesterday. You were rather obvious about it, you know—sitting there all day long."

"I was not trying to hide. If I had been, you never would have seen me."

Callie suspected his claim was not hyperbole because David was not the sort of man given to boasting. As she thought back to the night when she had met him—when her first impression of him had been that he was completely average looking—it was difficult to believe this was the same man. Callie now knew that David Remington was the farthest thing from ordinary.

"*Tsk, tsk,*" she teased. "No work all day yesterday and here you are again in the middle of the day. Do you really have a job, David?"

"I would like tea and an apple tart," he said, ignoring her banter.

Callie smirked and turned to go, but his voice stopped her. "One more thing. There is a dinner I need to attend in a few weeks. And I want you to accompany me."

"A dinner?"

"It is at the house of a prospective business associate. Evidently some of the others are bringing, er, companions."

She narrowed her eyes and dropped her voice to a whisper, "Whores?"

"There might be whores, although at least one man will bring his wife."

Callie hated how grateful she was that he had not said *other whores.*

She nodded. "Very well."

"How much?" he asked.

Callie stared at him hard, looking for some sign of… *something*—that he cared if she was the one who accompanied him, or if any whore would do.

As usual, she could see nothing in his flat, inscrutable gaze. "This time I don't want money."

His dark eyebrows lowered. "What do you want?"

"I will tell you tonight. At dinner." And then Callie turned and left *him* wondering for once.

It felt good.

Chapter 12

Callie had just descended the stairs and entered the foyer when there was a rap on the door. She opened it and smiled at the young lad who usually delivered their dinners.

"Good evening, Ned," she said, taking the basket from him.

"Evenin', Miss Fowler."

"If you wait, I will fetch some money."

"Naw, Mr. Remington already paid." He pulled his forelock and sauntered off.

Callie carried the heavy basket to the kitchen. They had been eating there, instead of the dining room, as the house never seemed to get warm, no matter how much coal they heaped on the fires. It was the coldest winter she had lived through and the night before she had slept in both her nightgown *and* her flannel dressing gown after David had left.

She had considered using one of her *lapses* to point out the dining room would be a lot warmer if David would only buy some heavy drapes and carpets. But she'd decided that she liked the kitchen—it felt cozier than the echoing, empty dining room—so she'd saved her precious lapse.

Callie smirked. But now she didn't need to worry about lapses anymore.

She left the basket in the kitchen and then lit a candle and went down to the cellar, which had no gaslight like the rest of the house. In addition to a bottle of wine, she brought up eight shriveled apples, which she would use to make some tarts tomorrow, which was Sunday and the one day the tea shop was closed.

When she reached the top step, she saw David had arrived and was unpacking the basket.

"I'm having wine," she said when he went to pour two glasses of ale. It felt odd to speak and for a moment she cringed.

But he just nodded and stoppered the jug and then wordlessly held out his hand for the bottle.

Opening her wine was a tiny courtesy, but it was still far more than he would have done a few weeks ago. Callie hated how much she liked it. The last thing she wanted was to develop a *tendre* for the man.

Once they were seated with plates of food, David said, "What do you want instead of money."

It was all she could do not to laugh at this proof that her words had been at the forefront of his mind all day.

Callie, too, had been thinking about what she wanted. What had begun as a whim to toy with him had taken on meaning during the past few hours as she had conceived of at least five changes she wanted to make. She had already decided that she would settle for two of them.

But David did not have to know that.

"I want five things," she said, earning a look of disbelief that was oddly satisfying.

"Five," he repeated flatly.

She nodded and took a sip of wine.

"What are they?"

"First, I want you to remove your clothing when you—"

"No."

She looked into his eyes and saw the ember of something burning behind the wall he had built between himself and the world.

"At least you gave it some thought before rejecting it," she joked.

He didn't acknowledge her sarcasm. "What are the other four?"

"It makes me feel like a whore when you just… *fuck* me and leave."

He frowned. "You are a whore."

Callie dropped her fork with a clatter. "That is unkind."

Genuine confusion creased his brow. "Former whore?"

He was so hopeless that it was almost amusing. But it still hurt. "I am a woman, David—your lover, as it happens. I now work in a tea shop, so I am also a waitress. In the past I volunteered at an orphanage and taught French and geography and a half-dozen other subjects—so I am also a teacher. And yes, for nine miserable months I was a whore. But I am no longer one."

"You sold yourself to me."

Callie clasped her hands together to keep from hurling her glass of wine at his head.

He held her gaze for a long moment before sighing and asking, "What do you want me to do after I fuck you?"

"Right now, I'd like you to fling yourself out the window."

He opened his mouth, but then closed it.

Callie suspected she should be grateful for what he did not say. Instead of continuing to chastise him, which appeared fruitless, she decided to explain, without sarcasm. "After you've come to my bed and given me pleasure, which you invariably do, and have finished taking your own, I would like to have some sort of… human connection."

"I don't know what that means."

Callie was suddenly very weary. "Just stay in my bed for a while and listen to me talk."

"I won't wish to talk when I am balls deep inside you," he said.

Callie couldn't believe that her face heated at his crass words. How was it that she could still blush? "No," she said patiently, "I do not expect any conversations while we are engaged in coitus."

His eyebrows knitted and he stared for so long she thought he was going to say *no*. But then he pleasantly surprised her and said, "Very well. What is the third thing?"

***

David took a bite of roast beef—which was not nearly so flavorful, tender, or juicy as the one Calliope had made—and masticated with some effort while he waited for her answer.

"I want to know something about you?"

"What?" he asked, immediately wary.

"Just… anything. All I know is that you like chess, you go to work at the Exchange, and you are *extremely* libidinous."

David almost smiled at that last part. "Those are the most relevant details."

"That might be so, but perhaps you could share some *irrelevant* details. Like where you are from, whether you have any family, have you always worked at the Exchange doing— what is it that you do there?"

"I buy and sell shares in companies."

"Oh. So you are not actually employed there?"

"No."

She stared at him for a long moment, clearly expecting him to say something.

David considered what she was asking for. She would not like the truth of who he really was, where he really came from, and what he had really done for the special department of the army that had employed him for decades.

Not only had he signed documentation prohibiting disclosure, but he had no interest in discussing his past.

As for the time before he joined the military? That was a period in his life he had not thought about for decades.

He had no interest in discussing *anything* except chess. Or perhaps sexual matters. He somehow doubted either of those subjects was what she had in mind.

David *did* know enough about her to recognize that militant glitter in her blue eyes. She would not give way on this as she had with the matter of him removing his clothing.

He sighed. "Fine. I will answer *some* questions."

She smiled at him, the skin at the corners of her eyes crinkling slightly. "Thank you."

David felt an odd squeezing sensation in his chest. He rubbed it and frowned down at the meat on his plate.

"Is something wrong, David?"

"I wonder if the roast beef has gone off."

"It tastes fine to me."

It must be something else—the ale, perhaps—that was causing the uncomfortable cramping sensation in his chest.

He pushed his plate away and said, "What is the fourth thing?"

She looked from his uneaten food to him. "Are you unwell? It is not like you to—"

"I am fine," he said, crossing his arms.

"You don't need to snap at me."

"I didn't."

"You just did it again."

David gritted his teeth. "Answer my question, Calliope."

Her eyebrows arched, but she merely said, "I might want to do something other than play chess every single night of the week."

"Like what?"

"Perhaps we might go somewhere—just once a week," she added hastily, no doubt seeing how little he cared for her suggestion.

"Go where?"

"There is skating now at the—"

"I don't skate."

"What about a symphony? The opera? A museum? The park? A theater?"

David chewed the inside of his cheek, considering what would be least unpleasant.

"Just try it once," she wheedled. "If you don't like it, we don't have to do it again. Besides, it's not as if it is forever. I am only here for another four weeks."

David felt another twinge in his chest. "Four weeks and two days."

She laughed. "Four weeks *and* two days."

"Fine," he said, unaccountably irritable. "I will go out. But you will have to choose the activity as I have no knowledge of such things."

"Astounding," she said.

He squinted at her. Was she twitting him?

She dropped her gaze and hurriedly said, "So, the fifth thing is—"

"No. That is enough. More than enough."

Rather than argue, as he had expected, she smiled. "Very well. I accept your proposal to accompany you to your business dinner."

Thank Christ. David would have paid five pounds rather than endure such a grilling again.

"Don't you like your dinner?" she asked.

"No," he said, absently rubbing his chest. "You should not eat it, either. I think something is wrong with it."

"It tastes fine to me," she said, taking a bite, and smiling as she chewed.

***

David was balls deep inside Calliope when he first noticed the blood. He stiffened—for a fraction of a second believing he had hurt her somehow—but then realized it was her menstrual blood.

"Is something wrong?" she asked.

David stared in rapt fascination at his glistening red shaft.

"David?"

"Nothing is wrong." He slid back in, concentrating on the sensation—was it different? He didn't think so.

She pushed up onto her elbows and looked down to see what had attracted his attention.

"Oh no! I'm terribly sorry," she said, trying to crab-walk away from him on her hands and heels.

He caught her by the hips and held her easily in place.

"What are you doing?" she demanded when he hilted himself again.

Was that a serious question?

David decided to answer it. "I'm fucking you," he said, pulling out slowly, his bloody shaft causing his already tight ballocks to throb.

"You should stop," she said, agitation clear in her voice.

He paused. "Why? Does it hurt?"

She looked astounded by the question. "No, it doesn't hurt, but it's—it's unholy—"

"Unholy?" he repeated, diverted by her choice of word.

"You're smiling! Well, not a smile. More of a smirk—but very, very faint."

"Did you think I was incapable?"

"I did, actually."

He snorted.

"And *laughing*," she murmured. "Will wonders never cease?"

He ignored her teasing, staring down at where they were joined, sliding in and out of her tight slick cunt, entranced. "Is it uncomfortable?"

"No," she admitted, chewing her lower lip and obviously discomposed. "But that's not—"

"Does it feel different?"

"No." She hesitated. "Yes." She scowled. "I don't know! But that's not the point!"

"What is the point?" he asked, thrusting back in.

"It's not natural. And it is… disgusting."

"I am not disgusted," he said, and then glanced up at her. "I don't want to stop." He couldn't keep his gaze from where they were joined. "I like it."

"Why does that not surprise me?" she muttered. "Mrs. Jenkins will be horrified."

"How will she kno—oh, she takes the laundry." He shrugged. "So throw the sheets away," he said, fucking her slowly, bottoming out each time and withdrawing almost all the way so he could admire his slick red cock.

"The sheets are expensive! I can't do that."

"Then I will pay her more to launder them," he said, already bored with the subject.

"Is that your answer to every problem: money?"

David ignored the question.

The overhead gas lamp was on, but he wanted *more* light. Somehow, he suspected that she would object if he paused to turn on the gas lamps beside the bed.

Instead, he lifted her knees until they were bracketing her lush tits and then spread her thighs wide and angled her so that he could see what he was doing.

"I… can… barely… breathe," she huffed a word between each thrust.

David shifted, so that his shaft ground against her clitoris each time he hilted himself.

She instantly stopped complaining about her inability to breathe and moaned. "Yesssss." Her back arching off the bed after a particularly deep thrust. "Yes, yes… right… *there*."

David's hips drummed with brutal precision, filling the room with her grunts and the sound of wet fucking. He wished he could remain inside her all night long and never come, but his balls were already drawing up tight to his body. He would not last long.

A moment later she was convulsing around him, her cunt as tight as a vise around his shaft. He did not stop thrusting as he usually did, but fucked her through her orgasm, his own not long behind.

His eyes fluttered shut when he reached his climax but he forced them back open, raw, primitive lust surging through him as he pumped her full of his spend, ejaculating so hard that he had to bite his lip to keep from moaning.

The sight of her blood-smeared slit stuffed full of his cock was the most sexually arousing sight David had ever seen. His balls ached from how hard he had just come, but his cock, rather than softening, remained as hard as iron.

Astounding!

David wanted to fuck her again. And again.

***

Callie rinsed the cloth until the water no longer ran pink. She considered climbing into the tub and turning on the noisy shower bath, but David was in the bedroom, and she had been the one to demand a half-hour of conversation.

Not that she could think of anything to say at the moment. She was still rattled by the past hour.

He had never softened after his first climax.

Instead of pulling out, he had taken her again—far longer and slower the second time, his expression rapt as he'd stared at where they were joined.

Callie had heard of men who liked *blood sport*, but they were rare and she had never been with one.

A far more common male reaction when confronted with a woman on her menses was anger or disgust. Indeed, she'd heard of patrons who'd become violent and struck a whore who'd taken a client without realizing they were about to begin their courses.

Lots of women—Callie was one of them—were not regular enough to predict their cycles. She had been fortunate up until now. Usually, she experienced cramping that let her know her time was near.

Perhaps she had not noticed the signs this month because of all the other emotionally draining events in her life.

David's reaction had been both unnerving and yet, at the same time, strangely liberating.

Callie had often thought there was something wrong with the way society viewed a woman's menses.

On the one hand, there was a cult of motherhood that believed a woman's main purpose–and duty—was to bear children.

On the other hand, the entire process was derided as unclean and considered shameful and something to be hidden.

Callie rinsed the cloth one last time and then inspected herself in the looking glass to ensure she was as respectable-looking as a naked female could look.

When she returned to the bedroom David was lying just where he'd been when she left him, staring at the ceiling, his cock—astoundingly—still hard.

"This cannot be normal," she said, without thinking first.

But he just glanced down at his erection and then at her and shrugged.

Callie knelt beside him and reached for his blood-smeared rod. His body went stiff—all of it—when she took him into her hand and wiped away the evidence of the past hour. He was just as hard when she was finished as he'd been when she'd begun.

There was obviously something wrong with this man. More than a few things, probably.

***

David stared at the ceiling, waiting for the barrage of questions to begin once Calliope had returned from the bathroom.

She looked up at his face and bit her lip as she finished wiping his prick.

"What is it?" he asked.

She pointed to a spot on her naked chest, just below the base of her throat, and said, "You have some, er, blood on your shirt.

He was amused by how nervous her own menses appeared to make her. "So?"

"Don't you want to take it off and—"

"No." He jerked his chin at the cloth in her hand. "Get rid of that and come back here. Your half-hour begins now."

Callie pulled a face at him, dropped the cloth onto the floor with a wet *splat*, and laid down alongside him, propping her head on her hand. "Why do you hate talking so much?"

"Why do you like it so much?" he countered.

"Remember that *you* were the one who asked me to start talking again, David. You were even willing to pay me."

He sighed, annoyed that she was correct. "Get on with it."

"So, where are you from?"

"England."

She laughed and the sour meat he'd eaten earlier roiled in his belly. He rubbed his chest absently.

"What city or town?"

"Just in the country—not in any town."

"You grew up in a rural area? That's interesting," she said.

He grunted.

"Don't you want to know why I think that is interesting?"

"I'm sure you'll tell me."

She laughed again.

Again, his belly clenched. Could his body be responding to her somehow? Obviously, he became erect for her, but this other reaction was something different. And not welcome.

"I think it is interesting because I have never actually spent any time at all in the country."

David had nothing to say to that.

"Do you have any family?"

"No."

"Did you grow up an orphan?"

He opened his mouth to lie, but then could not make himself do it. He hated lying. Which is why he usually avoided conversations like this one.

"Yes."

"What do you—"

"Enough."

She jolted at his harsh tone. "Very well. What do you want to talk about?"

Nothing, he almost answered, but then realized that would be a lie, too. There was one subject that he had thought about more than once recently. "What was it like being a whore?"

· She rolled over and swung her feet off the bed. "You can leave," she said, her back to him as she strode into the dressing room.

David sat up. "But there are another sixteen minutes remaining."

"I don't have any other questions."

David pondered her reaction rather than getting up and leaving—which is what he had wanted to do for the last fourteen minutes—and decided he must have insulted her, but he could not ascertain why.

He was still pondering the matter when she returned wearing a dressing gown.

"You're still here."

He ignored her comment; obviously he was still there. "Tell me why that question angered you."

She put her hands on her hips. "Why should I?"

"Because I am curious." And curiosity was not something he felt often. Except she seemed to bring it out of him.

"Ah. Curious, eh? Well, now you can experience what it is like when another person *won't* satisfy your curiosity."

"Are you saying you won't answer me?"

"Yes."

David rubbed his temple. Soon he would have a headache; he could feel the signs.

"I'm tired, David."

That was direct enough for even him to understand.

He tucked away his now soft cock and buttoned his trousers before standing and striding toward the door. He set his hand on the handle but didn't turn it. Something—he had no idea what—did not feel finished. Or right. Or maybe finished right.

But he had no idea what, if anything, to say.

"Please turn off the light when you leave," she said.

He hesitated only a few seconds before doing as she bade him.

Back in his room—which was cold and dark as he never bothered to have a fire—he sat down on the bed, which was the only piece of furniture other than one nightstand, but did not take off his clothing.

Instead, he sat in the darkness and pondered what was missing—or wrong—and why the ache in his chest had only grown worse as the evening had progressed.

Chapter 13

On Sunday, Callie had the kitchen to herself all day as Mrs. Jenkins had the day off.

She slept late and by the time she wandered down to the kitchen it was almost eleven. David was not lured down by the smell of eggs, ham, and toast she cooked, so she assumed he had left early to do whatever it was that he did when he wasn't trading shares.

With an entire day to herself, she decided to cook a traditional Sunday dinner like the kind she'd always made for her and her father. She had purchased a small roast, potatoes, and leeks on her way home from the tea shop yesterday as well as a jar of Devon cream, which was currently sitting outside to stay cool.

She started the bread rising just after one o'clock.

Once the potatoes were peeled and the tarts were already baked and cooling, she pulled out the old copper tub she'd found tucked away in the enormous still room and spent several hours reading a ridiculously melodramatic gothic novel while heating the water for the tub the way she had done for most of her life: one bucket at a time.

It was just before five when she poured the second-to-last canister of water into the tub.

She had fetched several towels earlier and hung them off the big chrome bars on the sides of the massive cookstove, which threw off more heat than the tiny thing Callie had grown up using.

When everything was ready, she stripped down right there in the kitchen and climbed into steaming hot bliss.

Something about lounging in a tub was special. The shower bath, as nice as it was, was also a race against time. There were only about seven minutes of water before the tank ran out and the water became frigid.

Callie washed her hair first, rinsing it clean with the canister of hot water she'd reserved for that purpose and then reclining and closing her eyes, mentally calculating what she needed to do in the two hours or so before dinner.

The kitchen was so warm and the bath water had gone from being too hot to being just perfect.

And she drifted off to sleep.

****

The delicious smell led David to the kitchen, but he froze in the doorway at the sight that met his eyes.

Not just tarts cooling on the counter, but Calliope bathing in an old tub he had never seen before. She was asleep, her full pink lips parted, chin just above the water, full breasts floating like twin moons.

David instantly got hard. He wanted to take her then and there. Spread her legs over the lip of the tub and bury himself to his balls.

But he had been the one to set the schedule and no part of it had included pre-nine o'clock fucks in the kitchen, so he restrained his urge. Barely.

The smell of what was cooking in the oven had his mouth furiously watering and he had to keep swallowing. He closed the door silently to keep the heat in the kitchen and leaned back against it, his gaze riveted to her face.

Looking at her mouth reminded him of last night and the way she had sucked him. His already hard cock throbbed. If he hadn't already known he was defective and deviant in every way a man could be broken and twisted it might have bothered him how much he had liked the sight of her blood on his prick.

Instead of feeling any shame, he had woken up this morning as hard as a plank and proceeded to stroke himself off to the erotic, taboo memory.

David had been in the army for most of his life and although he had never become friends with anyone, time spent in a barracks meant that he had often heard men talking to each other about women. Boasting, mainly, but also discussing their likes and dislikes and women's bodies and what they preferred.

Like most things that came out of people's mouths the comments were either foolish, thoughtless, cruel, or all three. He had overheard more than he'd ever wanted about their sexual exploits. He knew from all their blather that fucking a woman on her menses would have been a nightmare for most men.

He had not just liked it. He had *loved* it.

David knew he would never *fit* anywhere. Would never have a wife, children, a family, friends, or any of those things that were so important to everyone else. But there was one way he thought he was more fortunate than most people: he liked what he liked without shame or concern. Right now, he liked looking at a naked woman asleep in a tub. Something about watching Calliope without her knowledge or permission made him like it even more.

He unbuttoned his trousers and pulled out his rock-hard cock. He could have come with only a few strokes, but he wanted it to last and last and so he worked himself to the edge and then stopped.

And he then did it again and again.

Each time he deprived himself of an orgasm the discomfort in his balls increased, until he was sweating with the effort of denial, his prick leaking like a tap and his sac a tight pouch drawn up close to his body.

He thought he'd been quiet—the effort leaving the inside of his cheek shredded—but Calliope's eyes flickered open. He watched confusion and the remnants of sleep battle awareness. And then her eyes turned to him. Her body stiffened, the action lifting her breasts further out of the water, the peaked tips thrusting high. Her blue eyes lowered to his hand, which was moving at a lazy, torturous pace.

"Come here," she said after a moment, one of the arms that had been lying on the rim of the tub slipping into the water and settling between her thighs. Her eyelids fluttered as her knees lifted above the water. "Closer," she ordered quietly, pointing to a spot near her head.

His hand fumbled as he realized what she meant and he closed the distance until he stood over her, the view of her body superlative.

David had already been primed to come, but the sight of her masturbating was enough to blacken his vision with need. Her slim fingers moved deftly between her spread thighs, her other hand pulling and pinching her nipples, and her mouth falling open as her back arched, pushing her breasts up higher as she stared at him. "Do it," she hissed. 'I want you to—

David's normal iron control snapped like a twig and the first jet of his spend landed on her chin and cheek; the next spattered her breasts. The sight was so erotic it made his knees weak as he painted her flushed torso and jiggling tits with splash after splash of hot spunk.

She suddenly cried out, body convulsing. David could see her fingers in her slit, they were no longer moving, but he knew she'd be keeping pressure on the base of her little bud, just the way she liked it, the subtle action drawing out her climax.

Had he thought last night was the most arousing sight he had ever seen?

He'd been wrong.

There were rapidly becoming too many erotic memories to count.

***

Carrying a heavy pastry box, Callie made several stops on her way home from the tea shop.

The first stop was at the butchers, where she bought yet another roast, even though it was an extravagance. But it was her birthday today and she had enjoyed the roast she'd cooked last Sunday so much that she decided to treat herself to a birthday dinner, even though she would need to cook it herself.

Thinking about Sunday made her recall the episode *before* the meal. Who would have guessed that mutual masturbation could be so… arousing?

Perhaps she might orchestrate something similar tonight as another birthday treat for herself?

Smirking at the thought Callie let herself into the house and then paused in the foyer, frowning. It smelled like somebody was already cooking a roast.

By the time she was outside the kitchen door, another smell teased at her nostrils. Somebody was baking a cake.

"Mrs. Jenkins!" she said, stopping in the doorway and staring.

The older woman looked up from large, lopsided cake she was icing and pulled a frustrated face. "You weren't to see this yet," she grumbled, turning back to her job.

"What is that for?" she asked, although she could guess.

Mrs. Jenkins snorted. "Himself said I could make you a cake. And then he ordered me to make you a birthday dinner, too." She cut Callie sharp look. "I won't be servin' it."

Callie laughed. "A birthday dinner!"

"Aye." Her eyes dropped to all the packages Callie was carrying and she frowned. "Bought yer own dinner, eh? Told 'im that 'ee should tell you I was cookin'. Go on and put it outside and it will keep," she directed, pausing her work to open the pastry box Callie had set on the table. Her face fell when she saw the fancy cake inside. "That's nicer than mine."

"Oh, but it won't be nearly as good. I much prefer your cake," Callie assured her, touched by the woman's efforts. "In fact, why don't you take this one home to your family?"

"I couldn't—"

"I insist. Your delicious cake is the one I want on my birthday."

"Well, I suppose I could. But only if yer sure," Mrs. Jenkins said, staring covetously at the beautiful confection from the Duke's Crumpet. It was an expensive cake, but the owner offered her employes any items that didn't sell at half the price, and so Callie had been unable to resist.

"I am sure," she said. "Take it with my blessing."

The older woman quickly took the box and tucked it away in one of the string shopping bags she always brought with her. She looked at Callie and made a shooing gesture. "Go on and rest. Himself will serve dinner."

"What?"

Mrs. Jenkins's wrinkled face twisted into something between a grin and a smirk. "Aye. 'Ee's already been in 'ere lookin' for cutlery and whatnot." She snorted. "Just like Mr. Jenkins, couldn't find 'is arse with both 'ands without my 'elp."

Callie briefly enjoyed the image of David searching for his own arse with Mrs. Jenkins's assistance and laughed.

She left the other woman to her work and went in search of David.

A quick peek into the dining room showed that he had indeed set the table, although the forks were on the wrong side.

Callie left it as it was and found David in the bookless library, sitting at the desk and reading, something she had not seen him do before.

He glanced up at the sound of the door opening and hastily put the book into one of the drawers and stood.

"Thank you for the dinner and cake," she said, nonplussed by the courtesy. He had never stood before when she'd entered the room. Was this something special for her birthday?

"I will serve the meal," he said abruptly, ignoring her thanks.

"Mrs. Jenkins said you would. That is kind of you."

He shrugged.

"What was that book you were reading?"

He stared at her for a long moment, but then bent, opened the drawer, and handed her the book. It was an English copy of the *Traite de Lausanne*, one of the earliest books describing chess openings. Her father had owned a copy in French, along with numerous other chess books that were far more modern and useful.

Callie looked up and smiled. "Learn anything interesting?"

"I only bought it today." He said stiffly, and then cleared his throat. "The schedule for tonight will be slightly different."

"Oh?"

"As it is your birthday, I thought we could eat and after dinner you could have your gift. And then you could decide what to do for the rest of the evening." He hesitated and then added—almost grudgingly, "We do not need to play chess. Unless you want to."

Callie was speechless.

"Mrs. Jenkins told me—at some length—about birthday traditions," he said dryly.

"What do you usually do on your birthday?"

"Nothing."

Why did that not surprise her? "When is your birthday?"

His jaw flexed. "I don't know."

"You don't know when your birthday is?"

He made an exasperated sound and strode toward the door. "Dinner will be served at the usual time, but in the dining room rather than the kitchen. Only for tonight. That was Mrs. Jenkins's idea, as well," he said, and then opened the door and left.

Callie stared. David didn't know his own birthday?

***

Mrs. Jenkins was an excellent cook and the meal was delicious.

David obviously thought so as well since he was on his third plate. How a man who was so muscular and lean could eat so much was a mystery to Callie.

Callie finished eating her single portion long before him but, for some reason, she enjoyed watching him eat. He had tidy manners, for all that he put so much food away. He systematically demolished the contents of his plate, his dexterous hands cutting small pieces of roast and adding a piece of roasted parsnip to every bite.

His hands were one of his nicest features. Not that she'd ever seen anything else except for his face and cock. Those were nice, too, but she pondered the possibility of getting him to take his clothing off tonight, given that he was being so generous for her birthday.

She leaned across the table and squinted as she suddenly noticed something. "Are your knuckles swollen?"

He shrugged and took a drink of the ale he preferred, not that he ever had more than a glass with his meal.

Callie gave an exasperated huff and held out her hand. "Let me see."

His chewing froze and his velvety brown eyebrows descended.

She wiggled her fingers. "You have to do it because it is my birthday."

He sighed but extended his hand.

Callie was amused that her argument had worked on him. Who knew a birthday could be so powerful? Her humor drained away quickly when she examined his hand. It wasn't just bruised, it was swollen and there were also scrapes—some quite deep—that were still fresh enough to be oozing blood.

She glanced at his other hand and saw it was in the same condition.

"What happened?"

He pulled his hand back and put another bite of food in his mouth.

"Have you been… fighting?" she asked.

He finished chewing and swallowed. "Don't you have any jewelry other than that?"

Callie glanced down at *that* even though she knew what the simple gold chain and cross looked like because it was the only part of her old life she'd clung to.

"Why? What is wrong with it?" she demanded, fingering the delicate cross and glaring up at him.

"Nothing. But it is the only thing you wear."

"Strangely enough, whoring does not require an extensive jewelry collection."

He gave one of his grunts of assent, not registering her sarcasm. Yes, she was certainly becoming an expert on translating his wide variety of non-verbal responses. Callie had noticed that sarcasm, teasing, and humor were not things he had much appreciation for.

"You will need a gown and something nicer than that necklace to wear to this dinner. The men are wealthy and their wives and wh—companions will likely be well-dressed."

She didn't miss his near use of the word *whore*. It impressed her that he'd even bothered to catch the slip, especially as she believed that he honestly did not comprehend why the word offended her.

"If you don't like my clothing and jewelry and want me to wear something different then you will have to buy it," she retorted.

His own clothing was expensively but plainly tailored, lacking the dash and style that made garments fashionable. His hair was simply cut and he wore no jewelry other than a plain gold chain and a watch that was functional rather than ornamental.

"I will give you money to buy what you need," he said, and then stood and removed their plates to the sideboard, where the cake waited.

David brought it to the table and then carefully cut an *enormous* piece.

"You should take that for yourself," Callie hastily said. Before he could cut another monster, she added, "I want a piece that is a third the size."

Without any comment, he cut the second piece far smaller.

Once he was seated and had commenced eating, she recalled the conversation they'd been having. "How much?"

He swallowed, wiped him mouth with his napkin, and said, "How much what?"

"How much money will you give me for clothing?"

"How much will a new gown and some better jewels cost?"

"It depends on how nice you want me to look."

His gaze roamed over her as he considered her statement, the small furrow of concentration between his eyes amusing her. He might be strange, but she had never known a man—not even her father—who focused on her so completely. True, he often ignored her comments and questions, but when he did listen, he listened with his entire being.

"I will accompany you so that I can choose what is necessary," he finally said.

She snorted. "You don't trust my taste?"

He ignored her question and lifted another piece of cake into his mouth.

"When is this meal to take place?"

"It is four days hence."

"That doesn't leave much time for clothes shopping. Especially if I need to get the garment altered. One of those days is a Sunday, when the shops will be closed. And I work every day until three-thirty."

He chewed and swallowed before saying. "You will provide me with a garment so I can buy the correct size. It should not take too long to go in for a fitting so you can get any necessary alterations."

He was probably right. Still…

"Have you ever bought women's clothing before?"

"No. But I purchase my own clothing."

She raised her eyebrows.

"What? It cannot be so different."

Callie wanted to argue—she would have heartily enjoyed a shopping trip, something she'd not had in over a year—but she was a sweaty mess after a day's work and would need to go home to clean up and change her clothing before she'd feel comfortable shopping. That would mean even less than an hour-and-a-half.

She would have to leave it up to him.

Callie enjoyed the idea of David attempting to navigate the complex world of women's dress boutiques. It was simply too entertaining. It was unfortunate she would not be there to see it.

She nodded. "Very well. Blue is my favorite color."

He gave her a blank look as he finished the last bite of cake and then pulled out his watch. "You have seven minutes to finish your birthday cake and then I will take you to see your gift."

"I thought I was in charge of tonight's schedule?" Callie laughed at the sudden look of chagrin that flickered across his face and pushed her plate away. "I am too full to eat this right now. Where is my gift?"

"In the cellar," he said, coming around the table to pull out her chair.

Callie didn't know what shocked her more, the chivalrous gesture or the information that whatever he'd bought her was in the cellar.

Chapter 14

Callie's jaw almost came unhinged as she stared at the bleeding bruised man on his knees. "David! What is this?" she shrieked.

He blinked at her question, obviously perplexed. "It is John Carlton."

"I *know who* it is. I just meant—Good God! What is he doing here?"

"This is your gift," David said, looking from Callie to Carlton and back. A faint furrow formed between his eyes. "Don't you like it?"

She looked into Carlton's pleading eyes and gave a hysterical laugh. His mouth was stuffed with something and then bound with a piece of cloth to keep him from speaking. And there was a telling wet stain on the front of his trousers.

"What in the world am I supposed to do with him?"

David turned and took something off the rickety table that was piled with odds and ends. He held out his hand. "Here."

She stared at the riding crop and recoiled.

"Take it," he said.

She didn't realize she was shaking until she extended her hand. He laid the crop in her palm but it slid through her fingers and fell to the floor.

David crouched down, picked it up, and held it out again. His lips slowly turned down at the corners when she didn't take it. "You don't want to punish him for what he did to you?"

"P-punish him?"

"Whip him bloody, the way he beat you."

Her jaw sagged. "I—I can't do that!"

"Why not?"

"I just—I just could never strike anyone."

He looked nonplussed by her admission. After a moment, he said, "Do you want me to do it for you?"

She turned back to Carlton, the man who regularly featured in her nightmares.

He looked pitiful *now*, but he had been leering and jeering and cruel when he had bound, beaten, and brutally sodomized her. Callie had been in so much pain that she had not been able to walk for three days.

"Calliope?" David said. "Do you want me to punish him for you?"

"Yes." The word slipped out of her mouth without her even realizing it. "I mean—"

But David was no longer listening. He tossed the whip onto the table and drew a knife from somewhere on his person.

"You aren't going to kill him!"

He winced at her shriek. "No," he said and then bent and with three deft flicks cut the ropes on Carlton's bound hands and feet and the rag gagging him.

Carlton immediately started babbling. "Oh, God! Thank you! I knew you'd see reason."

"Get up," David said.

Carlton struggled to stand, but his legs must have fallen asleep while he'd been kneeling.

"How long has he been down here?" Callie asked, suddenly noticing the stench in the room.

"He snatched me just outside my business," Carlton said in a whiny tone. "I don't know how long I've been down here. It was daylight when—"

David grabbed him by the arm and, even though the other man was at least three stone heavier, he jerked him to his feet.

"Are you letting him go?" Callie asked, disgusted by the disappointment that stabbed at her.

"No. I only bound him for you," David said, stepping away from Carlton, who was standing, if a bit unsteadily.

David went back to the table and pulled off his four-in-hand and then unbuttoned his frock coat and waistcoat and shrugged out of both before draping them over the back of the table's only chair.

Carlton's expression turned from pleading to ugly with shocking rapidity. He rolled his shoulders, all signs of the puling pathetic victim of only moments before gone. He grinned viciously as he shook out his arms and stretched his legs.

"You want to fight, do you? Think you can take me?" He laughed, limbering up, his movements dauntingly supple for a man who'd just been tied hand and foot. "I suppose you have a few more knives on your person—maybe a pistol? Why don't I get the same benefit?"

David pulled knives—four of them—and a pistol from various places on his person and set them all beside the whip.

"I'm supposed to trust that's all of them?" Carlton demanded.

David ignored him and pulled out his pocket watch with one hand while unclasping the chain with the other. He glanced at the face. "You have exactly one minute before we start."

Carlton hooted. "I don't need a minute," he snarled, bouncing up and down on the balls of his feet and jabbing the air with worrying speed. "I've won more than a few championships in my day. Heavy weight." He cast a derisive gaze over David. "I'd say you're pushing medium—maybe even light."

David handed Callie the watch. "Tell us when it is time," he said, and then reached behind his neck and pulled his shirt over his head.

Callie's jaw dropped and Carlton paused his bouncing and jabbing to stare.

As she had suspected, there wasn't an ounce of fat on his body and his exquisitely defined muscles flexed beneath skin that had once been the same pale shade as his face but was now a horrifying patchwork of red slashes and shiny pink circles that looked like dozens and dozens of healed burns.

And he had no nipples.

"Jesus Fuck!" Carlton took a step back and stumbled, tripping over his own feet in his haste to get away. "What the hell happened to you?" he demanded, staring in horrified shock.

David laid his shirt over the rest of his clothing and turned to Callie. "What time is it?"

"Ten more seconds," Callie said in a hoarse voice, unable to look away from his mutilated torso.

Carlton shook himself out of his fugue. "I'm going to wipe the floor with you, you freak." He pulled his torn shirt over his head, revealing the thick, muscular torso that made Callie's gorge rise.

Carlton slapped his ridged, flat abdomen with both hands. "Take a look at a real man, you uppity bitch!" His eyes glittered with malicious promise and he threw his balled up shirt at her. "When I'm done with him, I'm going to bend you over that bench, shove my cock into your hole, and fuck your arse so hard you'll not shit right for—"

"It is time," Callie said.

The words were barely out of her mouth when David moved in a blur and Carlton flew backwards and slammed into the shelving on the far wall, old bottles and jars raining down on him like a shower of glass.

Callie looked from the fallen man to David, who stood as still as a statue, his breathing as even as ever.

Carlton shook his head, wincing at all the glass, his eyes unfocused as he glared up at David. "Aye, yer fast, I'll grant ye."

"Get up," David ordered stepping back to give Carlton room.

Carlton shoved unsteadily to his feet, shaking his head again. "You—you suckered me. I wasn't—"

This time it was Carlton who moved like a flash. If it had been Callie he'd attacked, she would have been unconscious or worse, but David was ready. Rather than punch the other man, David stepped toward him as he came charging and slid an arm around his neck, somehow managing to flip him over, slamming Carlton flat on his back.

It must have knocked the air from his lungs because his eyes went wide with terror and his mouth opened and closed like a fish out of water.

David calmly turned away from him and went to the table that held all the weapons. When he returned, he held the whip.

He kicked Carlton's boot. "Get up."

Carlton skittered backward like a crab, making a gasping sound as he finally drew in some air.

"Up." David kicked his leg again and the other man howled.

"Awright! Awright!" Carlton pushed slowly to his feet, clinging to the remains of the shelving behind him to stand.

David turned to Callie. "Where did he whip you?"

Callie stared from Carlton to David. Things had moved so *fast*. One moment Carlton had been so arrogant, so sure, so—

"Calliope!" David barked. "Where?"

"B-back—on my back and bottom and shoulders," she stammered. "M-mostly my bottom." He'd whipped her so badly that she'd bled for days and still had scars.

David turned to Carlton. "You can turn and take your whipping like a man or I can make you turn."

Carlton opened his mouth but blanched as he stared at David.

And then he slowly turned.

David closed the distance without hesitation and brought down his arm.

When Carlton screamed and tried to run David kicked his feet out from under him and then whipped him again as he crawled over broken glass.

David's arm rose and fell, the sound of leather on flesh punctuated by screams. Over and over, until Carlton was sobbing.

Finally, David paused, stood up straight, and shoved his hair off his forehead, the action making muscles all over his scarred torso flex and contract. "Take off your trousers," he said, his voice flat and calm.

Carlton squirmed until he was on his back, his hands held out in front of him. "Please! Have mercy! You're out of your bloody—Argh!" He screamed when the whip came down across his bare belly.

David hooked a hand under the waistband of Carlton's trousers and yanked so hard that buttons flew and fabric tore.

"Bloody hell!" Carlton yelled, grabbing for his pants.

But David whipped Carlton's hands and the man shrieked again and yanked them away, his trousers dragging to his knees as he tried to crawl away.

"Now remove your drawers," David said.

"Please," Carlton cried piteously. "Ain't this enough? Can't you show mercy?"

"Did you ask for mercy, Calliope?" David asked.

Memories of that night rose up inside her like bile. "Yes," she whispered.

David raised his arm. "Drawers down, now, or I'll whip your face bloody."

"Stop!" Carlton screamed, covering his face. "I'll take 'em off!"

"Do it. Now."

His hands fumbled as he shoved the drawers down a few inches.

"Turn over," David ordered.

Tears running down his cheeks, Carlton obeyed.

"David?" Callie said.

"Yes?"

"You don't have to do this. He's—he's learned his lesson."

David's eyebrows arched high, his dark eyes widening. It was the most emotion he had ever exhibited. "Did you not hear what he just threatened to do to you only a few minutes ago?"

"Yes! Yes, I heard. But—I—he didn't—I—" Callie broke off, no words left.

His mouth compressed into a straight line and he turned away from her.

Carlton had crawled to a corner while they'd talked and was cowering, hunched over.

"Please," he begged when David turned to him.

"Calliope has punished you enough," David said in a cool, detached voice. "But I have not. Turn onto your belly like the cur you are."

But Carlton merely sobbed and babbled, drawing his body more tightly into a ball.

David brought his arm down hard, the whip landing on Carlton's forearms.

Carlton screamed.

And David's arm rose again.

And again.

And again.

And again.

****

David handed the hansom driver four times his normal fare. "Drop him off behind Carlton's—you know the brothel?"

The driver was wide eyed and trembling as he looked from Carlton's bloody body to David's face and nodded. "Aye, aye. I know it."

"Why are you staring?" David asked. "Are you thinking about sending the police here?"

"No! I wouldn't do that! Honest I wouldn't." The man pointed a shaking finger at David's forehead. "Ye—ye've some blood."

David grunted and turned around, leaving the man staring after him. He entered the house through the servant door and locked it behind him. When he turned, he saw Calliope standing in the doorway that led from the cellar to the kitchen.

She was as pale as snow and there was a slight tremor in her hands as she held out his pistol. "Here. The rest are over there." She gestured to where his clothing hung over a chairback and his knives and whip were in a pile on the table where they usually ate their dinner.

David got dressed and once he'd tucked away all his weapons he turned to her.

She had not moved and was still wide-eyed.

"Are you scared?" he asked, needing some help reading her expression.

She swallowed and nodded.

"Of me?"

"A—a little."

"I would never hurt you," David said, only realizing when he said the words that they were true.

How… astonishing.

She gave a shaky nod. "I know."

He studied her for a moment. It was her birthday and he knew those days were special to most people. He had already given her a gift. What else was expected?

"You did not like the gift?"

She gave a strange sounding laugh, her face a study in emotions he could not decipher. "I should not have liked it," she said. "But I did—and that is what scares me. Because I liked it. A lot." Her tone was awed and confused and something else. Her eyes rose to his and he noticed her pupils were very large. "It—it was a good gift, David."

David was bemused by the relief he felt at her words. "Are you too scared to play chess?"

Her jaw dropped, and she laughed.

And she kept laughing.

Why was she laughing? Had he done something amusing?

Why were people so inexplicable?

***

Callie had to struggle to stop laughing, even though nothing was funny.

David stood across from her, looking like a confused, overgrown, blood-spattered boy.

"You're upset?" he finally said.

She nodded. "But that is not all I am."

"What else are you?"

Callie was so horrified by her reaction that she couldn't bear to say the words out loud.

Instead, she stepped closer to him, until they were almost touching and took his wrist with one hand and lifted her skirts

183

and petticoats with the other, glad she'd not opted for a bustle tonight.

When she placed his hand over her bare mound his nostrils flared and his pupils expanded.

"Why did it get me wet to see you beat another man?" she whispered.

He curled his middle finger and lightly strummed around her clitoris, his touch so confident and possessive that a brutal bolt of desire almost drove her to her knees.

With another of his sudden movements he dropped into a crouch.

"Hold up your skirts," he ordered.

Once she'd taken them with both hands he parted her lower lips with his thumbs and closed his lips over her engorged bud.

She moaned and shifted the gown so she could see him better.

His dark eyes stared up into hers as he sucked her toward an orgasm so fast that it made her dizzy.

Callie cried out as a wave of bliss crashed over her, surrendering to pure sensation.

The aftershocks of her climax were still rolling through her body when David suddenly stood, turned her around, and then bent her over the table. His chest covered her back and he slowly slid his thick cock into her convulsing flesh, stretching and filling her, drawing out her orgasm.

He grabbed a fistful of hair and yanked her head back, arching her neck painfully. "You like violence, Calliope," he muttered in her ear, his hips beginning to flex, fucking into her the way a pugilist threw punches: hard, fast, and savage. "It made you wet to watch me beat a man half to death."

Callie whimpered when he leaned forward and caught her ear with sharp teeth, biting her hard enough to make her cry out.

"Just think how wet your tight pussy would be if you had allowed me to do what I wanted to do." He punctuated his words with a sharp thrust.

"Wha—what was that?"

"I wanted to kill him for what he did to you," he hissed.

God help her, the words sent a shudder of desire straight to her sex.

"Perhaps I should have fucked you in front of him first?"

She squeezed her eyes shut at his utterly shocking suggestion, heat flooding her face even though he couldn't see her.

"I think you would like to be fucked in front of other men. Perhaps you would enjoy dropping to your knees and sucking my cock. After you serviced me, I would offer to let them use you."

Callie groaned.

"You would like that because you enjoy humiliation. But you already know that about yourself, don't you Calliope?"

He drove painfully deep and kept her pinned and full, his fist tightening in her hair. "Answer me."

"Yes," she gasped.

"Yes, what?"

"Yes, I—I like it when you humiliate me."

He gave a grunt of satisfaction, released her hair, and then spread her cheeks, smoothing the taut, wet skin that was stretched tight around his thick shaft. "I will never share you with other men, Calliope. You are mine." He slapped her buttock hard and then spread her again, withdrawing until only his crown was inside her. "This tight cunt is mine alone to fuck." He slammed into her and pushed the tip of one finger into her arse. "All your holes belong to me. *You* belong to me."

Again and again he spanked her, until it felt like her bottom was on fire.

"I did not like thinking about Carlton fucking you. It… annoyed me."

Callie heard more than just anger in his voice. She heard, for the very first time, jealousy.

"I do not like the thought of *any* other men fucking you or touching you."

This time she most certainly heard jealousy, and something even more interesting: confusion, as if he didn't know what he was feeling or why.

He eased a second finger into her arse as he pumped his cock slowly in and out of her pussy. "These holes are mine," he growled, his free arm sliding around her waist and pulling her tight. "This body is *mine*."

Rightly or wrongly, Callie thrilled at David's possessive words, which were almost enough to make her come.

His attention was like an aphrodisiac to her.

And she was beginning to fear that she would do anything to have more of it.

.

Chapter 15

A few days after Calliope's birthday David was up in the attic reading the letter he'd just received. It contained only four pieces of information: the location of the shipment, the number of wagons needed, a date, and a destination.

David already had a trustworthy carter who owned a number of wagons, so he was prepared. The shipment would arrive at two o'clock in the morning the same evening as his business dinner, and it needed to go to a destination nine miles north of the City.

It was inconvenient that the shipment was on the same night as his dinner, but it was late enough that—

David heard the door slam—from three stories up—and the distinctive sound of feet pounding on the naked wooden stairs.

He quickly put the letter into the portfolio and then dropped it into the hiding place he had created by cutting a square section of wood flooring. By the time he had dragged the small rug over the hole the footsteps were coming from the corridor.

"David!" Calliope shouted.

David scowled as he hurried to set the table and chair on top of the rug. He had left the door open, believing he was going to be alone all day.

He should have known better.

Only by running did he reach the doorway just as she did.

"What is wrong?" he demanded, alarmed when he saw her bright red cheeks, wild eyes, and heaving chest. He glanced behind her to see if somebody was chasing her.

"You—you—arrogant, interfering—"

David took her shoulders. "What is wrong?" he said more sharply.

"I have been given the sack, that's what's wrong." She squirmed to get out of his grasp and David allowed it.

She reached out and grabbed his wrist, lifting his hand. "I see your knuckles are swollen again."

"Oh."

"Oh? *Oh*? Is that all you have to say? You beat one of my customers half-to-death and say *oh*?"

"He wasn't even close to death." David *knew* he should have threatened the man against saying anything. It had been a foolish oversight and now—

"Why?" she shouted.

"I should have threatened him with a more severe beating if he said anything," David admitted.

She stared at him as if he were something that crawled out of the sewer.

"What?" he demanded, his skin unaccountably warm and prickly.

"You beat that man because you saw him grab my bottom, didn't you?"

"Yes," he said, puzzled that she had to ask.

Her jaw sagged, but he saw… *something* in her bright blue gaze.

"Did it make you wet?" He reached out to cup her mound over her clothing.

She slapped his hand away and—once again—David allowed it. Mostly because it wasn't pleasurable to touch her pussy with so much cloth between his palm and her bare skin.

He wanted her naked. The urge to lick and suck and fuck into her soft, tight heat was so strong that his vision blurred.

David needed her. Now.

But it wasn't nine o'clock.

***

Callie had never felt so many conflicting emotions in her entire life.

First, there was fury and fear at being sacked.

Second, there was more fear and frustration at the thought of having to go through the painful process of finding another position.

Third, was horror at the story her employer had told her— that the idiot groper was so damaged that his hand—the one he'd used to pat her bottom—would never function properly again. And that was just one of his injuries. His family had spirited him away to a private sanatorium, where he was expected to reside for weeks.

Fourth, and more upsetting than the other three combined, was the immediate, almost crippling, jolt of arousal she'd experienced when she understood what had happened.

Callie was just as bad as David—just as sick.

She stared into his flat, emotionless eyes, terrified at how quickly she had fallen under the thrall of this dangerous man.

"Now that you no longer work there you can accompany me to buy your dress," David said.

Callie laughed. Because… what else could she do? "I am so pleased that my unemployment is convenient for you."

His eyes narrowed and he regarded her silently for a moment before saying, "I have not found the clothes buying process as straightforward as I anticipated."

"Why?"

"It seems that I underestimated the sheer number of decisions required to select a woman's gown."

"Not the dress, David. Why did you track that man down and hurt him?"

Something that looked like unease flickered in his flat gaze but was gone too fast for her to be sure. "His behavior was inappropriate."

"So you beat him badly enough that he will likely spend at least a month recovering?"

David shrugged, almost as if he were embarrassed, and then something else—some more powerful emotion—seemed to flow through him, strong enough to make the nostrils of his narrow nose flare and his jaw flex. "And because he was touching what is *mine*."

There was no mistaking the expression in his eyes now: it was raw, raging, masculine dominance.

And there was no mistaking how it made her already swollen sex throb and slicken.

"You—you can't do that again, David."

"I will not have to as you are no longer working there."

She gave a helpless laugh. "I will have to get another job, David. I can't just—"

"I will pay you."

"To do what?"

He shrugged. "To fix this house."

"To do *what*?"

He frowned and gestured with one arm, moving enough that she could see a sliver of the attic he had made such a to-do about. It looked like an empty space, just like the rest of the house.

"The house needs… things," he said irritably.

"Things?"

"Rugs, drapes, furniture, more servants… *things*."

"You want me to be your housekeeper?"

"No," he answered immediately. "You can engage one of those, as well. And maids and a cook and a manservant to run your errands. I want you to make this house look—" he broke off, obviously floundering for the right word.

"Like a normal person lives here?"

He gave a startled bark of laughter. "Yes. Like that."

"And you will pay me to do that?" It frankly sounded too good to be true.

"Yes."

"How much?"

"How much were you earning at the tea shop?"

"There were my wages but I also made extra."

"For allowing men to fondle you," he said in a flat, tight voice.

Callie's face colored. "That—that's not true. They paid extra because their tea was always hot and I served their food quickly."

"I will pay you double your wages."

Callie did not leap at the offer, but pondered it, as if anyone in their right mind would even need a fraction of a second to take the job.

He sighed. "Triple."

"I'll do it." She chewed her lower lip to keep from grinning like a fool, and then said, "You must be very rich."

He shrugged. "We must go find a dress."

As usual, he was unwilling to be derailed from his objective.

Callie glanced down the front of his body and set her hand over the stiff ridge fighting to tear out of his trousers.

He hissed in a breath and she looked up, needing to tip her head back to meet his gaze, which was no longer flat, but hot with need. "What about this, David?"

The muscles in his jaw flexed. "It is not nine o'clock."

Callie smiled, genuinely amused. "We have just negotiated a new bargain. We no longer need to wait until nine o'clock. You can fuck me whenever you want.

His pupils flared. "But we will still play chess at eight."

It was a statement, not a question, but Callie said, "Of course."

The words weren't even all the way out of her mouth before the world spun as he turned her to face the wall.

"Skirts up," he ordered.

Callie quickly pulled up her dress and petticoat. She heard the sound of a door shutting and a key being turned in a lock and was both exasperated and amused that he was taking the time to lock his precious room before taking his pleasure.

His hand closed around the back of her neck and he held her pinned to the wall. "Skirts *all* the way up—I want to see that pretty arse of yours."

Was it pitiful that she loved knowing he thought her bottom was attractive?

His hand landed with a sharp *crack* on her left buttock and she yelped, more from startlement than pain.

He kicked her feet apart. "Did you enjoy it when that little prick put his hands all over you, Calliope?"

"Yes," she lied.

A truly terrifying roar came from behind her. "Are you trying to make me jealous?"

"No," she lied again.

"Liar." He stroked two fingers through her slick folds. "You are soaking wet. It makes you hot to tease me."

"No."

He reached around her and swatted her mound.

Callie yelped.

"Do not lie to me again."

"No, David."

He massaged her engorged bud, applying the perfect amount of pressure, until she was shuddering with need.

"Look at you," he murmured, his breath hot on her ear. "Thrusting your arse at me like a bitch in heat. You want me to fuck this tight, juicy cunt, don't you?"

"Yes, yes, yes," she chanted, finally telling him the truth.

He immediately removed his fingers.

Callie whined. "Dav—"

"Hush," he ordered, giving her buttock another stinging slap before rubbing her clitoris, this time with the hot, slick head of his cock.

Callie gave a groan of pure pleasure.

"You will take what I give you and be grateful for it. Do you understand?"

"Yes, David," she all but sobbed, so crazed with lust that she could hardly squeeze out the two words.

He grunted and then gave her what she desperately needed, the stroking of his hard, silky shaft against the sensitive bundle of nerves driving her quickly beyond her control.

The moment the first contraction seized her in its powerful grasp David positioned himself at her entrance. "Come all over my cock," he snarled, and then thrust into her so hard that he lifted her off her feet.

Callie whimpered at the cruel invasion, pain and pleasure becoming hopelessly entwined.

"Does it hurt?" he asked in a harsh voice, ramming himself balls deep again and again and again.

"It hurts…and I love it, David."

He growled and his mouth closed over her neck as he bit her, his hips pumping, the punishing thrusts making her orgasm last and last.

The pain from his sharp teeth should not have felt as good as it did and Callie was distantly aware that the man currently plundering her body with such carnal violence had yet again shown her a disturbing facet of herself.

David liked administering pain.

And Callie loved suffering for his pleasure.

***

If there really was a Hell, David was now sure that it was filled with women's clothing shops.

He sat rigidly on the delicate pink silk settee and stared unseeingly at the men's journal—about hunting, a sport he despised—waiting for all the giggling and chattering that was occurring behind a pink silk curtain to cease and for Calliope to emerge.

This was the third shop they had visited. The first two had been insufficient for what he had in mind. The gowns in those shops were the sort worn by women who worked in tea shops. Or whored. What David needed was a gown for a wealthy woman of leisure. Of course he had no idea what that looked like, exactly, but he was sure he would know it when he saw it.

He had investigated Edward Fanshawe—the man who would be bringing his wife to Smith's dinner party—and the industrialist was married to a well-known painter and had once been married to a marquess's daughter before, scandalously, granting his first wife a divorce. Fanshawe was rich, perhaps one of the wealthiest men in Britain, and his wife would be garbed in only the finest.

David had also investigated Banks. The volume of gossip about all Banks's whoring and mistresses was staggering and made him wonder when the man ever found time for work. According to the mindless drivel in the scandal sheets, Banks kept three mistresses mounted and still spent most nights in brothels. But Banks must be good at what he did because he too was wealthy.

As for Mr. Smith? David had discovered nothing at all about him, which is exactly what he had expected to find. Smith—or whoever he really was—wasn't the sort of man who wanted attention. David knew that because he was the same sort of man.

"How about this one?"

David looked up at the sound of Calliope's voice.

He was distantly aware that his mouth had fallen open and the modiste and her two assistants were tittering about something.

"Is it too bright?" Calliope asked, furrows of worry creasing her brow as she gazed down at the celestial blue silk hugging her luscious tits while leaving her shoulders bare, the full skirt floating around her like blue mist.

David swallowed and then croaked, "No."

"Are you sure?" she asked, staring at her reflection in the cheval glass, her hands absently smoothing the fabric at her waist, which had been laced to an erotically tiny size.

Normally, David was completely lacking in imagination. At the moment, however, he could easily visualize her spread out across her bed with that skirt baring her—

"David?"

His head jerked up. "Yes?" he demanded, unhappily pulled from his pleasurable imaginings.

"You really like this one?"

Good God. Could there be any doubt in her mind about that?

David nodded, his throat too tight to produce even a *yes*. It wasn't just the gown that had muddled his senses, it was the red, raised areas all over her throat that entranced him. Teeth marks and love bites and three bruises that must have come from his fingers.

His marks. He had never seen her in anything with bare arms or such a low neck. Tonight he would add even more marks. Even if he could not see them, now he knew what they looked like beneath her clothing and—

"I think *monsieur* approves," the annoying French shopkeeper said, the amusement in her voice obvious even to a dolt like David.

"We'll take it." He tossed aside the journal and stood, not caring that his cock was—for the second time today—thrusting at the placket of his trousers.

More tittering ensued when the shopgirls saw the obscene bulge, complete with a large wet stain, courtesy of his profusely leaking prick.

Calliope looked up at him, evidently the only woman out of the four who hadn't noticed his erection. "But this is only the first one, you haven't seen the peacock blue and—"

"She'll have the others, too," he said, withdrawing a card from his notecase and thrusting it toward the modiste. "Have them sent to this address." He jerked out a nod. "Go change out of that now," he forced himself to say, before he lost what few wits remained to him, bent her over the uncomfortable settee, and fucked her for the entire world to see.

"But I don' t need so many gowns, David. Unless there is—"

He gave her a gentle push toward the pink curtain and turned to the hovering Frenchwoman once Calliope had disappeared.

"How much?"

"She will need ze proper gloves and a warm wrap—I 'ave just what she—"

"Fine. Add whatever she needs to go with it." He tossed a thick wad of notes onto the desk. "Send me a bill for the rest."

The Frenchwoman's eyes threatened to bulge out of her head at the sight of all the money, making him think he had perhaps overpaid. He didn't care. Seeing her in that gown had been worth twice the amount.

The modiste came alarmingly close to him and whispered in an overloud voice, "*Monsieur* needs a jeweler, yes?"

"Monsieur does," David admitted, vaguely entertained by the predatory look in the woman's eyes.

She took a card from behind the desk and handed it to him. "Only four doors down," she said, all but shoving him from her shop. "You come back in an hour, yes?"

"Yes, I will come back in an hour," he said, imagining just how much damage the woman could do to his bank account in that time.

David suspected it would be the best money he had ever spent.

***

Callie propped herself up on her side, studying David's profile as he recovered from his climax. He had taken her mouth tonight, although she strongly suspected that what he'd really wanted to do was take her arse.

Based on the way his cock was still half hard the night was young so she knew he'd have more of his favorite perversion before it was over.

She was feeling just as aroused tonight, although it was easier to hide it. But the truth was that she'd never had anyone stand up for her the way David had.

True, it was violent and criminal and he was fortunate the groper's family hadn't come after him—they still might—but it was such a visceral reaction from a man who never showed any emotion.

Did it mean that he cared for her? Callie wasn't sure. In fact, she wondered if he was even capable of affection. Before meeting David, she wouldn't have thought it was possible for a person *not* to care, about something, at least. She had met kind people, selfish ones, and more than her share of cruel ones. But never before had she met an emotionless one.

Callie turned to him. She had discovered that she got the best answers to her questions when his brain was still a bit frazzled by his orgasm.

"Thank you for all the clothing." When he didn't respond, she said, "I really only needed that one dress." She had left the shop with five—Madam Lucille had run amok the moment David stepped out the door—along with undergarments and gloves and a madly luxurious fur-lined cloak that Callie had insisted on asking David about rather than simply allowing the Frenchwoman to sneak onto the increasingly long list of garments.

"Yes, she will have the cloak," he had snapped, clearly eager to get out of the shop and away from Madam Lucille.

And if Callie had felt a bit wistful that they'd not had time to go to a jeweler, she had quickly chastised herself for being greedy.

It was obvious that he didn't want to talk about the clothing, so she said, "You never answered me today. Are you wealthy?"

He turned to her slowly, his eyes glinting with distant amusement. "I am comfortable. Why?"

Her face heated. "I just wanted to know how much I have to spend on the house."

"Spend whatever is needed."

That seemed dangerously vague. "I don't want to beggar you."

His lips twisted just the slightest amount. "You won't."

"It would help if I had a budget to work within."

The humor disappeared, replaced by boredom as he turned back to the ceiling. "I'll let you know if I have any concerns about your spending. Just buy the items the house needs—and engage enough servants—and have all the bills sent to me."

She would remind him of that order if he raised objections to her spending later. "Do you own this house?"

"No."

She thought that was all she would get, but he added, "I have first option to purchase if anyone else were to make an offer."

"Will you be staying in London?"

Again, he turned to her. "Why?"

She heaved a sigh. "It's just conversation, David— remember you agreed to it?"

"I remember."

"So?"

"I don't know."

"This house doesn't feel very… lived in."

"I haven't occupied it for very long."

"How long?"

"Eight months."

"Where did you live before?"

"Somewhere else."

She flopped onto her back and groaned. "You can just leave if you don't want to answer."

"I did answer you; it just wasn't the answer you wanted. And I'm not ready to leave. I will want you again."

"Tell me something I do not already know," she groused.

"How would I know what you know?" he asked.

She snorted. "It's just a figure of speech."

They laid side-by-side in silence.

For once, it was David who broke it. "Don't you have any family other than your father?"

"No."

Shockingly, he chuckled and Callie rolled over to stare at him. If he had smiled, it was already gone. But there were wrinkles around his eyes and she noticed, for the first time, there were silver threads in the closely cropped hair at his temple.

"How old are you?" she asked.

He shrugged.

"What? Is that a secret, too?" she taunted.

"I don't know how old I am for certain, but I suspect I'm somewhere around two-and-forty."

Her lips parted in shock. This was a man who planned his life down to the last minute and detail. How could he not know his age? But then he'd said he didn't know his birthday, hadn't he?

Callie wanted badly to pry, but she knew he would rebuff her.

He suddenly turned to face her. "How old are you?"

"Twenty-one."

They stared at each other in silence. Strangely, it felt almost comfortable.

"You were at Brook's for nine months?" he asked.

"Yes," she said, amazed that he had been listening and remembered.

"That is the only place you worked?"

"Yes."

"Why did you choose that one, as opposed to some other place?

It wasn't an obnoxious question. There were hundreds, if not thousands, of brothels of various sizes in England.

"I had heard that he wouldn't let in men who were diseased—even if there was just a rumor." She snorted. "Not because Brook cared about the women there, but he liked to use us, too, so he didn't want to catch anything. I also liked that he didn't sell virgins—well, not young girls, at least. Although he would certainly charge a premium for a woman who was new to the trade." He had made a goodly sum selling Callie's hymen.

"Is that where you lost your maidenhead?"

Callie was amused by the archaic turn of phrase. She was also impressed that he seemed to have chosen it with the aim of making the question less insulting. Was he becoming… kinder? She couldn't help feeling that he would have been less subtle even a week ago.

"Yes, it was. That is a stupid phrase—*lost one's maidenhead* as if you just leave it lying around like a glove or a hatpin."

"Did Brook offer you to the highest bidder?" he asked.

Callie shied away from her memory of that horrid night—first the inspection, then the sale, and then… after. "Yes. Have you taken part in such an auction?"

"I do not want a virgin," he said with his usual candor. After a pause, he added, "I frankly do not understand the obsession with them."

Callie shrugged. "The man who bought me said he only took virgins because he was afraid of disease. But I'm not sure I believe that." She remembered her first time all too well—when she allowed herself to think about him. He had not just purchased her virginity; he'd wanted to buy her services for two entire weeks—exclusive. Callie had noticed how his interest in her had waned as the days passed. He'd become cruder, crueler, and rougher, until he'd looked at her as if she were a used up, broken toy once the fourteen days had passed. He came back to Brook's the next time there was a virgin for sale and looked right through Callie when they passed in the corridor, not recognizing her.

"What do you mean?" he asked, pulling her back from the distasteful past.

"I think some men just want to be the first to take something from a woman. I think they like to see the pain in a woman's eyes the first time a man enters her because it makes them feel powerful—like a conqueror—and big. They enjoy the tears they cause."

His jaw flexed slightly. "What was the name of the man who bought you?"

Callie squinted, and then laughed when she saw where he was headed. "Oh, no. I don't think I'll tell you that." The man was an important M.P. She could only imagine how much trouble David would land in if he started bloodying his knuckles on powerful men.

She deliberately changed the subject. "When did you lose your *manhead*?"

His lips twitched. "When I was thirteen."

She looked for some sign that it had been unpleasant— Callie knew men and boys could be raped just as girls and women were—but he seemed almost… relaxed.

"I never saw you at Brook's before that day," she said.

"That was my first time there."

"Where did you go before?"

"Nowhere. At least not for a long time."

He was still staring at the ceiling.

"How long?"

"A while."

That sounded like the end of *that*.

"What made you choose Brook's?" she asked, her question an echo of the one he asked her.

He hesitated so long she thought it was another question he wouldn't answer, but then he said, "One of the men you will meet at this dinner recommended it. He said it was clean and the women seemed happy."

"Happy." Callie gave a bitter laugh.

He turned to her. "Was he wrong?"

She considered his question. It would have been unfair to say *yes* out of hand. "Everyone there disliked at least some of the work. There were a few customers who made it bearable. Some women had favorites—"

"Did you?" he asked.

"Did I what?"

"Did you have *favorites*." He said the word as if tasted foul and he couldn't wait to spit it out of his mouth.

Callie stared at him. "Are you blushing?'

He scowled. "*No*."

She smiled.

His scowl deepened. "*This* right here—this sort of misunderstanding that always occurs in any conversation, especially with a woman—is why I don't like to talk."

Callie's smile broadened. "No."

"No, *what?*"

"No, I didn't have any favorites. I just had less unbearable clients." Her smile fell away. "And I had a few who were…a nightmare."

"Like Carlton."

"Yes."

The silence stretched between them and she wondered if he was recalling what they'd done the night after he'd beaten the man half to death.

"I was an oddity at Brook's for several reasons," Callie said a few moments later, even though he'd not asked. "I was well-educated and a twenty-year-old virgin. Most of the women had been in the trade, as they call it, since twelve or thirteen." She shook her head. "It sickens me how many Englishmen think nothing of debauching a child. At least I was of age and had a choice." She pulled a face. "Although I suppose it was a rather limited one. I hadn't planned to stay there forever, you know. I'd saved enough to purchase passage to America. I was only staying long enough to save some money so I'd have time to find a job—*not* whoring—when I reached my destination."

"America?"

"Yes. It seemed far enough away that I wouldn't encounter some man I'd serviced."

"Surely you wouldn't need to go so far?"

"Maybe not, but it also seemed like a fresh start. And I heard it was easier there to find work—that employers didn't expect sterling letters of recommendation, that it was… freer."

"I think you might be surprised," he said, his tone wry.

"You've been to America?"

He hesitated, but then nodded.

"Where? When? Why?" she laughed, "Sorry, but I've not met anyone who has been there. Tell me about it."

"It is bigger and newer, but there are people who give the orders and people who take them, just like here."

That sounded grim. "What were you doing there?"

He turned away again, but not before she saw his eyes shutter. "Nothing good."

Callie didn't want to ask, but at this rate she would never learn about him if she baulked every single time he did his best imitation of a clam. "Won't you tell me what you did that took you to America?" Although she was beginning to have her suspicions.

His jaw worked, flexing and relaxing, flexing and relaxing. "I was in the army."

"The American army?" she repeated, flabbergasted.

"No, ours."

"But…why were you in America? We haven't been at war with them for almost sixty years."

"War is not the only reason our government sends soldiers to foreign soil."

She lowered her voice—as if they were in danger of being overheard, and said, "You were a spy?"

"I did not say that."

No, he hadn't, but she would have to be an idiot not to guess what he meant. She left the topic alone—for the moment—and said, "Have you been to a lot of places?"

"A few."

"Where?"

He gave her a sideways look.

"What? I'm asking where you went, not why and what you did."

"France, Prussia and some of the German states, Russia, Brazil, Mexico—"

"Goodness! Why, you must have been in the army a long time."

His jaw flexed. "Twenty-eight years."

"But… you said you were forty-two. That would mean—"

"I joined when I was thirteen."

"*Thirteen*! Is that even allowed?" A stupid question, because he'd just said it was. Twenty-eight years! It was longer than Callie had been alive.

He turned to her, the look in his eyes hot, his pupils large. "I'm done talking."

Callie sighed. "Is our half hour over already?"

"I want to fuck you."

"You have such a charming way with words."

"I will let you choose. Should I fuck your cunt or your arse?"

She shivered at the crude words—and the way he was looking at her. It was the same look Callie had seen on his face when he was devouring her apple tarts, as if he had never seen anything more desirable in his life.

"A choice? Why are *you* so thoughtful tonight?" she teased.

He merely waited, his dark gaze riveted on her face.

"David?"

"What?"

"Do you like to hurt me?"

His pupils, already large, flared. "Yes."

It was suddenly hard to breathe. "I—I like it, too."

"I know," he said, without any hesitation. "Arse or cunt?"

She rolled on to all fours. "My arse." It wasn't her favorite, but he had been kind to her today and she wanted to do something to make him happy. Not because she had to, but because she wanted to give him something *he* liked.

***

David looked down as he penetrated Calliope's tight body. He had always liked watching what he did when he had sex. He was astounded by his appetite these past weeks. Indeed, he would not have believed his body was capable of so many ejaculations every single night. Not that he came much after the first time. But the subsequent orgasms were so painfully pleasurable that he almost enjoyed them more.

He withdrew slowly, inch by inch, and then slammed in hard enough to make her cry out.

Over and over he took her. He had already come in her mouth earlier, so he was in no hurry now. He could fuck her for hours. Perhaps he would.

His cock looked obscene stretching her tight pink hole and his hands looked large on her tiny waist. Her body was every man's fantasy, an hourglass made human, without any of the annoying frippery women usually used to shape their figures, just soft, yielding flesh.

He spread her cheeks even wider and spat on where they were joined, amused when she hissed in a breath, her shoulders pressing harder into the mattress, her hips lifting and canting, as she presented herself, silently begging him to take her deeper. Her response was a far cry from the way she had been that first night, when her body had clenched with intoxicating fear at the thought of being anally penetrated.

While David missed her fear, her eagerness to please him as well as her complete submission to his demands more than made up for the loss of it. He knew she would allow him to do anything he wished to her—and not just because he would pay for it.

She was obviously genteel—the daughter of a professor would be, wouldn't she? But her sexual preferences were as lewd and crude as his own. It was a heady combination and one David had never encountered before. He had only ever been with whores, and never the same one more than a few times.

Not for any particular reason, but because he had never been interested enough to seek out the same woman on a long-term basis.

In the past, women had been nothing but vessels for him; warm, tight holes to fuck and fill and then immediately abandon once he had satisfied his needs. Sometimes, when he had been in the mood for more, he had sought out brothels that permitted his peculiar…inclinations. On those nights he would spend a few hours whipping or spanking a willing whore before taking his release. But those women had obviously submitted to him for money rather than inclination. Never had he found a woman who craved humiliation and pain. David was finding Calliope's neediness addictive. Indeed, his hunger for her was worrisome. It was fortunate she would only be in his life, and his house, for a few weeks more.

David thrust aside the thought and stared down to where they were joined.

He knew that Calliope had not really wanted him to take her arse tonight, but she *had* wanted to thank him for the clothing. Her emotions were as easy to read as the large headlines that newspapers liked to employ.

He could have told her the truth, that he had received far more pleasure from seeing her in that gown than she had. As for the money he had spent? That meant nothing to him. Money was only a gauge of how accurate his predictions were—how good he was at what he did. Not the killing and maiming that he'd done for Queen and Country, but the buying and selling and speculating.

It was only since meeting Calliope that David had been glad to have plenty of money.

After all, without money, she never would have stayed with him.

Chapter 16

The morning after their trip to the dress shop David left early but made sure to leave Callie a letter with an official banking seal and her name. It authorized her to spend to her heart's content and have the bills sent to him.

Halfway through her first day at her new *job*, Callie realized that taking charge of a huge house was going to require a great deal of thought, time, and effort. At least if she was going to do it properly. It had initially seemed like she was getting the better of the bargain, but the more Callie pondered all that she had to do, the more she realized that she would be working far more hours for David than she had ever done at the tea shop.

She had believed the job of spending his money wouldn't just be simple, it would also be easy and enjoyable. But once Callie had the purchasing power, her expectations subtly shifted. She now had so many choices to make that it was harder than *not* having any money.

Well, not quite, but close.

"More maids?" Mrs. Jenkins barked when Callie mentioned hiring a parlor maid, a chamber maid, and a scullery maid.

"Yes. Mr. Remington wishes to engage a full-time staff."

Mrs. Jenkins's eyebrows shot up so far it looked as if they might launch right off her forehead. Whether she was disconcerted because Callie had referred to David by his surname when she usually just called him *David,* or because David wanted a houseful of servants, Callie wasn't sure.

"Am *I* to be consulted?" Mrs. Jenkins asked, her fists on her hips.

"I *am* consulting you."

"Who said I wanted a fulltime position?"

"Do you?"

Mrs. Jenkins stared for a long moment and then said, "I might."

Callie wanted to roll her eyes. "If you want it, you must tell me because the position of cook is one that I will need to fill otherwise."

"I just said I might, dint I?"

"I am sure Mr. Remington would be very pleased if you agreed to work fulltime."

Mrs. Jenkins grunted, no doubt a habit she'd picked up from David. "As it 'appens, I might know a footman and some maids. But I don't know no 'ousekeepers nor butlers." She said the last two words like they were diseases a person contracted while engaging in unsavory activities in foreign climes.

"There will need to be somebody to direct the servants, Mrs. Jenkins."

"I reckon I've been doing that already."

Callie told herself to have patience. "Are you saying that is something you would want to continue doing?"

"For proper wages."

And so it went.

After two hours of bargaining and prodding and cozening, she had a cook/housekeeper and the names of three maids and a footman, all of whom would come for interviews on the morrow.

None would live in—that was one thing David had specified—which suited Mrs. Jenkins down to the ground as she had Mr. Jenkins and numerous small Jenkinses at home.

By the time two o'clock came around—the time Callie would have been finishing up work at the tea shop—she was exhausted.

With Mrs. Jenkins gone for the day—the housekeeper had refused to assume her new duties until the beginning of the following week, yet another concession she'd extracted from Callie, who felt as though she'd just spent the morning haggling with a fishmonger—Callie decided to treat herself to the luxury of a bath. Although it really wasn't much of a luxury if one had to heat and haul the water oneself.

Tonight was the dinner with David's business… prospects? Partners? And so she wanted to look her best.

She was also beside herself with eagerness to wear one of her new dresses. She had tried them on again at home, but this would be the first time she would wear one in public.

Callie closed her eyes and considered what she should choose, reveling in the wealth of choices.

The next time she opened her eyes it was to find David watching her. She blinked at him. "Oh. I must have fallen asleep."

"Yes."

"You know it's not normal to spy on people while they sleep."

"Yes," he said again. "I want to watch you touch yourself like you did the last time," he ordered, his command suddenly making the water—which had cooled while she slept—much warmer.

Callie deliberately lifted a hand from the tub and touched her shoulder with it.

David rewarded her with one of the tiniest smiles in the history of humankind.

He dragged a chair closer to the tub and sat near enough that she could have touched him. "Put your legs over the side and spread your cunt for me."

Her pulse pounded at his command and she stared into his unreadable eyes as she obeyed.

His cold gaze slid down to her hips when she emerged from the water.

Callie was not surprised to feel slickness when she parted her lower lips. Just seeing him was enough to get her wet; hearing him make vulgar demands was even more arousing.

"Stroke that beautiful pussy."

Her heart threatened to beat out of her chest at the rare compliment.

David came even closer, the chair making a loud *scritching* sound as he inched across the floor, until his face was less than a foot from her crotch. He stared at her exposed sex as he caressed her flank, buttock, and thigh, all of which were taut with the effort of keeping herself raised up.

Callie's sheath clenched around nothing, needy and empty. She was so desperate for the feel of him—his thick girth—inside her, that she couldn't help begging, "Please, David, I need something inside me." She flexed her buttocks to raise herself even more.

And still he only stared.

"Make yourself come," he ordered.

Her finger was in motion before the last word came out of his mouth. His intent, rapt stare and increasingly labored breathing were more stimulating than her own hand, the hunger on his normally expressionless face the best aphrodisiac.

Only when she began to come unraveled did he touch her, lowering himself until he sucked her clitoris into the exquisitely soft heat of his mouth.

Callie cried out as the first contraction shook her body and he roughly shoved two fingers into her achingly empty sheath, drawing out her orgasm, until she thought she'd go mad with sensation.

He released her sensitive bundle of nerves but kept his fingers inside her, slowly fucking her as she clenched around him, the waves of pleasure gradually diminishing, until she felt replete in a way that only came from sexual release.

When her hips began to shake from the effort of holding herself up on the edge of the tub, he withdrew his fingers, licked them clean, and then splayed a hand over her belly and pushed her down into the tub.

Callie hissed at the now cool water.

Without speaking, David stood and fetched one of the towels she'd stacked by the stove and then returned to the tub and held out a hand, lifting her to her feet. Once she was standing, he wrapped her in the warm cloth and buffed her skin until she was rosy from the friction.

He tossed the towel aside, spun her around, and then shoved down her shoulders. "Bend over and grab the side of the tub."

Callie obeyed without hesitation and he nudged her feet wider. She felt the thick, hot head of him at her entrance just before he slammed into her. He took her fast, his thrusts so violent that water sloshed onto the kitchen floor. Just when his body began to shake, his climax almost upon him, he withdrew from her, leaving her empty and wanting, her clitoris pulsing with need, even though it was far too sensitive from her last orgasm.

He used his cock to slick moisture from her cunt to her back hole. "You are drenched," he muttered, the wet sounds of each stroke carnal evidence of his claim.

Callie stiffened when he finally slid his hot, hard crown back and back until it nudged against her tight pucker. And then he matter of factly dipped two fingers inside her cunt and smeared the moisture around her hole.

He pressed against her pucker but did not breach her.

Callie bit her lip as she anticipated the sharp ache of penetration.

"It will go better for you if you relax your muscles."

As if she didn't already know that.

He leaned forward, covering her back with his chest, the wool and buttons of his suit coat chaffing against her hot skin. "But it will feel better and tighter for me if you don't."

His selfish threat sent a pulse of desire through her that was so strong her knees weakened.

"You like that. You want to suffer for my pleasure, don't you, Calliope?"

God save her, but she *did*. Callie bit her tongue until it bled, refusing to give him the satisfaction of owning her shameful desires.

His dry, cruel-sounding chuckle told her that he didn't need her admission to know it was the truth.

"I shouldn't even bother to slick my cock before I fuck you. I should just ram myself into you dry."

Callie shuddered at the threat. Part of her willed him to carry through on it, but the other—wiser—part was grateful when he continued to wet himself with her juices and lubricate his fat crown.

"Clench your hole nice and tight for me, Calliope. Give me your pain," he hissed in her ear and then bit the side of her jaw, his teeth clamping down until she whimpered, sharp, eviscerating desire shooting directly to her sex.

He thrust inside her then, roughly breaching the tight ring of muscle—made even tighter by her clenching—and ramming deep.

Callie moaned at the agonizing invasion and he rewarded her with a bite on her nape, his hips not stopping until his groin pressed against her spread cheeks, until he was so deep that she felt as though her insides were in danger of being rearranged.

"So nice and tight for me," he praised, his cold, toneless voice fiercely arousing even as her entire body shook from the painful ache and stretch.

He reached beneath her and caressed her swollen sex, giving an almost inaudible growl of appreciation at how wet she was for him.

And then his hips began to move, slowly at first, giving her every inch with each thrust.

Rather than relax her body and ease her own discomfort, Callie kept her passage tight for him, shaking from the effort it took to maintain such control.

The involuntary groan of pleasure that tore from him was every bit as satisfying as the skilled fingers currently stroking her clitoris. Callie was shocked at the pulse of pleasure in her core and the warm gush of arousal that slid down her thighs at even that small amount of praise.

"You could come from me fucking your arse," he said, the wonderment in his voice no greater than her own.

Callie squeezed her eyes shut in shame, even though he could not see her face. What was wrong with her that she reveled in such base, cruel treatment? How had David managed to plumb the depths of her soul so quickly and effortlessly, finding parts of her that even she had not known existed?

"You *will* come while I fuck you," he said, the astonishment that had briefly colored his voice gone, his tone once again flat and coldly determined as he flexed his hips and pushed harder, as if there was any more room for him. "I cannot get deeply enough inside you," he muttered, grinding his pelvis against her bottom.

The pad of his finger rubbed the base of her swollen nub and Callie began to shake, her eyelids fluttering. It was too much…she couldn't resist any longer. She was going to—

The delicious pressure disappeared.

"Not yet," he said, the words hot on her ear. "Not until I say." He nudged her head to the side and dropped his mouth to her neck, grazing her throat with his sharp teeth as he slowly withdrew his cock almost all the way. "I want you to feel me even when I am not *here*." He punctuated the last word with a thrust that forced a hoarse cry from her. He continued to stroke her, but avoided any contact with her clitoris, the sensual deprivation making her grind her teeth with frustration.

Callie had to lock her arms on the tub to keep from going headfirst into it as his hips pounded into her so savagely that she would be feeling him for days.

"I want to be as deeply inside you as you are in *me*," he hissed, and then his wicked finger resumed its stroking with a vengeance.

Callie came hard, only vaguely aware when David reached his own climax.

Even in her bliss Callie was stunned that she had orgasmed while being anally penetrated, an activity she had always loathed and feared in the past.

But no matter how good it had felt—*still* felt—Callie wasn't sure she was pleased by yet another sign that she was too far gone to depravity to ever lead a normal life.

Even though the position was not the most comfortable one for her, Callie hated it when his chest lifted off her back and she sighed with disappointment as he slowly withdrew from her body.

Shockingly, he trailed kisses from the bite on her nape down the knobs of her spine, the action so uncharacteristically gentle and almost… loving that she felt a fluttering in her belly.

Tenderness? From David?

Before she could stand up, he set a hand between her shoulder blades and held her in place. "Stay as you are," he ordered. "I have something for you and you will wear it until I say you can remove it." A cold and hard object prodded against the hole he had just stretched and filled. "It will give me pleasure to think of you full of my spunk while we dine at the house of this rich and powerful man and all his friends." He pressed the thick bulb just until it pushed past the tight ring of muscle. "Beautiful," he murmured.

Callie squirmed at the painful stretching.

David's palm sharply stung her left buttock. "Stay still," he said, and then proceeded to fuck her with the hard object, probing her again and again and again.

Callie bit her lower lip and held her body motionless, her obedience earning her a guttural grunt of approval before he pushed the object all the way inside her, a flange at the end stopping it from penetrating her any deeper.

He caressed from her plugged hole to her shamefully wet sex and thrust two fingers inside her while he used his other hand to play with her clitoris and work her toward an orgasm with an ease that she almost hated.

Just when she began to shake, the pleasure building toward a climax, he removed both his hands from her body.

"Please, Davi—*ah!*" she yelped when he slapped her buttock *hard* three times.

"No begging or I will use my crop on you."

Callie's swollen, primed sheath tightened at his cruel threat and the ripple of pleasure that followed made her realize that she could easily make herself climax if she just—

"And no orgasms until I give you one," he said, and then leaned close and added, "If you come without my permission, I will tie you face down on your bed and whip you, Calliope."

She clenched so hard that—for a moment—she feared she wouldn't be able to control herself.

"Up," he ordered, pulling her to her feet, his strong fingers massaging the knots from her back and shoulders, rubbing her with such skill that her knees soon felt boneless. Just when she was about to melt into a puddle, he stepped away to fetch another towel, once again wrapping her up. This time, he turned her so that she was facing him.

"Eyes on me," he said, rubbing her skin until she was warm and rosy. His cold, dead gaze flickered over her face, but this time Callie could sense the intensity that simmered just beneath the surface. He was not as self-possessed as he seemed. Something had… discomposed him.

What?

His jaw flexed, as if he were about to speak, but then he released her, and shutters snapped shut over his already veiled gaze. "Wear the gown you showed me," he ordered, and then turned on his heel and left her alone in the kitchen, the heaviness in her bottom matched by an increasing heaviness in her chest.

Chapter 17

Callie was digging through the meager contents of her jewelry case when the door to her room opened and she turned to find David on the threshold.

They examined each other like duelists at twenty paces, neither moving.

He was dressed in evening blacks that were far more fashionable than the ones he usually wore and she wondered if he, too, had purchased new clothing for this dinner.

His coat was closely tailored to his frame and emphasized his broad, muscular shoulders and tight, narrow hips. He always looked good to her—when had she stopped thinking of him as ordinary or average?—but this ensemble clung to his hard, powerful body like a second skin, the rich black wool flattering his pale skin and dark brown eyes.

David broke out of the mutual daze first and it wasn't until he was right in front of her that she saw he held a box in his hands.

Callie felt a leap of excitement in her chest as she looked from what was obviously a box from a jeweler's back up to his face. "What, er, I mean where did this come from?" she asked stupidly.

"I went to a jeweler while you were with that rapacious dressmaker. It was no coincidence that the man she recommended was her husband. She must have sent one of her clerks over with a description of your gown because he was lying in wait for me and already had this out on his counter when I entered his shop."

Callie took the heavy box, a wave of shyness washing over her. She caught her lower lip with her teeth and looked up at him from beneath her lashes. "You did not have to do this. I have things I could wear."

His gaze flickered dismissively over the necklace and earrings—paste—that she had just laid out on her dressing table and then he turned back to her. "Open it."

She lifted the lid and gasped at the dazzling blue stones that sparkled up at her. "Oh, my," she murmured, reaching out to tentatively stroke one of the glittering blue gems. There was a bracelet, ring, necklace, and earrings.

"Do you like it?" he asked.

Callie's eyes darted upward and she smiled but had to blink away her tears. "It's beautiful."

He lifted the necklace from the box and went behind her, his fingers light and deft as he fastened the heavy clasp, which looked like a serpent head and was a work of art in and of itself.

"What are those tiny stones set in the clasp and around the bigger ones?" she asked, sliding the ring—which fit perfectly—onto her finger and turning it to and fro to admire it in the light.

"It is called marcasite and the larger stones are sapphires." He came around to the front of her and repositioned the necklace until the clasp sat on her bare shoulder. "The jeweler told me it was meant to be worn on the side, so it is visible," he explained, and then reached for the bracelet and clasped that around her wrist.

Once he was done, he stood back. "Put on the earrings."

She screwed them into her ears with shaking hands and once they were on, she met his gaze.

He nodded slowly. "The jeweler chose well."

Callie gave a watery laugh, a tear escaping and sliding down her cheek before she dashed it away with the back of her hand.

"Why are you crying?" he asked, his forehead furrowing. "Is it not what you wanted?"

She threw her arms around his neck, aware that he stiffened—and not in the usual place—at her impulsive touch. She kissed his cheek and whispered, "I love all of it—the gown, the gloves, the fur cloak, the bejeweled slippers, and the gorgeous sapphires. Thank you."

His muscles relaxed slightly, although he didn't seem to know how to return her embrace, but merely stood like a wooden totem, his arms hanging tensely at his sides.

Callie stepped back and then made a fuss about straightening his necktie before looking up at him. "You—er, these jewels must have been expensive."

He raised one eyebrow in the maddening way that he had.

"I am not asking how much," she hastily assured him. "I'm just—well, do you want them back?"

"What would I do with them?"

"I just meant… this wasn't something we negotiated for."

His jaw tightened and then he said, "They are a gift." He turned away before she could respond.

Callie stared at the doorway he'd just stalked through. Had she insulted him with her question?

***

Callie was relieved that she wasn't the only whore at Mr. Smith's dinner table that night.

In fact, the only married couple was Edward and Nora Fanshawe.

Callie had read about Mrs. Fanshawe, who was a painter of some renown and evidently had an *interesting* past. There were many rumors swirling about, and some suggested Mr. Fanshawe had met his wife in a brothel.

Wherever the two had met, they were a striking couple. Mrs. Fanshawe was as slender and pale and frosty looking as an icicle while her husband was a massive, brooding hulk of a man. The only time his hard, pitiless gaze softened was when his eyes rested on his wife, who returned his possessive, loving glances with heated looks that belied her icy exterior.

Callie felt a sharp twinge of envy at the affection the two obviously shared. It must be wonderful to be loved so fiercely by a man.

The dinner party was comprised of fifteen people as Mr. Smith, their host, was the only man who'd not brought a companion. Instead, Mrs. Fanshawe sat at the foot of the table and did the honors usually associated with a hostess, the two sharing the easy familiarity of close friends.

The meal itself was delicious and extravagant and Callie did not recall ever having eaten so well in her life. She did not do the food justice as she was too enrapt by the conversation flying about the table to eat very much.

Callie had been seated between two men who could not have been more different. Stephen Chatham, on her right, rarely spoke a word after their initial introduction although she felt his reserved gaze on her often during the meal. He had remarkable gray eyes that were huge and heavily lidded and the penetrating intelligence in them made her feel as if he could see right into her head. He wasn't exactly handsome, but at well over six feet—with massive broad shoulders that tapered to slim, muscular hips—he was strikingly attractive.

Mr. Chatham's companion spoke as little as he did and was breathtakingly beautiful, her hourglass figure so lush that Callie was amused to see several of the men around the table stealing glances at her again and again throughout the meal.

On Callie's other side was Gideon Banks, a man Callie recognized from Brook's. Thankfully, he had never been her client and did not recognize Callie.

Banks was an exquisitely beautiful man—the most handsome she had ever seen—and also the sort of blatant sensualist who made her feel uneasy.

While Mr. Chatham made her feel like he was inspecting the contents of her head, Banks was only interested in her body and stripped her naked with his first glance. Callie suspected that he was a connoisseur of women and could easily and accurately assess women's bodies even if they were swathed in heavy layers of sackcloth.

While he was witty and charming and lovely to look at, she did not find his company very restful or relaxing.

David might be surly, remote, and taciturn, but at least he was direct when he *did* speak. And—for all his shortcomings when it came to communication—he had been honest in his dealings with her.

Conversing with Banks for even a short period of time made Callie realize that she didn't just tolerate David's awkward ways but had actually come to appreciate many of his characteristics.

Chatham and Banks knew each other and Banks teased the other man relentlessly throughout the meal, not sparing so much as a glance or word for his own companion, a tiny blonde woman who was every bit as beautiful as her angelic-looking companion. If the other woman was offended that Banks ignored her throughout the meal in favor of Callie and Mr. Chatham then she was too well-trained—or too relieved—to show any displeasure.

Something told Callie that being Gideon Banks's mistress would be an extremely taxing position in more ways than one.

All through dinner Callie was intensely aware of the large obstruction inside her. If somebody had told her six months ago that she would enjoy having her arse plugged full of a man's spend, she would have been horrified. But something about David's possessive, dominating behavior—not to mention the quiet, almost smug, looks that he gave her from time to time across the table—kept her on the edge of arousal all night.

Once again David had shown her how he knew her body's desires far better than Callie did.

While part of Callie's mind castigated her for being such a deviant and enjoying his bizarre behavior, another part was relieved that she didn't need to hide anything with him. He had already seen her darkest most depraved desires and had not so much as blinked.

"—don't you agree, Miss Fowler?"

Callie blinked at the sound of her name and realized that Mr. Banks had been speaking to her. "Er—"

A low, almost rusty-sounding chuckle came from her right side. "It seems as if Miss Fowler was thinking of other, more interesting, matters than *you*, Gideon," Mr. Chatham said.

"I'm so sorry, Mr. Banks," Callie said to the blond god, her face likely a flaming scarlet.

But Mr. Banks looked delighted rather than offended. "Please don't be, Miss Fowler. You are instantly forgiven as you've managed to do the impossible and make Chatham laugh. I believe it might be the first time I've heard that rare sound this year." He grinned at his friend, who merely regarded him with a sardonic smirk.

Callie opened her mouth but then didn't know what to say as she looked from Banks to Chatham.

Thankfully, Mr. Chatham took mercy on her. "Just go with your first instinct and continue to ignore Banks, Miss Fowler. It really is the wisest decision."

Aside from Mr. Banks and his teasing, the conversation at the dinner table was lively and far more risqué than she suspected was normal at most houses on the respectable square. Callie wondered what Mr. Smith's neighbors made of him. She decided that whatever they thought, nobody in their right mind would ever show the man anything other than courtesy.

Although Mr. Smith was the consummate gentleman to all his guests—millionaire and whore alike—he emanated the same quiet aura of danger as David.

Mr. Smith, Callie decided, was not the sort of man a person wanted to cross.

All the men at the table oozed wealth and power and it stunned Callie just how well David fit in among them. The jewels he had given her tonight made her realize what everything else—such as his casual disregard for money, for example—should have told her some time ago: David Remington was rich. Very rich.

It was odd that a person would never guess just how wealthy David was based on his behavior or person. While he dressed in quietly expensive clothing, he did not own fancy carriages—or any carriage at all, although she had seen him ride a very fine horse a time or two—nor was the house that he leased the home of an especially wealthy man.

Callie got the distinct impression that money did not matter to him.

Yet another way in which he was unlike anyone else she had ever met.

When the sumptuous repast was over, Mrs. Fanshawe stood. "Ladies, shall we retire to the sitting room and allow the gentlemen to enjoy their port and cigars?"

As Callie got to her feet to follow the women from the dining room the heavy, now warm, obstruction inside her back passage shifted, sending a pulse of pleasure to her sex. She stole a quick glance at David and saw he was staring at her with a coldly knowing gaze that caused another wave of pleasure to ripple through her.

David did not allow Callie to wear drawers, so her slick thighs slid against each other as she walked, the feeling naughty and sensual. Her body had never in her life felt so aware, as if she possessed more than the requisite number of nerves.

No matter how much Callie was enjoying this rare evening of company, she was still eagerly anticipating whatever he had planned for them when they returned home.

"Are you related to Mr. Smith?" one of the women asked Mrs. Fanshawe in a quiet voice as they made their way down a hushed corridor.

"No, Smith and I are old friends," Mrs. Fanshawe explained with a private smile.

"How come he doesn't have somebody here tonight?" a lovely redhead asked, her eyes glinting hungrily.

"I don't know why he has chosen not to have a companion present, Dora," Mrs. Fanshawe said coolly, her tone discouraging.

Callie had seen Dora eyeing their host repeatedly throughout dinner, all but ignoring Mr. Nance, the man who had brought her.

Nance was a wealthy banker whose name was often mentioned in the *Times* as an influential force not only in the world of finance, but also in government circles.

He had the silver hair of a much older man but his face was not old and Callie thought he was probably close to David's age. His evening blacks were easily the most stylish of any of the men at the dinner table. Even their host, Mr. Smith—a man who *oozed* elegance and refinement—was not as cultivated and urbane as Mr. Nance.

Nance was lean and tall and well-proportioned and Callie found his sharp, austere features attractive, if a bit daunting. While he lacked the dangerous quality of men like David and Mr. Smith, the aura of quiet, confident power he wore like an invisible cloak was more than a little alluring.

Amazingly, Nance was also pleasant, courtly, and polite, which made for an appealing combination. It was her experience that rich and powerful men treated everyone who was not their social equal as inferior beings. She knew instinctively that a woman under Nance's protection would never have to fear harsh, demeaning, or cruel behavior.

In Callie's opinion, all of that combined to make Nance the second most fascinating man at the table that night, which made Dora's dismissive behavior toward her wealthy benefactor all the more perplexing.

Rather than look annoyed by his companion's blatant interest in Mr. Smith, Nance had appeared lazily amused by Dora's flirtatious pandering toward their host.

Callie herself had spent a mortifying amount of the meal sneaking glances at the *most* fascinating man, David Remington, who drew her like a lodestone.

Ever since he had mentioned the dinner she had wondered how he would behave in company. After all, it was fine and well to grunt at one's whore, but grunting at one's dinner companions would not portray him in the right light to men he wished to do business with.

She'd watched him all night not just because of the sexual pull he exerted on her, but also because he appeared almost normal while he conversed with the women who flanked him on both sides, listening to their chatter with polite interest and occasionally commenting to keep the conversations moving. Callie had been floored by his bland, civilized expression, one she never could have imagined on his face.

Initially, she had been annoyed that he *could* be social and polite when he wanted; just not with her.

But it hadn't taken much thought to understand that what David showed her was his *true* face, not a mask he'd obviously created to deflect unwanted curiosity or attention.

As much as Callie was drawn to him, it was undeniable that he was equally affected by her presence. Over and over during the meal she had felt David's dark gaze on her, their eyes briefly meeting and heat arcing between them.

Callie had hoped nobody else had noticed the brief interludes. And then she'd been irked at herself for feeling shame at exchanging lustful looks with the man who was paying for her. Did she somehow think she was better than she was? After all, she was a whore—just like most of the women at the dinner.

She glanced at the other whores as they whispered and peeked around the luxuriously strange house around them, following Mrs. Fanshawe like eager children.

Although Callie had lived in a brothel for nine months she had almost never worked alongside other women while servicing a patron. Oh, there had been the occasional man who'd wanted two women, of course, but for the most part, she had only ever gossiped with Flora in their shared room or snatched a few minutes here or there with some of the others, usually around the rickety table in the kitchen where they'd eaten hasty meals in between customers.

Tonight was a unique experience for her and she realized that becoming a rich man's mistress was something she had never considered before, although that seemed to be what she'd become now without even trying.

The women tonight were sleek, rested, and expensively clothed and groomed so it was obviously a much less demanding life than brothel work. But Callie could not help wondering if any of these women ever became attached to their wealthy lovers. How many of their protectors were married or soon would be? Did it bother them?

Thinking about David taking a wife and having children made her feel restless, hostile, and nauseated at the same time.

Working in a brothel had been hell, but watching a man she cared about have another life—a legitimate, respectable life that Callie had been raised to believe she would have—would be even worse.

Callie shook the pointless thought away. None of that was an issue for her as David had made it clear that she would be gone from his life on December twentieth.

She wrenched her thoughts away from the man, noticing that while she'd been gathering wool, Mrs. Fanshaw had led them down a black, gray, and white corridor into another room that was—yet again—black, gray, and white.

The only color in the large drawing room was provided by the artwork on the walls.

And oh, what artwork it was! Everything—from the paintings to sculptures to other *objets d'art*—was highly sensual or overtly sexual in nature.

Callie could not stop gawking, her gaze again and again returning to the huge canvases that dominated one wall of the cavernous room.

The women quickly broke into groups, four of them settling in one of the seating areas and commencing to whisper and giggle, their comfortable behavior telling Callie they knew each other well.

Mrs. Fanshawe and a Frenchwoman named Nathalie Dupont were engaging in stilted conversation, so Callie chose to join them rather than the others.

Nora Fanshawe's smile was unexpectedly warm given that the woman looked so cold. She had some of the palest skin and lightest blonde hair that Callie had ever seen.

"Miss Dupont is a native French speaker who has not been here very long," Mrs. Fanshawe explained, and then translated what she'd said in flawless French for the other woman.

Callie was not surprised that she was bilingual as her accent was refined, as were her manners.

"I would be pleased to converse in your language," Callie said in French, earning an amazed look from the Frenchwoman while Mrs. Fanshawe seemed to take her knowledge in stride.

Callie said to Mrs. Fanshawe in the same language, "I have read about your art in the newspaper, but I've not had a chance to see any of it. Do you display your work in galleries or other places open to the public?" She was genuinely interested to see some of her paintings now that she had met the woman.

"I do not have anything at the moment—my next showing will be next year." She gestured to the wall Callie had just been staring at. "Those four are mine."

The canvases in question were male nudes, the subjects in all four were a huge, muscular man who was visibly erect and quite well-endowed.

Callie wrenched her stunned gaze from the paintings and smiled at the artist. "Mr. Smith must be a big admirer of yours and I can see why. They are powerful paintings."

Nora Fanshawe chuckled. "Thank you. Smith is a collector of mine. If I am not careful, he will buy everything I paint."

Miss Dupont frowned. "But why do you not want him to buy all he wishes?"

"I like to think of more people getting to see my pieces."

It was clear the Frenchwoman did not understand that reasoning.

"Do you paint portraits, as well?" Callie asked.

"I take the occasional commission, although my husband would prefer that he be my only subject."

"Those are Mr. Fanshawe?" Callie asked.

"Yes."

Miss Dupont and Callie both stared at the canvases.

They were clearly of the same man. He was naked and his cock was huge and erect. The subject's face was not visible, but the general build and dark hair were clearly those of Mr. Fanshawe. In one of the paintings, he was having sex with a woman who was obviously not Mrs. Fanshawe.

Her Villain

What a fascinating couple.

Callie wouldn't have thought that she would enjoy looking at depictions of the male form given how often she'd been forced to see naked men in the past year, but the paintings were undeniably arousing.

How nice it would be to reproduce one's lover on canvas. Providing one's lover ever took off his clothing when making love to one, of course.

But why was Callie thinking about that?

David wasn't her lover; he was her employer, a temporary employer, at that.

And a generous one, too. Thanks to the jewels he had just given her, Callie could leave tomorrow if she wanted. If she sold them, she could pay for a fine cabin on a ship to America and have plenty of money left over when she got there.

For some reason, the thought wasn't nearly as exciting as it should have been.

***

David's mind hummed with possibilities as they rode home in the hansom. The men he had met tonight had brains that fit so well with his own it had been slightly unnerving.

Oh, they didn't lack the essential human skills and emotions that he did, but their thoughts about investment and financial growth were complementary.

He had especially enjoyed the conversation he'd had with Stephen Chatham and Edward Fanshawe. Both men were without affectations and spoke with a directness he could appreciate.

Gideon Banks was… Well, suffice it to say that the man took a great deal of concentration to converse with. It was true Banks had a brilliant mind, but unfortunately only about five percent of it was focused on business while the other ninety-five seemed consumed by women. Or, more accurately, fucking.

Smith was too difficult for David to read to be entirely comfortable in his presence. And the man's house had made him feel uncomfortable with its complete lack of color. He much preferred the gradual changes Calliope had effected, which were both attractive and comfortable rather than ostentatious.

"David?"

He turned to her. "Yes?"

"I'm sorry about earlier—when I asked you about the jewels."

David held her gaze, recognizing her apology as genuine, if somewhat confused. Well, she was not the only one. His reaction had confused him, too. He ignored her apology as he had no idea what to say.

After a moment, she spoke again. "I enjoyed the dinner tonight. I especially liked Nora Fanshawe," she said. "Did you see her paintings in the drawing room?"

"Yes." David had found the eroticism so powerful as to be almost overwhelming, especially the one where Fanshawe was fucking a woman who was clearly not his wife. Had Nora Fanshawe imagined that scene or had Fanshawe fucked another woman while his wife had painted them?

It was intriguing. And titillating.

Enjoying that painting was understandable, but he had also become aroused from looking at the others, which were all naked paintings of Fanshawe alone.

David had met men in the army who preferred men to women, but he had never understood why. After seeing the paintings tonight, he could see the beauty in the male form.

There certainly wasn't any beauty in David's form.

"Did you like them?" she asked.

"Yes."

"So did I."

He felt an odd churning in his belly at her admission. Did looking at the paintings make her want to fuck Fanshawe? David supposed he could ask.

He decided it was a question to which he would rather not know the answer.

"Did you know that Mrs. Fanshawe met Mr. Fanshawe in a brothel?" she asked.

"No."

"He was a patron and engaged her to live in his house because he did not wish to share her with other men."

David could certainly understand that impulse.

"They seem to be very much in love."

He had no response for that.

"Have you ever been in love, David?"

That was a very easy question to answer. "No."

"Me, neither. Although I thought I was, once."

His curiosity, which had been slumbering deeply, reared its head. David wanted to know more, but he wasn't sure how to go about it. If he asked who the man was, she would probably worry that David would find him and beat him. At the moment, that seemed like something he would enjoy.

She let her head rest against the seatback and stared at the roof over their heads.

David had just decided to ask the man's identity when she saved him the effort.

"He was a young lecturer at the same university as my father. He was a poet." She suddenly laughed. "Or at least that is what he aspired to be."

"What happened?" he urged when she stopped.

Her head rolled in his direction, until she could see him. "My father died." He saw her throat flex. "I thought—I thought this man might rescue me like the heroes in his poems seemed prone to do when they weren't making grandiose declarations of love." She closed her eyes. "But it turned out that he was only good with words, deeds seemed to come harder to him." She opened her eyes again. "And so I became a whore and developed a dislike for poetry."

David wanted to ask the man's name—where he lived— and then hunt him down and make him suffer for the stricken look in her eyes.

He felt a touch on his hand and looked down to find her gloved fingers over his.

When he looked up from their joined hands to her face, he saw that she had closed her eyes again and there was a slight smile curving her full lips.

His stomach roiled uncomfortably, pitching as if he were on the deck of a ship. Or standing too close to the edge of a cliff.

Perhaps something at dinner had disagreed with him.

Chapter 18

Callie had just finished drying herself after the quick shower bath she'd taken and was under the covers on her bed, shivering. Although the fire had been burning from earlier in the day, she had forgotten to bank it before leaving for dinner and the room was so cold that she could now see her breath.

She slid a finger between the lips of her pussy, both shamed and amused when she felt how wet and slippery she was even though she had just left the shower bath.

The plug still weighed heavily inside her and the insistent throbbing in her sex made it feel bigger and harder than ever.

David had seemed quieter than usual in the hansom on the way back from the dinner. If she didn't know better, she might have thought something had disturbed him tonight. He'd seemed indifferent to her apology, so she must have been mistaken about his reaction to her question about the jewelry.

Of course he wouldn't be offended. To David Remington, Callie was a whore and he was the man paying to fuck her. Just because he was generous with his money didn't mean he cared about her. It was clear even to a fool that David Remington had no use for all his wealth. He didn't buy anything for himself other than food and clothing.

Callie doubted that he would even notice the changes she had already made in his house. Small things like putting down a few rugs and hanging some drapes she had found in the lumber room, which had held all sorts of interesting items.

When the new servants started work the next week she would get help and distribute some of the pieces of furniture stored away. Whoever had lived here before had excellent taste and there were several quality pieces.

In any case, Callie needed to keep the thought firmly in her mind that David was nothing more than her employer and this was just a job. And a well-paying, easy one, at that.

She shivered again and rubbed her arms to keep the goose pimples at bay.

The door opened and David turned the gas to the maximum flame before entering. When he saw her under the blankets, he frowned. "Is something wrong?"

"I'm freezing."

He shut the door behind him and went to the fireplace.

As Callie watched, he threw on all her kindling until there were flames dancing and then he emptied the coal scuttle onto the fire.

Callie gasped. "That is my fuel for a week!"

He stood, turned to her, and brushed off his hands. "Why was your fire not burning?" he asked, looking and sounding more displeased than she had ever heard him sound before.

"I just forgot to bank it before we left." She smiled. "I was so excited about the dinner party."

He ignored her attempt at humor. "You should have a fire burning at all times."

"That seems wasteful as—"

"Do not gainsay me. I want you comfortable."

She blinked at that and even he seemed taken aback by his words.

"I like to have you naked when I come to you," he said, almost as if he were justifying the comment to himself.

"Yes, I'd gathered that," she said dryly.

He stared at her, pensive.

Callie began to lift off the covers.

"No. Stay beneath them until the room is warm."

"That might take a while," she warned even though she was grateful for his thoughtful impulse.

He grunted, looking almost uncertain.

"You could always get under the blankets with me," she suggested hopefully, already guessing his answer.

He merely stared.

Callie had to bite back a smile. He looked devilishly handsome in his evening clothes, but his expression was that of a boy who'd been deprived of the use of his favorite toy.

"Or you could just come and lie down beside me—on top of the bedding."

He pursed his lips, his dark eyes flickering over her and the bed.

"We could have the half-hour of conversation *now* as opposed to after. The room will have warmed by the time we are finished talking," she assured him.

He hesitated, but then gave an abrupt nod and strode toward the bed. It dipped under his weight and he propped himself against the headboard, fully clothed, arms crossed over his chest, staring straight ahead, his expression that of a martyr resigned to the torments of the Spanish Inquisition. "What did you want to ask me tonight?"

It was difficult not to laugh. He sounded as if he'd just been condemned to another afternoon in a modiste shop.

Callie decided that she would be merciful and not pry into his past for once. Instead, she asked about something that had been weighing on her all night long, both literally and figuratively. "When we were at dinner tonight did you think about the plug inside me?"

He turned to her slowly, his eyelids lowering over pupils that suddenly flared to life. "I scarcely thought of anything else. It was not conducive to discussing the syndicate's copper mine proposal."

She could not hold her laughter in.

David, predictably, looked perplexed by her amusement.

When she was once again in control of herself, she asked, "What did you think?"

"You are not asking what I thought about the copper mine," he said, something that *almost* looked like a glint of humor in his dark gaze.

She shook her head, smiling. "No."

His jaw worked slightly and his eyes flickered down her covered body and then back up again, until he met her gaze. "I thought about taking it out, filling you with more, and then plugging you again."

Callie completely lost the urge to laugh, her mouth suddenly as dry as a desert. She swallowed hard and moistened her lower lip with her tongue. He lowered his gaze to her mouth and stared, as if riveted, hungry flames dancing in his eyes.

"Did it make you hard to think of me full of your seed?" she asked in a lust-roughened voice.

"Yes."

Their eyes seemed fused by the heat arcing between them.

"Did those portraits of Fanshawe arouse you?" he asked.

Callie was startled by this unprecedented expression of interest in her thoughts—at least about anything other than chess "Yes."

"His cock is bigger than mine. Did you imagine what it would feel like to be fucked by something so long and thick and hard?"

Her heart pounded as if there was a herd of horses thundering in her chest. After an agonizingly long pause, she said, "Yes."

David growled and his nostrils flared. "Your cunt is so tight that he would split you in two. But you would like that, wouldn't you?"

"Ye—"

He moved in the lightning-fast way that he had, straddling her body, caging her between his arms and legs, their faces so close that their noses almost touched.

"I do not like thinking of another cock in your pussy." His black gaze dropped to her mouth. "Or in any part of your body.

It makes me—" he broke off, his eyes flickering restlessly around the room, as if an answer might be hiding on the bare walls. After several moments he pinned her with his inky black stare. "It makes me feel violent."

Callie could tell by the faint note of perplexity in his tone that he was unfamiliar with the emotion causing those violent thoughts.

She could also tell—by the rock-hard ridge pressing against her mound over several layers of blankets—that something about his current emotional state aroused him even as it unnerved him.

Now you know what it feels like to be me, she wanted to say.

Instead, she taunted him. "Are you imagining how my cunt would look stretched around such a huge cock?"

His eyelids fluttered slightly, his face taut as knots of tension rippled up and down his clenched jaw.

"He looked so huge that I would never be able to take all of it int—"

"*No.*" The word was a primitive snarl and David ripped the blankets off her body, exposing her suddenly scalding hot skin to the cold air.

His gaze swept down her chest and stopped on her mound. "Open your legs."

Callie eagerly complied while he yanked open his placket hard enough that she heard the fine suiting tear.

He took out his hard cock, which was not much smaller than Mr. Fanshawe's. Not that Callie had any intention of telling him that as it appeared to be inciting him in interesting ways.

David roughly stroked himself and stared down at her with a menacing glitter in his eyes. "Spread yourself. Show me how much you want me, Calliope."

She parted her lower lips and he hissed in a breath at the sight of her slippery, swollen folds.

Some internal struggle took place behind his eyes before he suddenly pushed her thighs wide and dropped down to one elbow, using his other hand to guide himself to her entrance. Rather than fill her with a savage thrust, as she had expected, he teased the tight entrance with the thick head, pulsing inside her shallowly.

He felt so good that she lifted her hips, desperate for more. "Please, Dav—"

David plunged into her and the effect of the sudden thrust was electric, every muscle in her body tensing at once as his long, thick shaft ground against the stone plug inside her, the combination of the two filling her pelvis to bursting.

"Fuck," was all he said, his tight ballocks pressed snugly against her sex.

Callie couldn't even manage *that* much. She was stuffed so full that she could feel his shaft pulsing against the heavy stone, making it throb. It was…

Callie wasn't sure what it was, other than exceedingly intense.

David partially withdrew, rising up higher on his knees while sliding his arms beneath her thighs.

"I want to see," he muttered, folding her legs against her chest, so that her knees framed her breasts.

Callie whimpered at the change in angle, which made her pelvis feel even fuller.

David grunted as he slowly withdrew, until only the tip of his erection was still inside her.

Callie immediately missed him—missed the pain and pressure of being so achingly full.

She had just opened her mouth to beg him to fill her again, harder and rougher, when his eyes darted from where their bodies were joined back to her face.

"Does it hurt to have both your holes filled at the same time?" he asked, his chest rising and falling faster than it normally did.

Callie shivered at his crude question and caught her lower lip between her teeth, holding his hot gaze for a long moment before nodding.

She was instantly rewarded by the slowest, most sensual smirk she had ever seen sliding across his face. It was such an astounding expression that for a moment she thought it was a stranger wearing David's face.

The smile fled in a flash and his gaze lowered back to where he teased her with only his tip. "Good," he said.

And then he proceeded to give her what she needed without making her beg for it.

***

Fucking Calliope with a plug inside her was one of the most pleasurable experiences David could recall. He could see by the lines of pain around her eyes that it hurt—and that made him even harder. She was suffering because it pleased him.

And that was an even better feeling than her tight pussy.

David pressed her knees harder, spreading her thighs until her sex was tilted toward the ceiling, affording him a superlative view of his shaft spearing her again and again and again. But as enjoyable as it was to watch himself penetrate her, it would not give her the friction she needed to reach her release.

And so, after a few more glorious thrusts, he reluctantly released her knees and dropped to his hands, angling his hips in a way that made her gasp. She was so ready—indeed, she had been even before David had entered her—that it took lamentably few thrusts to bring her to climax.

David paused while she clenched around him, the contractions bringing his cock into even closer contact with the plug, the tightening of her inner muscles giving her both pleasure and pain if the little choked cries she made were anything to go by.

He waited until the spasms faded to almost nothing before withdrawing completely and then lowering to his elbows and taking her engorged bud into his mouth.

"David!" she wailed, suddenly understanding that he was not done with her yet.

She tried to squirm away, but he held her thighs pinned wide and sucked.

For all her screaming and sobbing, he still managed to force two more orgasms from her body before she tangled her fingers in his hair and pulled so hard that his eyes watered.

"Please… no more. Please!"

David smirked to himself and released her.

She sighed and her body sagged with relief as he moved away from the tender bundle of nerves and proceeded to lick the rest of her.

Once he had cleaned every part of her, he gave her a leisurely tongue-fucking just to make certain that she knew who was master of her body. After all, it would not do to let her think she could manipulate him and evade orgasms merely by whining and begging.

David pushed up onto his knees, wiped his wet face with the back of his hand, and met her sated gaze. "Hands and knees," he barked, amused when she gave a sullen little huff but rolled over and assumed the position.

He shoved her knees apart and then pushed her shoulders down until her head was on the bed, bottom thrust in the air.

And then he spread the cheeks of her arse and looked his fill at that part of her he'd been fantasizing about all through dinner.

His full, aching balls boiled at the sight of her soft pink flesh around the cold, hard stone. David throbbed even harder at the realization that *he* had filled her with this unforgiving device. Calliope had not only allowed him to insert the plug—neglecting to engage in her usual haggling for more money—but, judging by her slick thighs, she *loved* it.

David knew, without a doubt, that Calliope would allow him to do anything he pleased to her body. And not because she had no choice, either. The jewels he had given her would afford her at least five years of living expenses—longer if she was careful.

No. The reason she would allow his debauchery is because she wanted it just as much as David did.

The thought was enough to make him ejaculate like an overexcited schoolboy all over her delectable arse. Only by sheer force of will was he able to leash his desire and focus his attention.

The plug was made from some sort of black stone that had been polished smooth. The odd little shop where David had purchased it sold many different sorts and sizes. The one inside her was of the smallest variety, but he already knew he would want to use more—bigger—sizes on her.

He took the flat black flange and slowly began to withdraw it.

She wriggled her bottom slightly and made a soft noise of discomfort.

David used his free hand to deliver a stinging slap. "Do not move," he ordered, secretly disappointed when she instantly obeyed. He enjoyed spanking her a great deal and always looked for any excuse to do so.

But then… did he really *need* an excuse?

David blinked at the captivating thought.

And then he gave her a second, even harder slap.

"*Ow!* What was that for?"

A tiny smile twisted his lips. "I do not require a reason, Calliope," he said in an admirably cool tone considering how aroused he was.

And then he spanked her again.

This time she muffled her cry and stayed still, as if she thought that behaving would spare her a spanking.

Not anymore.

David wrenched his thoughts away from the pleasurable contemplation of all the spankings he would administer and turned his attention back to the plug. He slowly eased the widest part out of her tight hole. As much as he enjoyed administering pain, the thought of damaging her was distasteful to him.

Her body, which had been rigid with tension, relaxed once he removed it.

David set the stone, which was deliciously hot from her body, aside and then slid a finger into her slightly stretched arse, pumping her gently but deeply, using his spunk to ease a second finger in and open her properly.

Only when she was writhing and moaning and pushing back onto his fingers did he replace his fingers with the head of his cock, slowly filling her, the tight clasp of her passage so exquisite that his eyes rolled back in their sockets.

He fucked her slowly, giving her every inch with each stroke.

"*Mmm,* David. 's'good," she slurred, pressing back against him.

Her moan and words sent a bolt of pleasure through him—not sexual, but something just as powerful. Maybe even *more* powerful.

She was right; it *was* good. Too damned good.

He felt too damned good.

David knew it would never last—nothing good ever did—but he could at least enjoy it for now.

And so he closed his eyes and let his head drop back while he savored the moment.

A question Calliope had asked him once—which had confused him at the time—suddenly came back to him. She had asked him if he was happy and David had not known what she meant at the time.

But tonight, he had done something normal and behaved just like tens of thousands of other people and shared a companionable meal.

And now he was in his home—safe and warm—with a woman who derived physical pleasure from the things he liked to do to her.

Right then—for a brief, fleeting moment in time—David finally knew what happiness meant.

He felt a rare pang of regret that it could not last.

As least not more than an hour.

Because that was when David would need to venture out of his pleasurable cocoon and into the cold, dark night so he could meet up with men who were planning to kill their leader and overthrow the government.

And David would help them do it.

Chapter 19

Several mornings later David was eating his breakfast and pondering the message he'd received last night about the next shipment he was to retrieve at the docks.

The message had not come from Sir Andrew, of course, but some other player in what seemed to be an ever-growing conspiracy around the assassination.

None of that was his concern. All David had to worry about was seeing that the shipments got to their destinations and making sure he was ready to carry out his job on December twentieth.

To the extent that David thought about Andrew Morton and his co-conspirators—which wasn't a great deal—he assumed their treasonous organization was widespread and reached the highest levels of society. That wasn't—

The door to the breakfast room opened and Calliope entered.

"Good morning," she sang out, her smile bright as she hastened to pour herself a cup of coffee.

David grunted and turned to the newspapers beside his plate, watching her bustle about surreptitiously from beneath his eyelashes. She was garbed in one of her older worn day dresses, which told him that her plans for the day involved the house, rather than going out and shopping.

He had planned to go into the Exchange for a few hours, but if she was going to be at home then perhaps she might need him for something.

Like what? Do you think she might need somebody killed? Or that she has some weapons to illicitly deliver? a sly voice whispered.

David blinked at the bizarre thought, which he was fairly certain was sarcastic, something he had very little familiarity with.

Well, the voice wasn't wrong; what in the world would she need him for? And when had she ever—

"David? *David?*"

He looked up at the sound of his name.

She was smiling quizzically. "You seem distracted this morning."

He just stared.

For some reason, his silence made her laugh. "I need to talk to you about something."

David wanted to groan.

"You needn't get that surly look on your face," she said.

If she was learning how to read his expressions that meant David needed to do a better job of hiding them.

"What do you want to talk about?" he asked warily.

"Remember you promised to spend an evening doing something different?"

"Different?" he said, although he suspected he knew all too well what she meant.

"Yes. Perhaps the theater or opera or a ballet?"

"I remember," he said grimly.

"Might we have an evening out this week?"

David glowered. Usually, that was enough to get her to lower her gaze and begin to shuffle uncomfortably. He must be losing his skill because she merely stared back.

"You promised."

"I *remember*," he repeated, even more grimly. "Fine. What night?"

"Three nights hence?"

"Fine," he said again. "What do you have planned?"

"It is a surprise."

David scowled. "I don't like surprises."

"It will be a *good* surprise."

When he hesitated, her smile faltered and she said in a quiet voice. "Please? Just this once?"

David filled his lungs to near bursting and then exhaled heavily. "Fine," he said for a third time.

Her smile was brilliant.

For a moment it felt as if the always chilly dining room had become warmer.

Ridiculous.

***

Calliope slid a surreptitious look at David and had to bite her lower lip to keep from grinning like a fool.

It had been a risk to bring him to his first-ever opera, but when she had heard there would be only one more night of *Das Rheingoldt*, she knew it was the perfect choice.

David had been rapt from the moment the curtain lifted and the powerful music of the composer Wagner thundered in the cavernous opera house, filling the huge space to an almost overwhelming level.

There was the added advantage that the opera was quite short—only one part of the Ring Cycle—and therefore an excellent first choice. Callie personally loved operatic performances, but many people did not and a lengthy opera would have been hellish if he had disliked it.

But the curtain had come down the moment before and after only a brief hesitation David had lurched to his feet along with hundreds of others and had clapped through three encores.

Now the crowds were beginning to disperse and he looked almost… bereft. Callie had briefly considered spending a sizeable portion of her savings to engage a box, but—at the last moment—she had been sensible and had opted for seats. They had still been expensive, but in her opinion it had been worth it.

Callie watched in silence as David slowly came back to the real world.

"Did you enjoy it?" she asked, even though she didn't need to ask.

His eyes narrowed slightly as they came back into focus and he regarded her with one of his unreadable looks. "Yes."

She couldn't help smiling. "I thought you might."

***

David felt…bemused. That was the only word he could think of that might describe it. He slid a glance toward Calliope, who was riding quietly beside him as the hansom cut through the London night.

She was wearing yet another blue gown, but this one a much darker shade than the one she had worn to the dinner party. Again, she wore the jewels he'd given her.

David had seen many women tonight and all of them had been dressed grandly and with fine jewels. But he honestly had not seen a more desirable woman in the entire building.

He had to admit that the night had not gone as he'd expected.

They had eaten an excellent meal—all his favorites cooked by Mrs. Jenkins as well as some apple tarts that Calliope had taken the time to make—and then he'd gone to his first-ever opera. His first performance of any kind.

He had dreaded the evening for days, but it had ended up being one of the most stimulating of his life. At least the most stimulating night that had not included sex.

While it was true that the music had transported him, it had also mined some emotions that he would not have believed existed. Emotions that were better left deeply buried.

As moving as the experience had been, David did not think he would want to go through it too often.

"I don't want to take off my cloak yet," Calliope said, shivering as they entered the foyer, where it was possible to see their breath. "Will you come with me to the drawing room, David?"

He paused and pulled out his watch. It was almost midnight. Evidently their schedule had been discarded for the evening. He put away his watch and looked up to find her watching him with an almost anxious look.

David wanted to take his coat, hat, gloves, and walking stick up to his room and put them where they belonged, but he could see she wanted him to come with her.

After the musical evening that she had just devised—mostly for his pleasure, he suspected—he decided he could live with the unease of his things not being where they belonged, so he hung his hat and coat on the rack.

When he opened the door to the drawing room for her, he paused on the threshold. After a moment, he turned to her. "What is this?" he asked, gesturing to the frosted cake sitting on the tea tray.

"I had one of the new maids stay late and bring this up at midnight," she said. "She is gone now and it is just the two of us."

He closed the door behind him and when she reached for the clasp on her heavy fur-lined cloak he stepped behind her and lifted it from her shoulders.

She turned to him, her lips parted in obvious surprise at the courtesy.

David was more than a little bemused himself, but he had seen Edward Fanshawe remove his wife's cloak the same way. Surely he had not erred?

But her astonished expression turned into a smile, so he assumed not.

"I thought we might have some cake and tea and a game of chess," she said, seeming to glide toward the tea tray, the layers and layers of diaphanous blue material floating around her. "Sit, and I will serve you."

David draped the cloak over the back of a settee and then took his usual seat at the chess table.

He felt mildly discomfited and knew it would be the changes to the schedule. And the fact that they never ate cake while playing chess. Indeed, the only other time there had been a cake had been for Calliope's birthday.

Was this some other occasion? Or did cake naturally follow after an evening of opera?

Christ. These social occasions gave him a throbbing in his temples.

"Here," she said quietly.

He looked up to see her holding out a cup and saucer. Already on the table was a plate with a huge slice of cake.

He took the tea from her and she met his gaze. "You told me that you'd never had a birthday celebration—that you have no birth*day*."

David had no desire to discuss that information, so he merely set down his cup and saucer.

Calliope gestured to the cake. "Everyone deserves a birthday, David. I took the liberty of making today yours."

He looked from her to the cake, his mind oddly sluggish.

Fortunately, she didn't seem to need a response.

Instead, she took her usual chair. "I believe it is my move first tonight," she said, and then moved the white king's pawn.

The board blurred in front of him and David blinked to clear his vision.

Watching the opera so intently must have strained his eyes and made them water.

Chapter 20

David stared at the board, replaying the moves as he always did. It was their third game—one more than usual.

When he had asked *why* Calliope was giving him a third opportunity to beat her, she had smirked and said, "Because it is your birthday and I'm giving you things that you can't or won't give yourself."

He had not argued. After all, the schedule was so destroyed as to be non-existent tonight.

Naturally, she had beaten him three times in a row.

Calliope stood. "Will you come to me in half an hour?"

David's cock—already hard from getting thrashed in three games—throbbed at her heavy-lidded gaze and he nodded.

He took the opportunity to bring his possessions up to his room and have a quick shave—his third of the day—as he had noticed that her skin was often red and scratched when he finished with her. While David liked to see his teeth and finger marks on her body, he did not like to see her creamy white skin become red and chafed.

He finished shaving and still had six-and-a-half minutes to spare and so he sat on his bed, closed his eyes, and recalled the opera from earlier in the evening.

Only when he heard the distant chiming of the clock from the drawing room—yet another of Calliope's recent additions— did David open his eyes and realize that he'd drifted without purpose for six-and-a-half minutes.

Her Villain

It was an evening for firsts.

And it appeared that was going to continue, because when he opened the door to Calliope's room, he was so startled by the sight that met his gaze that he paused on the threshold.

Calliope reclined on the bed, naked. Beside her in a neat pile were black leather straps with buckles on them.

David had seen those straps before—but not in this house—and had used ones just like them in brothels in the past.

He could not help noticing that the lamps on both nightstands were blazing, making the room brighter than ever—just the way David liked it.

And then his gaze moved to the item beside the lamp on one of the nightstands and his cock, already leaking with arousal, pulsed at the sight of the crop.

When his eyes slid back to her face, he saw that she was breathing through parted lips, a mottled flush spreading over her breastbone and up her throat.

He strode to the nightstand and picked up the whip, only noticing when he tested its heft that the initials D. R. were engraved into the silver ring just above the leather grip. He looked at her.

"Happy birthday, David."

"You bought this for me?" he asked rather stupidly.

She smiled.

David examined the whip more closely. It was well made, the craftsmanship far finer than the one he owned.

He looked from the whip to the black leather belts before moving back to her face. "The straps are to bind you and the crop is for me to use on you?" Yet another stupid question.

She nodded. "Another birthday present."

"I thought being bound and whipped frightened you."

She swallowed, her elegant throat flexing in a way that indicated nervousness. "It does. But…I trust you. And I want to please you."

David's balls tightened so hard at her words that he ejaculated just a little.

He reached out with the whip and ran the stiff keeper over her quivering belly down to her sex. "Open your legs."

She obeyed without hesitation and he lightly tapped her pussy lips with the crop, fascinated by the way muscles up and down her body clenched with each tap.

"Spread your cunt."

Her fingers were in motion before the last word was out and David gazed down at the glistening pink frills, his pulse throbbing in his cock.

He dragged the keeper through her folds until the square of black leather was slick with her arousal, and then lifted it to her mouth. "Taste yourself."

She blushed furiously, but opened her lips and licked the damp leather, her eyes holding his as she caressed the keeper with suggestive strokes of her tongue.

David growled. He wanted to whip her—to lay red stripes all across the canvas of her silky white skin—but he was too aroused. Too eager for her.

Too…excited.

As much as David hated to wait, he needed to ejaculate and dull the edge of his need before he used the crop on her.

He tossed the whip onto the bed and then took her left wrist and speedily secured the leather strap to the heavy brass frame, pulling until her arm was taut.

It took no more than a few minutes to tie both her ankles, spreading her legs as wide as her hips would allow—and then some—until she was powerless and vulnerable and completely open for his use.

David knelt between her spread thighs and dragged a single finger between the delicate petals of her sex, teasing and stroking and taunting her swollen folds until her greedy cunt was clenching, begging to be fucked.

His hungry gaze slid from her spread sex up over her quivering belly, lingering on the pulse that pounded in her throat before finally landing on her beautiful face.

She'd caught her lower lip with her teeth and her eyes were wide, more white showing than was usual.

David *knew* for a certainty that she was only now realizing how how utterly and completely she had put herself under his control by allowing him to bind her.

He could do anything he wanted to her body and she could not do a thing to stop him.

David felt a brief, dark flare of amusement at the predicament she had made for herself.

She gasped at whatever she saw on his face, her chest rising and falling faster, like a hare poised to flee.

But there would be no running away for Calliope, and they both knew it.

The raw fear in her blue eyes sent a violent wave of lust rolling through his body and David yanked open his placket, freed his cock, and then filled her tight cunt to the hilt.

She moaned and her muscles strained to arch off the bed, but he had bound her so tightly that only her head could move.

When she lifted her chin and bared her throat to him, David sucked and bit the tender skin, fucking her with all the finesse of a street cur mounting a bitch, penetrating her as hard and deep as he could with each stroke, grinding against the source of her pleasure and driving her to orgasm.

***

It felt odd to be bound so tightly that Callie could not move. The vulnerability was painfully arousing.

As was the feeling of David's hard, heavy body collapsed on top of hers, still hard inside her. Callie was confused as to why he had stopped without achieving his own climax.

She was also confused that he'd not used the crop on her. Or perhaps making her wait was his way of heightening the tension?

Callie was afraid of pain—afraid of *him*—but she wanted what he would do to her even more. Which made no sense.

What she had said to David was true: she trusted him not to hurt her. If he had wanted to hurt her physically, he could have done it at any time and she would not have been able to do a thing to stop him.

Callie trusted him. And it bothered her how much she craved and yet feared a whipping at his hands. The look in his eyes when he'd dragged the crop over her sex had been almost diabolical.

But that, too, had been arousing—his hunger for her. How had she managed to fascinate this powerful, dangerous, and seemingly untouchable man?

Callie felt his body tense as he quickly eased out of her body, turning his back to her as he fixed his clothing.

"I will whip you hard," he said, his back still to her.

Callie jolted at the sound of his voice and then shivered, more aroused by the flat, emotionless way he said the words than the actual words themselves. "I know."

"But I will not break the skin."

"You—that is—you can control that?"

"Yes. I can control that," he said, humor obvious in his voice.

Callie desperately wanted to see his face when he was amused, but when he turned around a few seconds later he was as unreadable as ever, if slightly more disheveled from his exertions.

"You've, er, done this to women before?" Callie couldn't resist asking, even though she knew the answer.

"Yes."

She burned with jealousy at the thought of him with another woman. The irony of her reaction did not escape her. Callie was a whore and it was almost certain that she'd had far more sexual partners in nine months than he'd had in the last twenty years.

"Why do you like administering pain?" she asked.

"Why do you like receiving it?" he countered.

"That is a question I have asked myself often," she admitted.

"And?"

"I don't know why. But I do know that I only like it with you."

The spasm of pleasure that shot across his face was quick and she would have missed it if she'd not been staring at him.

"So, why do you like it?" she asked.

He turned his head slightly, until his dark eyes were looking into hers. "Because it makes my cock hard."

Callie laughed and then glanced down at his tented trousers. "Your cock was *already* hard."

"That is because I am thinking of whipping you."

She swallowed, suddenly doubting the wisdom of what she had promised him. "Will I like it, David?" she whispered.

His pupils, already large, flared. "Yes. I will teach you to crave it, until you need it so badly that you will get wet just looking at the whip in my hand."

***

David released her from her bondage, untying only the straps on the posts. "Turn over."

Calliope obeyed after only a slight hesitation and David tied her face down on the bed, two pillows beneath her hips to lift her enough that he could easily and quickly mount her when the time was right.

Once she was secure, he stepped back to admire her. She trembled and her pale as cream skin sheened with sweat. She looked more beautiful than she ever had.

David ran a hand up one thigh, stroking his palm over the firm globes of her ass and allowing a finger to part her arse cheeks and caress the tight pucker between them.

She shivered beneath his touch, her hips vainly straining up to meet him, but again he had tied her too tightly to move.

As he stroked over her buttocks and imagined laying his mark on her, he noticed several faint lines.

David's eyes narrowed as he studied the slightly raised marks. If there was one thing he knew a great deal about, it was scars.

Fury, colder and stronger than any emotion he had ever experienced, slammed into him. These were scars from the whipping Carlton had given her.

His hand shook with the force of his rage and the crop trembled in his palm.

Once again, he tossed the implement aside. David was too angry to whip her. Not at Calliope, but at himself for allowing

Carlton to live that night. He'd heard the man threaten her, and yet he had yielded to her plea for mercy.

David would not make that mistake a second time.

Calmed by his decision, he lowered himself unto his belly between her bound legs, spread her cheeks, and gave himself up to the pleasure of making her squirm in another way.

***

Callie was not sure what had happened. One minute David was caressing her body, standing beside the bed with his crop in his hand.

The next, he was between her thighs and going after her arse as if it were roast lamb and apple tarts all rolled into one.

Not that Callie was complaining; she was greatly enjoying the tongue-lashing he was giving her. Her sex so swollen and wet from his enthusiastic ministrations that she wondered if she could once more climax untouched.

But a moment later, when David moved up her body, covering her back with his front and parting her slick folds with the head of his cock, she realized she wouldn't have to.

He pushed into her with agonizing slowness, making her aware of every thick inch, until his root was snugged up against her spread sex.

He caged her with his elbows, his body anchored deeply within hers, and then said in a low, rough voice, "I saw the scars."

Callie blinked. "That is why you stopped?"

She felt him nod against her.

"Why?" she asked, genuinely curious.

"I was too angry to wield a whip. I would have hurt you—badly." He flexed his hips, tilting them so that his shaft sank into her a fraction of an inch deeper. He gave a soft sigh of satisfaction and lowered his weight on her, the crush of his body deliciously erotic. "I am going to kill him."

Her cunt squeezed before she could stop it.

David groaned and rolled his hips, withdrawing slowly and then sliding all the way back in. "That excites you," he said, rather stating the obvious.

"Yes," she admitted, face flaming, "But that does not mean I want you to do it."

"Why not?" he asked, his tone distracted as his hips continued to rock into her, penetrating her almost painfully deep each time.

"Just—Because—*Urhg!* I don't know. I'm finding it difficult to concentrate right now," she admitted with some asperity. "Could we please have this conversation later?"

His body shook noiselessly.

"Are you laughing?" She twisted her head to try and catch his expression. But she was tied too tightly to move. Blast! Would she never see the man smile?

He did not answer her, probably because he did not lie. Instead, he increased the speed of his thrusts.

Callie groaned when he wormed a hand beneath her and massaged the base of her clitoris with the pad of his finger, working her exactly the right way.

He did not stop when she came, instead fucking her through her climax, his relentless finger circling and circling, until a second, far fiercer orgasm, washed over the first.

Only when she had completely come undone did he take his own pleasure, flooding her with heat.

"Calliope."

Callie struggled to lift her heavy eyelids, not recognizing the raw voice that had whispered her name. "David?"

But then another wave slammed into her. Her last conscious thought before euphoria carried her away was that she must have imagined it.

***

Callie woke with a jolt, the room completely dark. She felt beside her, not surprised to discover she was alone.

David had obviously untied her and covered her with blankets, and the fire was glowing a sullen red and heating the room.

It took her a few moments to recall what had happened.

He did not whip me. He saw the scars and was too angry at what had been done to me to take his pleasure.

She pulled her lip beneath her teeth, hoping to squelch the odd scratchy feeling at the back of her throat that heralded tears. She caught the sob, but felt a hot trail on one cheek, and then the other.

Callie did not know why she was crying.

Chapter 21

A light dusting of snow swirled around Callie's feet as she stepped from the hansom. It was creeping toward the end of December and the weather, until now, had been almost too cold for snow.

Time is running out…

The thought dimmed her joy at the beauty of the white flurries dancing along the sidewalk. Every day, when she woke up, she thought about how quickly the last few weeks had flown past.

David's house was beginning to resemble a home—or at least it had the trappings of a place that was lived in. It still lacked any personal items and she suspected that was because he simply did not have any. Even his bedchamber, which she had forcibly invaded in order to select drapes and carpets, had nothing except a dressing room full of almost identical suits and a bathroom with the minimum of toiletries.

There was nothing else, no photographs, no paintings, none of the sentimental knickknacks people usually accumulated while engaging in the business of living.

The room was exactly like David himself: spare, tidy, and giving no hint of the man who occupied it.

The door to the small bookstore opened before Callie reached it and Mr. Miller, the owner and sole employee of the shop, stood on the threshold.

"How are you on this fine, snowy day, Miss Fowler?" he asked as he shut the door behind her.

"I am well, sir. I have come to see if my books have arrived yet?"

"I have one of them, but the other is proving elusive." He turned and looked through a stack of books on his cluttered desk. "Ah, here it is. This is the newer of the two. I am optimistic about the older one, but you will need to give me another few weeks."

"I understand. I will check back in two—" Callie realized she would not be there in two weeks and shoved down the wave of unhappiness, forcing a smile. "Let me pay for both— no, I insist." She gave him one of David's cards. "Please have it delivered here whenever it arrives."

As Mr. Miller made change, she looked down at her purchase. It was one of her father's favorite chess books. She wanted to give something to David for Christmas—well, an early Christmas as she would be gone—and this seemed like a gift he might actually appreciate.

"Let me wrap that up for you," Mr. Miller said.

Ten minutes later she was headed toward a draper's shop that was supposed to have delivered several purchases a week ago and still had—

"Miss Fowler?"

She stopped and turned at the sound of her name, peering through the thickening snowfall at a stranger.

He tipped his hat, giving Callie an apologetic smile. "I'm terribly sorry to accost you like this, but I could not think of a better way to approach you." He held out his gloved hand and Callie saw there was a card in it.

She took it without thinking. The card contained his name—George Jameson—and an address that almost any person in Britain knew. Callie looked up once she had read it. "The Home Office? What do you want with me?" Had prostitution suddenly gained the interest of the Home Secretary while she hadn't noticed?

"It is about your, er, employer—the man who calls himself David Remington."

"What do you mean *calls himself.*"

Mr. Jameson gestured to a tea shop across the street. "Could you spare me ten minutes? If you do, I think you will be glad you did."

Callie hesitated, studying the tall bland-looking man. Why did even talking to this Jameson make her feel disloyal toward David?

"It is a matter of some importance, Miss Fowler."

She held his somber gaze and finally jerked a nod. "Ten minutes."

Chapter 22

avid lifted another bite of salmon to his mouth and studied Calliope's face, perplexed by her stilted behavior. He was even more perplexed by the fact that he noticed or cared. Other people—and their emotions—had never mattered to him. Except when they became inconvenient. But right now, he had a burning desire to know what she felt—*why* she felt—a certain way.

She was unhappy, from what he could tell.

It was irksome to care.

David had always suspected that emotions would be inconvenient, and here he was, falling prey to some after forty-odd years in the world. He should have guessed the woman was going to be a problem that very first night, when he couldn't seem to get enough of making her come. He had always made sure the woman he fucked were ready to take him—there were few things more unpleasant than trying to shove a cock into a dry cunt, after all—but never had David felt so compelled to pleasure a woman past the point of necessity.

Trouble. That's what Calliope Fowler was. It was just as well she would be leaving soon—before he had to do the job that would be the last of its sort in his career. He didn't need distractions now. He never needed them, but now less than ever.

"Is aught amiss?" David asked as she gazed at her plate of food as if something fascinating was occurring.

Her Villain

Her head jerked up and she smiled brightly. "No! Why do you ask?"

David almost laughed. The woman across from him was one of the worst liars he'd ever met. Now if he only knew why she was lying.

He merely stared, having realized long ago that silence and a harsh glare were guaranteed to get another person babbling.

She swallowed convulsively, reached for her wine, jostled the glass, and spilled some on the table.

"Oh, dear," she murmured, beginning to rise from her chair.

"Leave it for a servant to clean up," he said. "That is why I pay them all, isn't it?" he added when she hesitated.

She slowly lowered herself into her chair.

"You seem anxious tonight."

"I, er, I had a rather annoying day."

"What happened?"

"The draper won't be able to deliver until the middle of January."

Yet another lie. Normally, her lies would infuriate him. But these lies were so blatant, so… pointless—that it was difficult to work up any anger.

"I wanted to see the curtains up in the library before I left," she said.

David had not forgotten that she was leaving in less than five days, but he'd not dwelt on the matter, either.

He felt no shame admitting that he liked having Calliope live with him. Not only were the chess games the best he had ever played, but he greatly appreciated having access to her body every night.

And, bafflingly, David discovered that the house *was* more pleasant with carpets and drapes and servants and other…things.

"Have you purchased your passage to America?" he asked.

"Yes."

"What city will you be living in?"

"New York City."

David was glad that he'd asked about her plans before suggesting they extend their arrangement. She would have rebuffed his offer and these last few days would have been even more awkward than they already were.

He decided to put her out of her misery and gestured to her barely touched plate. "I see you do not have much of an appetite. If you are amenable, we could start our games early tonight."

"Yes," she said, her eyes sliding nervously from David to her plate. "Early."

"Is there any of that brandy left?" he asked as he came around the table and pulled out her chair.

"Of course. I bought a case when I saw you enjoyed it."

"I would have some of that." David had never cared for spirits before, but he had become quite greedy about this brandy, having a glass every night.

"The decanter in the library is already filled."

David stopped at the door and turned to her. "I appreciate you recognizing what I like and providing it for me, Calliope."

She smiled, although it was more of a grimace.

Or perhaps David was simply not reading her expression correctly. After all, she had insisted nothing was wrong.

He sighed, shut his mouth, and ushered her into the drawing room. It was time to play some games.

***

Callie chewed her lip bloody while David slowly drifted off to sleep in his chair. Even when his eyes had closed completely and his breathing had become disturbingly slow and deep she couldn't bring herself to move.

Finally, when the longcase clock she'd chosen especially for this room—so he would not need to get out his pocket watch—chimed nine o'clock and he didn't so much as twitch, she let out a shaky breath and stood.

"David?" she whispered.

Nothing.

"David?" she repeated, louder this time.

Still nothing.

Callie quickly checked his wrist, fear stabbing her at the possibility that she'd given him too much of the drug. But his pulse seemed strong, if a little bit slow.

She leaned down and kissed his thin, normally expressionless lips, which seemed fuller and softer in sleep.

And she brushed the thick dark hair off his forehead; he needed to visit the barber soon.

Something hot landed on her arm and she realized she was crying.

"Do it, Calliope—you coward!" she whisper-hissed at herself.

Without breathing, she reached inside his frock coat and felt around until she found the pocket where he kept his small ring of keys, wincing when they jingled.

But still, he didn't move.

Callie squeezed the keys hard enough in her hand to cause pain and hurried to the door. She found Edward and Nellie just finishing clearing the dining room. "Mr. Remington is taking a nap in the drawing room, please see that he's not disturbed."

"Yes, Miss Fowler."

She smiled. "And you may tell the other servants they can have an early night." She hesitated only briefly before adding. "Mr. Remington wanted to be the one to give you the news, but he is going out of town tomorrow and I shall not be here, either. He wishes you to take the next four days as a paid holiday."

Edward and Nellie couldn't stop the grins that took over their faces. "Please thank him for us, Miss Fowler."

She nodded and watched until they'd disappeared around the corner that led to the kitchen. And then she ran up the stairs as if the devil himself were on her heels. Her hands shook badly as she tried to unlock the attic door, missing the keyhole multiple times before she finally opened it.

There was gaslight up here, as well, although the fixture was functional rather than decorative. The room was almost laughably sparse. There was a table and chair and a rug beneath it.

The surface of the table held only blank paper, a pen, and ink. There were no drawers.

She looked around, suddenly frantic at what she'd done. There was *nothing* here. Callie had listened to that horrid man and believed what he had told her about David and it had all been lies!

She began to crumble inside as she stepped away from the table. As she did, the floor squeaked loudly, startling her so badly she yelped.

Callie gave a half-hysterical laugh of relief and then stared down at the thick rug beneath her feet.

A rug.

The rooms in the house—except for the lumber room—had not contained a single rug when Callie had arrived.

Heart pounding, she shoved the table and chair off the rug and dropped to her knees. "Please be nothing. Please be nothing," she chanted as she flipped up the rug.

At first, she almost missed it. Whoever had cut the square into the wood—David, probably—had done so with great care, using the gaps between planks to disguise most of the cuts. But there was a hair-thin line that didn't fit with the floor pattern. She grabbed the small penknife off the table and pried at the cracks, scratching the floor in her haste, but the wood plank came up. And beneath it, between the joists in the floor, was a slim oilskin-wrapped packet.

"No! Please, *no!*" she moaned. Callie was tempted to throw it onto the fire without reading it. Maybe if she destroyed it then David would not do what the Home Office agent said he was going to do.

Callie sank onto her bottom and unwrapped the packet with trembling fingers even though some part of her mind shrieked against it.

And then she laid the documents out on the floor and began to piece together a puzzle she wished she had never learned about.

Chapter 23

Waiting for dawn to arrive was the most difficult thing Callie had done in her life.

David's tidy stack of documents irrefutably proved what the man, Jameson, had said was true: David was going to assassinate Prime Minister Gladstone on the day Parliament closed.

There were more details, much of it too shadowy for her addled brain to decipher. But the crux was that a group of men supporting a member of the opposition party—a man who was never named in the documents—would take advantage of the fact that most parliamentarians were either gone already for the holiday, or on their way out of the city, to seize control of the tumult created by the assassination.

Not only that, but David had been shepherding illegal weapons into the country for weeks. Callie did not understand exactly what would be done with the guns, but she was certain that nothing good would come of it.

She had allowed herself an hour to cry, rage, and pace.

And then she had collected napkins and bedsheets and anything else that could be used as a rope—everything except the straps she had purchased for David's birthday, which she could not bring herself to use—and commenced to tie David to his chair.

Looking at him now, Callie suspected she might have overdone it. He was all but shrouded in knotted linens.

He had scarcely moved after she'd left to go to the attic, but another check of his pulse had assured her he would be fine whenever the sleeping draught wore off. Or two sleeping draughts, which is what she'd put in his brandy. She'd had the powder since her father had died. The physician had insisted she accept them, positive that she would dissolve into hysteria without them. Callie had carried them with her all this time, almost as if she'd known there would be a use for them.

The clock began to chime eight and she kissed David one last time and caught up her reticule, leaving a letter on the salver in the foyer before striding toward the door.

Jameson had said that she was to take any confirmation of what he had told her about David's involvement in the conspiracy directly to a man at Whitehall. He had claimed this individual would know what to do with the information.

Additionally, she was to have a letter delivered directly to the Prime Minister himself—including only the details of the assassination attempt, which was to take place during his brief address to journalists, which he typically made at the end of each week.

When Callie had asked why she should not just go to Jameson rather than the man at the Home Office—and why she needed to send a message to the Prime Minister, as well—he had told her he was being dispatched from the city to track down the most recent weapons shipment, hoping to discover more of the identities of the conspirators.

As for the message to their nation's leader, Jameson had looked slightly aggrieved as he'd confessed that it was not always easy to get through the men around Gladstone, so the visit she was making would be an extra precaution.

"I cannot believe his people—those looking after his security—would not take a threat like this seriously!" Callie had exclaimed.

"He gets dozens of assassination threats every week, I'm afraid. As a result, he and his people do not take them as seriously as they should."

It seemed inconceivable, but Jameson worked for the government, so he would know.

It was icy and frigid outside, the delightful snow from yesterday having formed an unpleasantly slick crust over everything. As cold as it was, Callie was sweating profusely as she watched landmarks flicker past the hansom window, the carriage getting closer and closer to Whitehall.

She could still turn back. She could keep David tied to that chair for the next several days, making it impossible to do what he had been paid to do. If that was truly how he earned all his money—killing—she would beg him to come away, to go with her to America and start a new life. He obviously had enough money. They could start over. Together. She didn't have to do either of her errands—

Callie groaned. Yes. She *did* have to speak up. If something happened to the prime minister or if those weapons were used for something heinous, she would never forgive herself.

All too soon the cab drew to a halt. Callie paid the driver and marched with determined dread into the building. Jameson had told her where to go—what to say, even. The only thing he had not explained was how sick with betrayal she would feel.

"If you turn over the plans, it will make matters easier on Remington," he had assured her. "You will be saving him from the noose."

Perhaps that was true, but Callie had a plan of her own.

The building was a bit of a maze and it took her longer than she had thought to reach the right department. She stopped in front of the desk where a very young man sat in an ill-fitting suit. The plaque on the wall told her this was the right place.

She cleared her throat and the man, his eyes rimmed with red from a night of too much entertainment and too little sleep, looked up at her, throwing back his shoulders when he saw her face.

"How may I help you, ma'am."

"I am here on a matter of great importance. I need to speak to Sir Andrew Morton immediately."

The man's eagerness to help turned condescending. "Do you have an appointment?"

"No."

"Then you will need to wait and—"

"I have proof of a plot to assassinate Prime Minister Gladstone."

And just as Jameson had said, her words worked like a magical password.

***

If the man outside the door had been supercilious, it was easy for Callie to see where he'd got that habit from.

292

Her Villain

Sir Andrew Morton had the thin, long, pointy features of a rat and a personality to match.

Although her words had caught his secretary's attention and got Callie into the room, it was immediately clear the man wasn't ready to believe her.

"This is a very serious allegation you are bandying about Miss—"

"Fowler. And I'm not *bandying* anything."

He gave her a gratingly condescending smile. "We get at least one or two threats every week, Miss Fowler. If you just tell me what you know, and how you—"

She leaned forward and hissed, "This is different. The assassination is planned for three days from now, when the prime minister gives his weekly speech."

Morton's face didn't change expression, but something in his superior gaze flared to life at her words.

"I see," he said. "That is, er, rather specific. Excuse me a moment." He stood and went to the door and Callie heard him say, "Do not disturb me for the next hour, Larson." He shut the door and then—oddly—turned a key in the lock.

When he came back, he didn't go to his desk but to the wall behind it.

Callie watched in astonishment as he pushed something and a section of the wooden paneling opened just like a narrow door.

Morton stepped inside and she heard the hum of voices but could not understand the words.

A moment later, Morton stepped out and closed the door behind him.

"I beg your pardon," he murmured, and then smiled at her. "Now, I have a few questions for you."

The hardness in his gaze caused ice water to trickle down her spine.

When she didn't speak, he sat in his chair and laced his hands together, laying them on the desk as he leaned toward her.

"How did you come by this information, Miss… er Fowler, was it?"

"I overheard it."

His eyebrows shot up. "Indeed. And where did you overhear it?"

"In a brothel." She'd come up with this story last night—without Jameson's assistance.

"I see." A layer of civility seemed to melt away and his gaze slid over her expensive, tasteful clothing as his mind reassessed who she was. "Where is this establishment?"

"I prefer not to say at present."

His jaw moved back and forth and then he said, "And who was speaking of this?"

"I do not know their names. It was two men who met—they must have been using the brothel as a way to hide their scheme. They talked about the assassination and about a shipment of weapons."

The color drained from Morton's face. "Weapons?" he repeated faintly.

"Yes. And it was the last shipment, so there must have been more."

His throat bobbed as he swallowed and his skin turned an unhealthy gray.

"Sir Andrew? Are you ill?"

He ignored her, took a set of keys from his pocket, and unlocked a desk drawer. When his hand came back up, there was a pistol in it.

Callie lurched to her feet, clutching her reticule in front of her, as if that might stop a bullet.

"Sit. Down," he snarled, all semblance of the urbane man gone. His face was distorted by anger—but by something else, too: fear.

Callie sat.

"Why did you come here? And do not lie to me."

"I came because I was told your office handled such matters for the prime minister," she answered truthfully.

He lifted the pistol and aimed it at her. "Don't. Lie."

"It is the truth. And—and if you think to hurt me in any way, I should tell you that I had a message sent to Lord Gladstone with the same accusations I've laid before you. I've also left a signed letter with a friend," she lied, for good measure. "In it, I swore to everything I heard. So, if anything happens to me, it will be delivered to the *London Times* and you will be listed as the last person I spoke to."

Sir Andrew's face seemed to fall apart, like a rickety structure hit by a sudden gust of wind. His cheeks sank in and the fire in his gaze was a dead cinder as he lowered the gun.

Callie sagged with relief.

But rather than put the pistol back inside the desk, Sir Andrew dropped it with a *clunk*, leapt to his feet, and fumbled with the paneling again.

Callie launched herself toward the desk a second after he turned his back, grabbing the pistol he'd abandoned on the desk. She pointed the barrel at the man's back as he slammed his hands against the panel in frustration, as if it refused to open.

The door to the corridor suddenly exploded open and Callie's scream was swallowed up by a deafening bang, the pistol jumping in her hands.

Callie forced her eyes open and sagged with relief when she saw Sir Andrew was still upright and evidently unharmed and that her shot appeared to have shattered the hideous bust on his desk.

Five large men flooded the room and three of them leapt on Sir Andrew.

Callie lifted her hands in the universal gesture of surrender, realizing only then that she must have dropped the gun after firing it.

One of the large men stopped in front of her, towering over her. "Miss Fowler?"

She nodded.

His huge hand closed around her upper arm. "Come with us, ma'am."

Callie went without any resistance.

Sir Andrew, however, shouted, threatened, and blustered.

"What is going to happen with him?" Callie asked her captor as he marched her down an empty corridor.

The man's face, already hard and frightening, shifted into even grimmer lines. "Nothing good."

Callie suddenly feared the same thing might be said for her.

Chapter 24

Callie had never been in gaol before.

It took only a few minutes for her to decide that she could have happily lived the rest of her life without the experience.

The first day was terrifying, endless, and awful.

But the second day was even worse. Because that is when she realized that she could very well spend the rest of her life in the small, cold, dark cell.

The guards would not answer any of her questions or even speak to her. The only thing that gave her any hope was the fact they had given her a blanket, a bucket of water, and food twice a day.

Judging by the cells Callie had been escorted past on the way to hers—all of which had been crowded and smelled like open sewers—she was receiving preferential treatment.

By the third day, her treatment seemed like an ominous sign. They could keep her there forever. Who would come look for her? Certainly not David. Thanks to her stupidity, he was probably in a cell somewhere nearby.

Callie had stopped praying after her father had died, when circumstances had forced her to choose a life of prostitution. But she prayed more in those three days than she'd done in all the years before combined. She made dozens of promises to God—as if she were in any position to bargain—and while she prayed for her own salvation, her most fervent pleas were reserved for David.

I know he is a bad man, Lord, but he has been so good to me. Well, not good, *exactly,"* she amended, *"but as good as he is able. And honest. I don't think he can help what he does because* you *made him with pieces missing and—*

Callie had to stop herself when she realized her pleading had turned to hectoring.

But wasn't that true? If God had made all of them, it meant he had made David, too.

Callie had long since realized that David was lacking something—several somethings—fundamentally human. But not until she had spent time in a cell with nothing to do but ponder the last weeks of her life—an activity that was far better than considering her bleak present and future—had she been honest with herself and admitted the truth: she simply did not care how *lacking* he was in those areas.

Indeed, there was no longer any use in pretending that she had not fallen in love with David Remington, or whatever his name was, warts and all.

Callie suspected that loving a man like David probably meant there was something fundamentally wrong with her, too.

Admitting her love for David was not the only subject that consumed her time.

Repeatedly Callie was tormented by the same questions. The worst one was, obviously, what would have happened if she had *not* taken action about the assassination. Would it have been possible for her to stay with David—provided he'd extended their agreement—knowing that he'd killed, or attempted to kill, the prime minister?

Each and every time she asked herself that, the answer was an emphatic *no*.

And even if she *had* been able to live with herself, there was the fact that people in the government—like Jameson—already knew about the plot.

Thinking about Jameson hurt her head. Why had he come to her? Why not send a message himself? He had used Callie for some reason, but—for the life of her, which it very well might be—she could not understand *why*.

Callie gave a weary sigh and paused her endless pacing, lowering herself onto her pallet—the only piece of furniture in the room, unless one counted the bucket. The straw-stuffed mattress stank and the blanket was thin, but it was still better than more thinking. She curled up on her side and pulled the blanket up over her, shivering not so much from cold as from dread.

If only she could sleep. If only…

The sound of metal clanging jolted Callie upright and she blinked into the gloom, cringing away from a large, dark figure limned by the light. "It is time, Miss Fowler."

It was the voice of the man who'd brought her there. "Time for what?" she asked, her voice dry from a lack of use.

"Time to come with me."

His non-answer infuriated her and Callie weighed the value of kicking and screaming and resisting, but decided her pride was worth more. Especially when she knew nobody would come to her rescue, or probably even hear her.

He took her arm again, but this time he walked her out a different route. They went through so many doorways and took so many corridors that she was quickly lost. The one thing she noticed was that her surroundings began to look cleaner and slightly more modern. Gone were the weeping stone walls of her cell and the dank smell of decay and neglect.

Her captor took out a large ring of keys and unlocked a door that opened on a hallway so luxurious and warmly lit that she closed her eyes against the burn of the light.

"Come," he urged, pulling her slightly resistant form into the hall.

They took two more turns and climbed a set of stairs, the hallways becoming wider and more richly decorated, until finally the man stopped in front of a grand set of double doors and knocked.

"Come in!" a voice called.

Callie stared at the middle-aged, pinch-faced, dark-suited man sitting at the desk, vaguely disappointed that he looked so mundane.

"He is waiting for you, Miss Fowler," the man—obviously some sort of secretary—gestured to another larger and more ornate door.

Her captor turned and left without another word.

"Go inside," the secretary said impatiently before returning to whatever he was writing.

She swallowed and opened the door.

The person at *this* desk was instantly recognizable and Callie froze on the threshold as she beheld the Grand Old Man, or so his admirers called him—while his detractors had nicknamed him *God's One Mistake.*

Mr. Gladstone smiled at her and came out from behind a vast desk, one of his hands sheathed in a glove—his practice after losing a finger—and the other stretched toward her.

"Miss Fowler, thank you so much for coming."

She almost laughed—as if she'd had any choice—but instead, she nodded, took his hand, and dropped a curtsey.

"Please, have a seat." He gestured to two chairs and sat beside her. "Well," he said, a faint smile pulling at his lips. "I consider myself fortunate that you count yourself among my supporters, Miss Fowler."

She blinked, her brain a bit fuzzy from having made the journey from a gaol cell to this magnificent office all in the span of ten minutes. "Oh, you mean because I wrote you that message?"

"Yes. A great many people would not have put themselves in the middle of such a dangerous situation."

Callie could have told him that she hadn't sent the message because of him personally. She would have sent it for anyone, be it prime minister or street sweeper. But she wisely kept that to herself, too.

"I already told Sir Andrew that I don't know who the conspirators are," she said. "I overheard it." She swallowed and then forced herself to add, "In a brothel."

The prime minister gave her a gentle smile. "I know exactly where you heard it, my dear."

"Er, you do?"

"Yes. You see, David works for me, Miss Fowler."

Her jaw sagged. "But…" Callie shook her head, too befuddled to finish.

He chuckled. "Yes, I know it seems a tangled ball of wool."

"I don't understand why one of your men—unless…was Jameson *not* working for you?"

"He was, too." A faint flush stained the papery skin of his cheeks. "I must apologize for using you, but we needed your actions to seem sincere."

Callie stared. "I don't know what you mean."

"I can tell you a little bit about it—not all, but some. Shall I start from the beginning?"

"Please."

"Without going into too much detail, I have known about a plot to, er, get me out of the way for quite some time. There is a piece of legislation that will shortly be passed that has attracted some powerful opposition. Once it is in place, it will give Britain's workers the right to legally organize for the first time in our history. Naturally, there are those that oppose it vehemently—men whose interests will be negatively impacted. Although I knew of the existence of this group, they were canny and kept to the shadows. I knew only of middle-echelon members like Sir Andrew.

"The plan to ferret out the ringleaders has been a long time in the making, Miss Fowler. The first thing that needed to happen was that David Remington was given a dishonorable discharge from the military—the charges against him manufactured specifically to frame him as a man who would be amenable to revenge against my government. It took a great deal of time and carefully planted seeds, but Sir Andrew approached him approximately two months ago. Over the past weeks, men like our Agent Jameson have tried to tie Sir Andrew to his handlers—we knew they existed, but they remained elusive. It was imperative we catch them before the assassination attempt"—he chortled—"for more than just the obvious reason. It was Jameson who came up with the notion of shaking up Sir Andrew and hoping that he could be made to drop his guard enough to send word to his superiors without using the usual secretive channels." He smiled. "Thanks to you, he did exactly that. Over the course of the last three days, we have apprehended the ring leaders and their plans have fallen apart. We've seized the cached weapons, and neutralized men who were a threat to not just me, but our system of government."

Her mind reeled at all he'd just said. "You used me."

"Yes."

Callie stared at him. "And David knew about this?"

Gladstone opened his mouth, closed it, and then nodded. "He knew part of it." He cleared his throat. "When the idea was presented to him, he objected to having you go to Sir Andrew alone."

"But he obviously changed his mind."

"No. David was provided with alternate information to encourage him to proceed with Jameson's plan."

"You mean you lied to him."

The Prime Minister looked pained. "I suppose you could put it that way. We had men surrounding Sir Andrew's office, Miss Fowler. You were never in any danger."

Callie wanted to tell him exactly how wrong he was, but she knew men, and this one was beginning to reassemble his armor after already showing her too much. Her opportunity to get answers would soon dissipate and she did not want to waste time on pointless recriminations.

"What do you know about David? Where does he come from? Who is he really?" Callie hesitated and then added, "And what is wrong with him?"

Gladstone was visibly relieved at the change of subject, but still, he hesitated. "David's story is not a pretty one—and there is not much we know about his past, either."

"I want to know."

His jaw firmed.

"I just spent three days in gaol and risked my own life because I thought I was saving *you*, sir. I think a little information about the man I betrayed is a small enough price to ask."

He sighed, but nodded. "David belonged to a very wealthy, powerful lord who'd been caught selling secrets."

"Belonged? You mean he is the son of an aristocrat?"

"No. I mean he *belonged* to this lord." Distaste flickered across his face. "The man in question was a traitor we'd spent years gathering evidence against. Once we had enough information to move against him, we apprehended him at his country estate. This man wasn't only a traitor, he was also a cruel, feudal master to the people living under him. The things our agents discovered—" Gladstone broke off and swallowed, his face actually paling. "David was living in the kennels, with the man's hounds."

"Wh-what do you mean *living* with them?"

"The master of hounds for this treasonous aristocrat said he went to feed the hounds one morning and discovered David sleeping among them, dressed in ragged clothing. The man thought David might have been three, maybe four, years of age. When the master of hounds told his employer about the boy, the lord had been diverted when he'd heard the child slept and ate with dogs." Gladstone coughed. "And so, he left him there."

"My *God.*"

Gladstone continued. "The servant we interrogated said the boy could speak, but they had only ever heard a word or two out of him over the years he lived there. Nobody had bothered to name him, just calling him *boy.* Naturally he developed a keen connection with the animals he lived with—not just the hounds, but his horses, too—and could direct and control them far better than the lord's trainer." Gladstone swallowed. "Evidently there were… difficulties when he insisted on going with the hounds on the hunt."

"Difficulties?"

"He did not care to see the dogs endangered by the inevitable vicissitudes of the hunt."

Whatever that meant. Callie did not care to ask.

"He was whipped for it, but even that didn't stop him, so they locked him in the kennel whenever the lord rode to hounds. When he escaped the kennel, they chained him *and* locked him in."

"My God," she said again. "How—how old was he?"

"It seems this started after he'd lived there five or six years."

Which would have made him eight, maybe nine, years old. Callie squeezed her eyes shut, but not in time to stop the tears. She forced them open and angrily wiped the tears from her cheeks. "Did *nobody* think to intervene?"

"Miss Fowler, I'm afraid that this sort of man did not tolerate interference. If his people had done anything other than what he'd directed them to do, they would have suffered."

What about David? Callie wanted to scream, but she knew an angry, shouting woman would get no further answers, and so she chewed the inside of her cheek to ribbons, and calmly asked, "How old was he when you finally took the estate?"

Gladstone looked away from her. "When we took control of the lord's properties David was… upset when he was taken away from the horses and dogs. But naturally he could not continue to live there. He fought like a wild beast, injuring several seasoned soldiers in the process, even though he could not have been more than thirteen or fourteen. He moved faster and with more confidence—and with a shocking capacity for lethality—than even our most experienced soldiers."

He glanced at her before once again looking away and continuing. "There were two choices: David could either go to an orphanage, or… the men could look after him."

"Men? You mean your soldiers?"

"Yes. It was decided that he would be brought to live in the stables at one of the barracks."

Callie opened her mouth, but Gladstone did not let her speak. "They wanted to put him in the barracks, Miss Fowler, but David refused to sleep anywhere but with the horses and dogs. If anyone tried to force him to do something he did not want to do…Well, the things he was capable of—his physical abilities were remarkable."

"You mean fighting?"

"Yes. To put it bluntly, he fought with the savagery of a street cur. And he was also able to escape almost any situation, damaging himself in the process if he found it necessary. The man in charge of him put David through the standard battery of testing for the army." He cleared his throat. "And then some not-so-standard tests."

"What does that mean?"

"That is not public information, Miss Fowler."

"You mean you taught him how to kill?"

"I don't think you expect me to answer that."

No, she didn't. Nor did she need him to answer.

"And then what happened to him?"

"He became one of our most valuable assets."

"Assets." She shook her head, disgusted but not surprised. "Why does he have all those scars? What are they from?"

Gladstone shifted uncomfortably. "That is not public information. And David knows that. He signed documentation to that effect, so he cannot tell you either."

Callie snorted. "Do not be concerned; he told me nothing. And then you discharged him from the military so you could use him again."

"His discharge was inevitable, Miss Fowler. He had been compromised—his identity exposed—during an operation. After that, his utility for the sort of work he specialized in came to an end. It wasn't his fault, but it meant that the only job he had ever known was effectively over. But this new assignment—infiltrating this traitorous group—was a way to make some good come out of his loss of cover."

"Some good for you, you mean."

"For the country."

Callie laughed.

The prime minister's mouth tightened and he got to his feet.

"What will happen now?" she asked, not ready to leave just yet.

"Nothing will happen. It is over. The sooner you forget all about it, the better it will be for you."

Callie recognized a threat when she heard one. But she had one more question. "What about David?"

Mr. Gladstone did not answer her. Instead, he went to the door and opened it. "Give Miss Fowler the packet that has been prepared for her." He turned to Callie. "I understand you will be going to America. This should make your journey more… comfortable and compensate you for any unpleasantness these past few days."

The secretary handed Callie an oilskin packet like the one she'd found beneath the floorboards in the attic. She did not need to open it to know this one would have money, rather than treasonous plots, inside it.

Callie looked up at the prime minister.

"I trust we understand one another?" he said, the steel in his gaze making her shiver.

What else could she say or do?

Callie nodded. "Yes. I understand." All too well.

"Goodbye, Miss Fowler." And then the Prime Minister stepped back into his luxurious lair and shut the door in her face.

Chapter 25

David stared down at Jonas Graham, the man he'd been beating for the last hour, and then glanced at the brass knuckles digging into the swollen flesh of his right hand and let the bloody tool drop to the table with a clatter while he flexed his fingers.

"Well?" David asked the other occupant of the room—Robert Melton—who was naked and bound to a chair but, as yet, untouched, although he was now liberally spattered with his co-conspirator's blood.

"I don't know anything—I keep telling you that," Melton whined. "I only received orders; I never saw anyone's face."

David stared.

"It's true." Melton was breathing so fast that David was astounded that his heart didn't explode in his chest.

David pointed to the bleeding unconscious man, and then to Melton. "You do not have a great deal of time to save yourself. Once Graham is dead, I am going to start on you."

A sob tore out of Melton and his eyes threatened to bulge from his head as urine trickled over the edge of his wooden chair and spattered on the floor.

"Give me the name," David said.

"I swear, I don't—"

David picked up the pistol from the table, placed it beneath Graham's chin, and pulled the trigger.

The *bang* was deafening, but David could hear Melton's screaming even over the ringing in his ears.

"*Swanson*!" Melton shrieked. "Swanson! Swanson! It was Swanson. That's all I know!" The last word was such a garbled sob that it was unrecognizable.

"Micheal Swanson, the MP?"

"Yes! Yes, Michael Swanson!" Melton glanced at what was left of Graham's head and then vomited.

David rapped on the door and then began unrolling his sleeves while Melton wailed, choked, and puked some more.

The door opened quickly and Jameson entered. The black eye that David had given him two days before had turned a lurid purple.

"I've got what I need," he said.

Jameson glanced at the two prisoners and swallowed hard before dragging his gaze back to David. "We can take it from here…sir."

David was amused by the honorific, even if the man couldn't keep the revulsion from showing on his face and in his tone. He was also amused by the way Jameson gave him a wide berth as he left the room.

He paid a visit to the lavatory and washed his hands, scowling when he saw the blood on his cuff. Yet another shirt ruined.

Once he'd cleaned up and shrugged on his overcoat, he left through the door that only a handful of people knew existed.

Her Villain

Although it was late, David knew Gladstone would want to hear the news about Swanson, even though it was news the prime minister could never officially acknowledge.

Nor could he ever acknowledge how David had extracted the information. Her Majesty's government did not condone torture or murder. Nor did it employ an entire office devoted to the extraction of information from uncooperative suspects.

In the eyes of the Crown, people like David did not even exist.

The corridors and hallways became increasingly wider, grander, and more luxurious the farther away he got from the soundproof interrogation chamber where he had spent far too many of his days and nights.

By the time he reached the elegant anteroom to the Prime Minister's office a few moments later, David felt as if he'd entered a brand-new world.

"He is expecting you," the secretary said, not asking for David's name or identification. It was late and the huge building was mostly empty. David suspected he was Gladstone's last appointment of the day—not to mention the sole reason the PM was still in London.

David opened the door and saw the older man standing in front of the fire, facing it.

"You got the last name?" Gladstone asked, turning around and lifting the cut crystal glass in his hand.

"Swanson."

Gladstone uttered a curse beneath his breath, threw back the contents of the glass, and sighed. "I am not surprised, but I am disappointed."

David said nothing. He was neither surprised nor disappointed in the traitor's identity. Nor did he care.

"So, that is that," Gladstone said, his mind obviously elsewhere.

"Yes, sir."

The older man's gaze sharped. "By the by, I saw what you did to Jameson's face."

David just stared.

"I have to admit I expected worse," Gladstone said with a chuckle, crossing the room to refill his glass. "Have you come to give me a black eye, too, David?"

"It crossed my mind, sir."

Gladstone laughed again, a deeper, belly laugh.

"Never fear. Your soiled dove was no worse the wear for a few days in custody and now she has a pretty packet of money to see her on her way to America." He gave David a curious, speculative look. "I met her, you know."

David's hands curled into fists and the temptation to thrash the older man was shockingly difficult to restrain.

"I was bowled over that she never gave up your name—not even after we kept her in gaol for several nights. She stood firm in her claim that she had overheard everything in the brothel where she worked."

"Why did you keep her locked up?" David asked, rage spiking at the thought of Calliope in one of the cells where so many were left to rot.

"You know why. She could not be allowed to go free until the worst of the threat was over. It was safer for her."

David wanted to argue, but it was true that it had taken three days to bring in most of the conspirators involved in the plot. Gaol probably had been the best place for her.

Gladstone settled behind his desk and regarded David with a brooding look before a slow smile slid across his face. He glanced at David's fisted hands. "Go ahead and take a swing at me. You would probably have time to get at least one hit in, but I am not stupid, David. After seeing what you did to Jameson, I made sure that Fender and Pike would be outside after you arrived. They are waiting for you to do something foolish."

David didn't tell the older man that he would only need one hit. That he knew exactly where to strike a man to end his life, a skill his own government had seen fit to teach him long ago.

But Gladstone wasn't worth hanging for. No politician was.

"Was that all you wanted from me?" David asked.

"For now."

"I am discharged, sir," David reminded him.

"I will be the judge of when you are finished, David." Something flared in the Grand Old Man's eyes—something cold and reptilian—but it was gone in an instant and Gladstone smiled charmingly. "But let us not quarrel. Christmas is in a few days, David. Congratulate yourself on another job well done and then go buy yourself something—or some*one*—and spend a bit of that money you are sitting on, like a dragon hoarding its gold."

David did not bother answering. Instead, he turned on his heel and strode from the room, ignoring Gladstone's laughter behind him as he pushed past the two brutes flanking the office door.

Rather than slink back through the dark narrow corridors like a rat, David decided to leave through the regular entrance for the first and last time.

It was late, dark, and cold, and the snow that had been threatening for the last day had finally arrived and was blanketing the city.

The freezing air felt good on his swollen hands and so he walked, not caring how long it took to make the trip from Whitehall to his house.

His mind was nearly as empty as the streets he strode through, his thoughts battened down tighter than the hatches on the ship Calliope would soon be on, if she was not already.

David felt a pang of something in his belly and wondered if the meat pie and ale Jameson had brought for him a good twelve hours earlier could be causing the sensation.

Well, he would be home soon enough and could forage in the kitchen for something to settle his stomach.

Several of the houses on his street had windows blazing and the sounds of late-night celebrations and laughter spilled out. Christmas parties, he supposed.

The windows of his own house were dark, not even a glow through the bedroom that he had begun to think of as Calliope's.

So, she had gone—at least from the house, and maybe even from Britain.

Had she lost her place on the ship while she was held in gaol?

David had purposely not asked her anything about her departure plan or schedule. He hadn't wanted to know.

Gladstone would have given her money—probably a great deal—to keep her from asking questions, so if she had not been released in time to board her ship at least she could afford to purchase a new ticket.

David felt the slightest twinge of… something as he opened the door, his gaze drifting to the flowers arranged in a bowl on the console table.

It had only been five days since he had seen them, but already they were fading.

He locked the door and slowly climbed the stairs.

For the first time in twenty-seven years, he had nothing on his horizon. Nothing to plan. Nowhere to go.

Nobody to kill.

Tomorrow was Saturday, the day before Christmas, so the Exchange would be closed and he'd not even have that to occupy him.

Not that he minded. For once, the thought of engaging in the mental puzzle of buying and selling and trading held little appeal.

Gladstone had been right about one thing; David was like a dragon with its hoard and already had more money than he could spend in five lifetimes.

David had no idea what to buy, what would make him *happy*. The brothels would be open and busier than ever. He knew that because he had gone to them before on Christmas and other holidays.

He did not think he would bother this year.

Would Calliope purchase a cabin now that she had money? Or would she mind her pennies and decide on the dreaded steerage?

David realized he'd stopped and was standing on the landing, staring at nothing while his mind wandered.

He firmly put all thoughts of the woman from his mind and strode to his room.

And then stopped abruptly when he saw the door was ajar.

He never left the door open.

If anyone was in there, they would have heard him enter the house. Even with the carpets Calliope had bought his bootsteps were audible.

He took the small pistol from the holster on his ankle and reached around the doorframe to flick on the gaslight.

A soft noise came from within.

"I am armed," David said. "If you are stealing something, put it back. Lift your hands over your head and exit the room and I will allow you to leave with your life. If you do not do as I say within the next five seconds, I will kill you."

"I am not stealing anything. Nor am I armed," a familiar voice said, although it was more high-pitched than usual.

David jolted at the sound of Calliope's voice and he stepped into the open doorway.

She was on his bed, naked, and laid out on her side, head propped on her hand.

"Hello." She attempted to give him a jaunty smile, but he saw her chin quiver when she eyed the gun.

David lowered the pistol to his side. "What are you doing here?"

She made a sweeping gesture down her naked body with one hand. "It is unlike you to ask questions with obvious answers."

He stared at her and was unsurprised when she started talking to fill the silence.

"I wanted to say I was sorry I left you tied up."

David lifted his knee and slipped the pistol back into the holster. "I let you do it."

"I know. Gladstone told me you'd been aware of the plan. Were you really unconscious?"

"No."

She snorted. "I think part of me must have known that." She took a deep breath, but then hesitated.

David knew where this was headed. He was fully aware of the average adult's compulsion to apologize. While he had never experienced the urge himself, that didn't mean he couldn't recognize it.

He did not need to hear it, nor did he feel compelled to offer his own apology for anything he had done. But it was something she needed to do, so he kept his mouth closed and let her get on with it.

"I'm sorry that I went to stop the…er, well what I thought was an assassination. I should have known you wouldn't do that. He told me everything."

David doubted Gladstone had told her everything, but he kept the thought to himself. He also could have told her that he not only *would* have carried out the assassination, but he'd done that and worse in the past.

"I misjudged you terribly," she said.

"That was the intention."

"I didn't really stop and think after Jameson talked to me. I just reacted—frantic and terrified and desperate to stop everything. I wish I had *thought* about it."

"You played your part the way you were supposed to."

"I didn't give them your name."

"I know."

"I would never have told them it was you."

David knew she believed that. He decided it was better that she lived in a world where men like him would never torture answers out of women.

She swallowed hard and sat up, wrapping the top blanket around her shoulders, making a mess out of his bed in the process.

"I thought you were going to America."

She stared at her hands for a long moment before looking up at him. "I know you probably won't believe me after I have betrayed you. But I love you. Even when I thought you were going to kill the P—*him*, I couldn't stop loving you. I just hoped that your plans would be thwarted. I didn't want you to be captured. I wanted you to get away. I am deeply sorry that I believed you would do that, but… there is nothing I can do to change the past and—"

"I don't love you."

Her lips parted and her eyes glassed over quickly, until a tear slid down one cheek. And then another. And another.

"I'm sorry. I will leave."

It was suddenly imperative that David explain something he wasn't sure he had the words for. But she was already sliding off the bed, preparing to go.

"I cannot love," he said, frustration boiling inside him at the inadequacy of words. "That is to say, I have never loved anyone. I am almost forty-two years of age. If I were capable of feeling such an emotion then it would have happened by now. I have concluded that I am not capable of it."

Rather than stop her tears, more slid down her cheek.

"I do not like to see you cry." David blinked as a thought—a feeling—struggled to emerge from somewhere deep inside him, buried beneath ancient layers of ice. He repeated the words, hoping that might speed the process. "I do not like to see you cry."

She roughly wiped the tears off her cheeks with jerky movements. "I'm sorry, I didn't mean to come here and blubber—"

David raised a hand, grateful when she stopped speaking. "I do not like to see *you* cry." He stared at her, willing her to understand what he was saying.

He recognized her expression because he had seen it on her face when she played chess. She was pondering, assessing, and discarding possibilities, her mind working like the efficient, elegant machine it was.

It took only a moment before she looked up at him with eyes wide. "Do you mean that you don't like to see *me* crying, as opposed to somebody else?"

Relief swamped him, the wave so overwhelming his knees were briefly weak. "Yes."

She swallowed. "And—and that is because you don't care about most people?"

David shook his head. "I do not care about *any* people. Except for you, Calliope. Only you. It is important to me that you are happy," he added, more to himself. "It bothers me if you are not happy. It angers me if anyone makes you unhappy." He met her gaze, the words inside him becoming trapped and garbled again. But David needed her to know and he wasn't sure he would ever get this close to telling her the contents of his mind—or even understanding what he felt himself—and so he forced himself to go on.

"I would kill for you. And I would die for you. And… and you make me want to come home," he added somewhat inanely, not sure she would understand just how singular that was, frustrated that his thoughts were so elusive. "And—" David ground to a halt again.

Instead of flailing in frustration, he thought about her behavior a scant moment earlier—her orderly assessment of the situation—and applied himself using the same methods he normally saved for his work or chess.

It did not take him as long as he feared to reduce the chaos of his thoughts.

"You are the only person who matters to me, Calliope."

The odd churning in his gut that had bothered him on and off for weeks suddenly disappeared. It was as if he'd expelled something that had been burning a hole through him and he felt the strangest expression shift the muscles of his face. It took him far too long to realize what it was. It was a smile. Or at least the closest he would ever get to one.

"Only you, Calliope," he repeated.

***

Callie stared—no, she gawked—not just at what he'd just said, but at the smile on his face. It was a tortured expression— and so fleeting a person easily could have missed it—but it was a smile, all the same.

For some reason, that only made more tears flow. She quickly wiped them away and patted the bed beside her. "Won't you sit?"

He hesitated, his gaze resting on the bed. After a moment, he came and sat stiffly beside her.

"Does it bother you that I messed up your bed?"

Again, he hesitated. "I am… glad that you are here."

His evasion was probably as close as he ever came to lying. And David being *glad* was probably as close as she'd ever get to any sort of declaration of happiness or affection.

Could Callie live with that?

She looked in his eyes, searching for… something.

But they were as flat and lifeless as they had been that very first day.

"This is how I have always been," he said, guessing the direction of her thoughts. "It is how I will always be. I cannot love you, but I can protect you and take care of you. I can see that you never want for anything. I can give you a life of comfort, ease, and material possessions." He suddenly reached out, his palm cupping her face in a gesture far gentler than any he had ever displayed. "I do not want you to go, but I am aware that I am not enough to keep a normal person happy. I can see what I am missing and I can pretend that I have it for brief periods of time, at least well enough to get by, but that is all it is: pretending. For you, I can do better when it comes to appearing normal and—"

"I don't want you to pretend," she said, setting her hand over his. "But I also don't want you hurting or killing people. For me, or for anyone else." She swallowed hard. "I know that is asking you to change, but—"

"This job was the last."

"Can you promise not to kill or maim people who might hurt me?"

He took so long to answer that she thought this would be one of those times when there wouldn't be one.

"I will talk to you before I kill anyone."

"Or hurt anyone."

He nodded. "Or hurt anyone."

Callie suspected that was as good as she would get.

"Do you want to marry me?" she asked before she lost her nerve.

"I will if that is what you want."

"Do you want children?"

"If that is what you want," he said again.

Callie smiled sadly, pained by his answer. "I'm not sure that is enough when it comes to children, David."

Once again, he pondered her words for a long, long time, the house creaking and settling around them.

He met her gaze. "If they are yours, then I will want them."

"They would be half yours, too."

He shrugged, any spark of life she had briefly seen in his eyes—or imagined—gone.

"Will you ever tell me about your own childho—"

"No." Muscles knotted up and down his jaw.

Callie thought of a child—an infant of three or four—sleeping with dogs, growing up living in a kennel—

Her mind rebelled against continuing down that road. Callie was disgusted at her own weakness, but the fact was that she didn't want to know.

She nodded at him. "Very well, I will not ask you again."

"What else is there that you would know? Now is the time, Calliope. Because when you are mine…"

He didn't need to finish the sentence; she knew what he meant. Once she was his, he would never let her go.

"Will you take off your clothes when you come to my bed?"

"I won't answer questions about the scars."

Coward that she was, Callie was willing to agree to that. "I won't ask any."

"Then I can do that—if you promise not to—" He broke off and gestured to the bed and the room and the two of them. "I need one place that is…" He floundered, once again searching for the right word, his very inarticulateness a sign of how agitated he must be. "Uncluttered," he finally said. "I cannot have anyone here. Not even you," he added, reminding Callie that she was in a category of one.

"I can agree to that," she said. "What about the attic?"

"I no longer have any need for the attic."

Callie stood and held out her hand. "Come to my room."

David hesitated. "Are you sure this is what you want? That *I* am enough for you?"

She smiled. "I am sure."

Her Villain

David took her hand and, without a word, followed.

***

David immediately felt lighter when they left his room behind. The knowledge that his bed was disarranged nagged at him, but he could push it to the very back of his mind. He would come and make it right later.

Right now, his cock—which had hardened at the sight of her—was aching and he needed her. Not just wanted her but needed her. He also needed several games of chess, but decided he would wait to broach that subject until after he fucked her.

When they reached her room, David released her hand, turned on her light, and tugged the blanket off her shoulders, folding it neatly. "Get on the bed—on your back."

"Will you remove your—"

He pulled off his necktie and her mouth snapped shut and she climbed up on the bed.

Her promise that he would not be expected to explain every mark and scar was a liberating one. David was not ashamed of his body—he didn't care enough about his appearance to feel either shame or pride—and he was glad to please her with such a minor concession.

Truthfully, he was also looking forward to feeling her naked body against his.

Her eyes roamed over him as he removed and neatly folded every item of clothing, setting it on his blanket.

When he was naked, her gaze lingered on his erection, a part of him she had certainly seen without clothing often enough. As always, the weight of her stare made him leak like a tap.

"I want you now," he said.

"Then have me."

David slid a hand beneath each of her thighs and spread her wide. "Grab the headboard and do not release it until I tell you," he ordered in a voice that was gravelly with need. He waited until she had wrapped her small hands around the narrow but strong copper spindles and then lowered his mouth to her cunt and proceeded to make her come. Over and over again. Not stopping until she was begging him.

"I can't do it again, David. Please."

"You can come once more or I will fuck your arse. It is up to you, Calliope. What will it be?"

She sucked in a lungful of air, hesitated, and then said, "My arse."

Interesting. As quickly as she had always offered her ass up whenever he had demanded it, David knew it was hardly her favorite activity. He had believed she was bluffing when she said she couldn't bear another orgasm. It appeared he had been wrong.

She deserved a reward for telling the truth.

"Release the headboard and grab your knees," he ordered, positioning the head of his cock at her entrance once she'd obeyed.

Calliope's smooth forehead furrowed. "But I thought you wanted—"

She yelped as he slammed into her tight body, penetrating her as deeply as he could go. Once he was hilted, he squeezed his eyes shut against the nearly overwhelming compulsion to fuck her hard and fast, fill her with his spend and claim her after so many nights without her. He wasn't sure he'd be able to delay his satisfaction as long as he wanted. Not tonight.

He opened his eyes and found her watching him.

"David?"

"I don't want to talk right now," he said, his hips pumping, driving into her harder, as if he could fuck any conversation right out of her.

He should have known better.

"I don't want to converse," she persisted, making arousing little whimpering noises with every thrust. "I… just…"

David stopped, buried deeply inside her, and scowled down at her. "What?" he demanded when she just stared up at him, finally silent.

"Just because you can't love me doesn't mean I don't love you."

He blinked. It was not what he had expected.

"You can continue," she said.

He snorted at that, but he resumed his thrusting, his second smile of the night—hell, of the year—stretching his face.

Beneath him, Callie laughed, the joyous sound filling the room.

Filling David.

***

David briefly slumped on top of Callie once he'd climaxed.

As usual, he didn't fall asleep or even rest for long before rolling over on his back, his breathing gradually slowing, eyes open and evidently staring at the ceiling.

Callie took the opportunity to roll onto her side and explore his body. The scars were even more brutal in the bright light than they had been in the kitchen and cellar that night. She reached out tentatively, but he didn't stiffen or pull away, so she stroked him.

Rather than tracing the scars she followed the fascinating musculature of his abdomen. For as much as he ate every night, there wasn't an ounce of fat on him. She flattened her hand and rubbed hard over the taut ridges, stopping just short of his, for once, softened cock.

He made a low near-purring sound and his hips lifted off the bed and into her touch when she stroked him again. It was like petting the belly of a dangerous animal—because that is exactly what he was.

If Callie stayed with him, married him, had children with him, she probably would never know him any better than she did at that moment. He was a solitary man of few words who liked food, fucking, and chess—and not necessarily in that order.

The young professor she'd once believed she was in love with had written sonnets to Callie's beauty, but when she had needed help, he had receded like fog. All words and no substance.

David would never write her poetry, or even read it, and he would never flatter her with pretty words.

But she knew with certainty that he would take care of her, never lie to her, and protect her with his life, if that ever became an issue.

As for his government work, Callie desperately hoped he was right and that part of his life was over as he believed.

Still stroking him, she allowed her gaze to wander up his body, past the scars and mutilation to his face. He had thrown back his head, luxuriating in her touch, the position baring the soft triangle of flesh beneath his jaw.

Her heartbeat so loudly at the sight that she was astounded that he didn't hear it. Callie knew this was a view of David that nobody else in the world ever saw. He was baring his throat to her, the ultimate sign of trust for a predator.

He was vulnerable, and Callie, out of everyone he had ever known, exposed that vulnerability.

Vulnerability wasn't love, but it was trust.

He was offering her devotion and trust.

And Callie decided she could live with that. Happily.

Chapter 26

Christmas Eve

David finished shaving and wiped his face with the still-warm cloth, clearing away the soap before inspecting himself to make sure he had not missed anything. Shaving was an activity he enjoyed. It felt good to scrape away the old growth, as if he were disposing of the past.

He thought about the message he had received just that morning, a summons to Whitehall for after the New Year.

Gladstone and his minions had not even waited until after Christmas to plan his next assignment.

David also thought about the promise he had given Calliope only last night—that he would no longer work for Her Majesty—and pondered the decision he would have to make soon.

If it were up to him, he would reject the summons. But David knew it was not up to him. Calliope, he suspected, had not discovered the truth yet: that David was nothing but a tool to be used by his masters. They would continue to use him until he was no longer of value.

Or until he was broken.

David was not sure what he would do, but tonight was not the time to make that decision. It was the very first Christmas Eve he had ever celebrated.

He finished drying off his body and brushed his hair before turning away from the mirror and going to the other room and donning fresh drawers, putting on the same suit he'd worn at dinner. He did not usually bathe a second time, but because it was Christmas Eve and Calliope had requested a loosening of his schedule—much to his chagrin—he had an hour between their last chess game and fucking.

As he knotted his tie his gaze went to the two boxes on his nightstand. He hoped they were adequate Christmas gifts. He had briefly considered asking Mrs. Jenkins about the suitability of the item in the small box—even David knew he could not ask her about the gift in the larger box—but the kitchen had been so crowded with servants that he had decided not to bother.

And so he had relied on his own judgment, which was less than sterling on the matter of gifts and celebrations and whatnot. Some part of his mind suggested that one of the gifts, at least, was more for him than it was for Calliope.

Well, it was his first Christmas. Doubtless he would do better next year.

He glanced up and caught sight of his reflection, his eyes widening when he saw the slight twist to his lips. What was wrong with him? He was practically giddy.

Once he'd composed himself, he gathered up the two packages and made the short journey to Calliope's room, his footsteps muted by the thick carpet runner she'd had installed on both the stairs and in the corridors.

He opened the door to Calliope's room and then froze on the threshold, vaguely aware that his lips had parted.

The overhead light was already blazing at full strength, as were the two on the nightstands. Some distant part of him knew she disliked being looked at under such bright lights, so she would only have set the stage this way for David.

He stepped into the room, his bootheels loud on the wooden floor. He frowned and looked from the bare floor back to the bed. "Why is there no carpet in here?"

Calliope widened her eyes and then laughed, gesturing to her body. "I went to all this effort and *that* is what you notice first?"

"That is not what I noticed first," he assured her, allowing his hungry gaze to feast on her body. She lay atop the blankets, naked except for the black leather straps she had already buckled around her ankles and wrists. Beside her, on one of the nightstands, was the riding crop that she had given him for his birthday.

The one David had never used.

"It's not really a Christmas gift as I gave it to you already, but—"

"It is a Christmas gift," he assured her, not telling her how often he'd regretted that he'd not used the implement on her that night. "And tonight I will use it. But not yet." He would make them both wait, Calliope growing more and more nervous, David more and more excited. The anticipation would only heighten the experience.

It took only a few minutes to tie her face up on the bed, as he had once before.

She watched him in silence, her chest rising and falling faster than normal.

David unbuttoned his placket and was about to take out his cock when she spoke.

"Your clothes."

He grunted. He'd forgotten that was now the way things would be. David had to admit he had enjoyed her skin against him the night before, so it was certainly no hardship.

He quickly stripped, folding everything on the dressing table before turning back to her.

Her lips curved with a wicked smile when she looked at his cock. "You are dripping," she teased.

David climbed onto the bed, but instead of shoving himself inside her, he positioned himself higher, until his knees were nudging her armpits.

He stared down at her wide eyes, which were fastened on his bobbing, leaking cock. "I am going to fuck your mouth," he said, although that was probably evident.

Calliope smirked. "I am going to break your unshakeable control."

David snorted, but suspected she was correct. "And I am going to make you come without touching your cunt."

Her lips parted in shock and David took that as an invitation, guiding his length into her hot mouth.

Holding her simmering blue gaze, David rolled his hips, pushing deep, until his sensitive crown stroked the back of her throat.

She moaned, her long blonde eyelashes fluttering as she opened wider.

Her submission was intoxicating, as was the hunger in her slitted gaze.

He'd been on the edge of arousal all day long thinking about tonight and his balls were tight and ready to empty their load, but he gritted his teeth and fucked her with deep, measured thrusts.

She knew exactly how to please him, her tongue cradling him and her plush lips thinned from the effort of protecting his shaft, her throat open and willing and speeding David toward his release too fast and too soon.

Triumph glittered in her eyes, making David recall her erotic threat of making him lose control and how close she had come to achieving it.

His lips twitched faintly as he stared down into the hot, lust-black gaze of the brilliant tactician who mastered him nightly across a chessboard.

Now it was time to remind *her* which of them did the mastering in the bedchamber.

David slowed his pace but kept her full longer with each stroke, his hips pumping so hard that each stroke squeezed a whimper from her chest, until her lungs would be screaming for air. But she never choked and she never turned away, instead angling her head to encourage deeper penetration, her sharp gaze rapidly clouding with animal need, her body more pliant with every thrust.

When he could fight his need no longer, he sheathed himself to the hilt and closed one hand around her neck. "*Yes.* Take it all," he hissed, reveling in the flexing of her throat as she swallowed every drop and milked him for more.

Her eyelids fluttered at his vulgar command and then her muffled moan vibrated up his shaft and David felt the unmistakable signs of her body tightening, back bowing, as Calliope gave in to her own orgasm.

David spared a few seconds from his own bliss to lock eyes with her as she came apart. Who was triumphant, now?

***

A dam exploded inside Callie at David's command, flooding her with euphoria tinged with wonder.

I climaxed not from any stimulating touch, but because I gave him pleasure.

How absolutely astonishing.

David lifted off her and rolled onto his back beside her, his hot, sweaty body pressed against hers, skin to skin.

Callie swallowed several times and reveled in the ability to breathe even though she missed the feel of him. Her lips felt bruised and she knew she'd have difficulty swallowing her breakfast tomorrow.

But she would eagerly take him again right now, if he wanted her.

David slid a hand between her thighs.

Callie hissed in a breath when he stroked her, thankfully avoiding her too-sensitive clitoris.

"You came while I used your mouth," he said, his voice smug.

David had every right to be smug. Indeed, she felt more than a little smug herself. "Yes."

He gave a rumble of pleasure. "That was a good Christmas gift."

Callie laughed. "I am relieved to hear it. You are not an easy person to buy a gift for."

David slipped from the bed and unbound Callie's arms and legs from the posts but did not remove the straps.

When she reached for the buckle on her wrist he said, "Leave it."

Callie cut him a questioning look.

"I am not finished using them," he said. "I have not forgotten my other gift, Calliope."

The relief she felt at his words perplexed her. Did she really want to be bound and whipped so badly? Had she actually felt hurt and offended that he had not leapt at the offer on his birthday?

Before she could ponder the matter too deeply David picked up the smaller of the two boxes he had set on the nightstand and thrust it into her hand. "This is for you."

***

David watched as Calliope pushed up until she was sitting. She looked from the box in the palm of her hand to him. "You bought me a Christmas present." There was something in her tone he could not identify.

He grunted.

Evidently it was the right thing to do because she laughed.

David had to admit he enjoyed making her laugh, even though he knew it was often at his own expense, rather than anything clever or witty that he'd said.

She opened the box and her eyes bulged. "Oh, David!"

Even a dolt like him could tell that was a very good *oh, David*.

She took out the ring and slid it onto her finger, moving her hand so the large marquis sapphire sparkled under the bold gaslight. "It is beautiful."

David ignored the impulse to preen. "I chose it this time, rather than allowing that dressmaker's husband to decide," he felt compelled to point out.

"You chose perfectly."

"It is not really a Christmas gift."

"Oh?" she said, still staring at her hand. "What is it for, then?"

"It is a wedding ring."

Her head whipped up and her eyes turned glassy.

David groaned.

She grabbed his wrist when he would have turned away, giving a watery laugh. "They are good tears, David."

Why did she have to cry at all? And why did it bother him? People beyond counting had cried and begged him for mercy, and their tears and words had meant nothing to him. Less than nothing. And yet her tears made him feel as if somebody had carved out one of his internal organs with a rusty blade.

"You really want to marry me?" she asked.

David could not have cared less about marriage, but he wanted her to stay, so that meant he wanted to marry her. "Yes."

Her chin wobbled, but she smiled. "When?"

"Whenever you like."

A small, secretive smile slid over her lips and she said, "I love my ring."

That didn't seem to require an answer from him.

Suddenly she pushed up onto her knees and held out her arms. When he merely stared, her smile faded. "I want to hug you."

He frowned.

"You do not like hugging?" she asked, her arms lowering.

He shrugged. "I have never done it."

"Oh, David!" she all but wailed. "That's terrible."

He opened his mouth to ask *why?* But her hands shot out and snaked around his waist. David allowed himself to be pulled closer, until her arms were like slender iron rings around his body, her head resting on his chest.

"I can hear your heart beating," she said.

"You sound stunned that I have one."

She laughed and pulled away to look up at him. "Did you make a joke, David?"

Rather than answer, David pulled her back into his arms. She felt good—small and fragile and yet warm and vibrant.

David decided that hugging was…acceptable.

No, *acceptable* wasn't the right word. Hugging was pleasurable.

Chapter 27

More Christmas Eve…

Callie thought David looked perplexed, but not displeased, by the hugging experiment, and so she pushed for more. "May I kiss you?"

The way David's jaw dropped at the question one would have thought Callie had asked if she could bugger him with a hay fork.

"Have you never kissed anyone?"

His eyes lowered to her mouth for a moment and then flickered back up, his dark gaze unreadable. "No."

No hugs? No kisses?

Callie had rarely kissed her clients, and then only because they had insisted, threatening to become ugly if she denied them.

She had always assumed that David had never kissed her because she was a whore. Why had she not guessed that was not the case, given what she knew of his brutal past?

She shoved down the sadness that threatened to overwhelm her and said, "Do you not want to?"

"I don't know how."

That made her smile. "It is not difficult."

He blinked slowly; his gaze speculative. "I will try it."

She patted the bed. "Sit here."

He sat and she straddled his thighs, lowering her bottom until she sat on his knees.

Considering the rest of his body, his face was remarkably unscathed. But there were fine lines around his eyes, which must have been from squinting because they certainly didn't come from laughing or smiling. There were also plenty of gray hairs mixed in with the brown. Most of the time David seemed strangely ageless to her, but right now, he looked like a man who had lived far too long without being kissed.

Without being loved.

She framed his face with her hands and his body stiffened beneath her, as if he were preparing to protect himself. He was skittish—at least for him—and she knew that any chance for future kisses would depend on the next few minutes.

Callie started slow, kissing and nipping his plush lower lip—the only soft part of his body—before lightly trailing the tip of her tongue over the seam of his mouth.

His breathing deepened and his jaw relaxed, his lips parting slightly.

She made an approving noise and gently sucked his lower lip into her mouth.

David's chest rumbled.

Counting that as approval, Callie slid her tongue into soft wet heat, lightly flicking and probing, caressing his teeth, gums, and the tender skin inside his lips.

He grunted and his hands closed around her waist while he tilted his head slightly to allow her better access.

Callie closed her eyes and gave herself up to sensual intimacy, teasing his tongue, luring him slowly, inexorably, into her mouth.

His fingers tightened, digging into her flesh as if he were building toward something.

Finally, he responded to her invitation, slowly at first, like an explorer carefully mapping unknown territory, his actions mimicking hers, until they were engaging in erotic jousting, his tongue stroking hers with increasing aggression.

She opened her eyes and was amused to find his dark eyes wide open. David Remington was not the sort of man to close his eyes and miss out on anything.

Callie decided it was time for something new, so she closed her lips around his tongue and sucked.

The effect on him was electric and he moaned, pulling her closer, his arms like iron bands.

David was a very fast learner and soon he was fucking her mouth with deep, suggestive thrusts that made her sex clench with the need to be stretched and filled.

When she pulled away to catch her breath David stared up at her, looking poleaxed—at least for him.

Callie smiled. "You like it?"

***

Kissing. Who would have thought shoving one's tongue into another person's mouth could be so erotic?

David had never even considered kissing anyone before. He certainly had never wanted to kiss any of the whores he had been with over the years. Indeed, the notion of kissing had always struck him as filthy and invasive. Even he could see that was rather ironic given his eagerness to put his mouth everywhere else on a woman's body.

Like in so many other ways, Calliope was different than anyone else.

Her mouth was so sweet—David swore that she tasted of apples—and instead of being repelled, he could not seem to get enough of her.

He also needed to fuck her again.

David reluctantly pulled away, breathing hard. "Mount me," he ordered gruffly, unable to take his gaze from her swollen red mouth.

She rose up high and took his cock in her hand, stroking the crown through her drenched sex before positioning him at her entrance and lowering herself slowly until he was fully sheathed.

David steeled himself against the intense pleasure and reached for her face, needing to taste her again. "Fuck me, Calliope," he gritted out, and then reclaimed her mouth.

It was sex unlike any he'd ever had. She rode him with slow deliberation, taking him all the way inside her and grinding her slick little nub against his shaft and using him for her pleasure in a way that made him want to fling her onto her back and fuck her like the crazed beast she was making him.

But he restrained his urge and let Calliope take what she wanted, how she wanted.

All the while, David plundered her mouth, reveling in being joined in two places.

She began to shake as her orgasm built and David slid his hands beneath her arse and lifted her up before turning and laying her on her back. He maintained the same slow rhythm she had used, stroking into her as he watched her face contort, her body clasping his cock almost painfully tight.

Only when she whimpered and begged that she was too sensitive did he have mercy on her and cease his thrusting.

David would not make a habit of giving in to her pleas, but he was feeling a strange tenderness toward her for reasons he could not understand.

He leaned back as he withdrew from her body, his gaze fixed on his still-hard shaft which was glistening with her juices. Although he was erect, David could not have ejaculated right now if his life depended on it. He did not mind. The ache in his balls—swollen yet empty—was sharply pleasurable. Besides, it just meant he could fuck her longer.

But when he looked up from his rigid prick, it was to find that her eyes were closed and her lips parted, her breathing soft and regular.

She had fallen asleep.

Rather than leave and go to his room, which is what he normally would have done, David lay down beside her and watched her sleep, patiently waiting.

After all, he had yet to enjoy her generous gift from weeks earlier.

Nor had he given her the second gift he'd bought her.

Chapter 28

Yet more Christmas Eve...

Callie opened her eyes, disoriented as she blinked around at the bright room. Was it morning?

When she tried to push her hair away to see the clock, she could not move her hand—either of them.

Or her legs.

That is when she realized she was face down, and she never slept that way. She twisted her head to the right and then the left.

"David?" she said, a stupid question as it was most obviously her lover across the room, naked and aroused, his hand lightly moving over his shaft as he sprawled in the leather wingchair she had recently placed there. "What—what is happening?"

He picked up the box he had brought earlier, which was on the table beside his chair. "I have one more gift."

She looked from the box to his face, lightly tugging on her restraints—or at least trying to, but again he had tied her too tight to move so much as an inch. "I will have a difficult time opening it."

His lips curved slightly. "I will open it for you." He flipped the lid up with one hand and reached into the large leather case and came out with something Callie immediately recognized, although she had never seen one that looked so... elegant.

347

"Do you know what this is?" he asked as he held the erotic tool in one hand and lightly caressed it with the hand that had just been stroking his cock.

"It is—" she stopped and cleared her throat. "It is a dildo." Callie had to clear her throat a second time before she could ask, "Are you going to use it on me?"

"I wanted to fill both your holes at once." He said the crude words without inflection, which only made them more arousing. "I know you would rather have another man's cock inside you while I fuck you."

"Yes, I would," she lied, deliberately goading the beast inside him.

His dark eyes kindled and his face went hard, his mouth thinning to a cruel line. "I will never allow another man to touch you. If one tries…" He left the threat unspoken and rose from his chair.

A terrified thrill raced through her bound, vulnerable body as he stalked toward the bed, his leaking erection telling her how arousing his body found the image of her taking another man, even though he hated the thought.

It was about damned time David experienced a taste of what Callie had been dealing with since the night she met him—which was getting wet about something she hated, which happened every single time he humiliated her or whenever she abased herself for him.

Although Callie had to admit she was hating it less and less…

He reached between her spread legs and slid the dildo between the slick petals of her sex, slowly pushing it inside her.

Callie grunted as the hard, cold stone stretched her hot flesh. It felt even more alien than the plug he had used on her—more of a delicious violation—and her inner muscles contracted around the unrelenting invasion.

His lips were suddenly against her ear while his hand held her full. "I am going to whip you and then I'm going to fuck your arse and pump you full of my seed. And then I am going to keep you plugged until my balls are nice and full, and then I will fuck you again. And again. As often and as hard as I want. *That* is your Christmas present." His breath was hot even though his voice was ice cold. "I gave you a chance to escape, to flee my unnatural appetites and start a new life far away from me, and you rejected it. Now you are *mine*. I am the only man who gets to look at, touch, lick, or fuck your body, Calliope. Understood?"

It was the most he had ever said at one time, and Callie almost climaxed on the spot.

"*Do you understand*?" He pushed the dildo deeper.

Callie gasped, her vision darkening with pain. "Yes, David."

He gave a satisfied grunt and eased the hard tool out slightly, wedging a pillow or blanket against it, so that it stayed inside her, even when he took his hand away.

When he walked around the bed, Callie turned her head to follow him.

He lifted the crop off the nightstand and stood beside the mattress, staring down at her with eyes as black as a starless night.

His hand whipped out and Callie tensed at the sharp, quick sting, the sound of the leather on her flesh more shocking than the sting.

His nostrils flared and he struck her again, and again. "If you tense your muscles, it will hurt more." His mouth curved into a smile so cruel that she clenched around the unforgiving stone buried deep inside her, sending pleasure rippling from her womb. "I will enjoy that, but I doubt you will," he added, stinging her again.

He did not just whip her bottom, but moved down her thighs, even landing a few strikes on the soles of her feet.

He did not even apply a fraction of his strength when delivering his blows and the feelings he built inside her could not have been more different than Carlton's crude abuse.

The stinging shifted so subtly to an aching that she wasn't sure when it happened, the crop landing harder but still not close to breaking her skin. Instead, a sensual throbbing swelled within her until her skin felt so hot she was sure she would burst into flame.

Her inner walls clenched again and again on the inhuman cock buried deep inside her and the orgasm that ambushed her went on and on and on.

It was as close to euphoria as she had ever been.

Just when she began to fly—as if she could actually leave her body—David muttered something and flung the whip onto the nightstand before straddling her hips and commencing to slick her back hole, careful to open her so that he wouldn't hurt her, even though he shook with need.

And then she felt the familiar hard heat of him pressing against her pucker. He entered her with one, long, slow thrust, not stopping until his ballocks pressed against her spread buttocks.

She bit her lip at the painful stretch, his big cock nudging against the unforgiving stone phallus in her sheath.

"So full," she whined, which only made him flex his hips and drive deeper.

He pulsed his hips, grinding his shaft against the dildo. "Beg me to fuck you, Calliope."

Callie had no shame when it came to him. She did not hesitate. "Please…I need you…*hard*, David."

He began to move before the last word left her mouth, reaching beneath her body to work another orgasm from her exhausted clitoris as he pounded her with a flurry of thrusts.

Callie cried out just as he pinned her to the mattress, his cock spasming as he pumped her full of heat.

"I love you, David."

The slurred words came out on a moan of pleasure and Callie was not sure that he'd even heard them until he bit the shell of her ear hard enough to make it bleed, and said, "I know."

His answer jolted a laugh out of her and Callie twisted until she could see the clock. It was well after one.

"Merry Christmas, David. Thank you for my gifts."

"Merry Christmas, Calliope," he said. And then added in a rough voice, "*You* are my gift."

It was, Callie knew, the closest David would ever come to declaring his love.

And it was more than enough, filling her with joy and hope.

Epilogue

Four years later

David stared down into the cradle, endlessly fascinated by the sight that met his gaze. For the life of him, he could not understand why he enjoyed looking at a sleeping child so much. Calliope said it was his new hobby, and he had to admit his wife was right.

Until the birth of his son almost two years earlier there had only been one thing in his life that he would have considered a *hobby*. Well, two if he counted fucking. But chess had been his only pleasurable pastime for as long as he could remember.

Now he had another, even better, hobby.

People who saw Marcus Jonathan Remington always commented on how his nose was like David's or his eyes were like Calliope's and all sorts of other drivel.

But David could not see it. To him, Marcus looked only like Marcus.

David had watched his son's growth with rapt wonder and had enjoyed each and every stage of it: the way Marcus had drooled and put everything he could grab directly into his mouth; how he had, before he could walk, conceived of an ingenious way of half-crawling, half-pushing his body to propel himself toward something that interested him, right up to his current and far more mobile stage, where he ran and grabbed and babbled in his own mostly indecipherable language.

There was no way of knowing what might catch his son's attention, and David—who was not normally a wagering man—often placed private bets with himself as to what Marcus might become fixated on next.

The only thing about his son that did not give him pleasure was Marcus's complete lack of self-preservation instinct. It bothered David so much that he came up to check on him several times most nights, just to assure himself that Marcus was safe.

There was a nanny and a nurserymaid, of course, but they both slept like the dead. Marcus, on the other hand, was often awake. Like right now. And he was staring at David.

And smiling.

"Papa," he said.

Papa had been his first word, spoken when Marcus was fourteen months old. David had worried that was unusually late, but Calliope—far more comfortable with all matters concerning their child and child rearing—had convinced him that children were all different and not to fret.

She had been correct. Once he had spoken his first word, it was as if a dam had been breached and Marcus said new words every day, speaking more and more over the past six months.

David stared into his son's blue gaze and saw a trust so complete that it made him feel anxious and unworthy.

Right now, David was a god to his son. The slate was still blank, waiting to be filled. Never in his life had David experienced terror, but he suspected that was what he felt when he considered all the ways he could fill Marcus's slate with bad things.

After all, David's own slate was indelibly scarred and cracked—why would he be able to give anything better to his son?

Even David, as damaged as he was, must have once looked up at somebody's face and trusted completely.

And been betrayed.

Marcus's eyelids began to droop, but David could tell his son wanted to keep them open and fought against sleep.

"I thought I would find you up here," Calliope said softly as she came to stand beside him, her warm, soft body pressing alongside his. "Well, look who else is awake," she said in the silly voice that most people seemed to adopt with infants.

"I did not wake him; he was awake when I got here," David felt compelled to say.

Calliope looped her arm through his and molded her body to his. "He is a night owl like his papa."

"I think he is bored, that is why he's awake."

His wife laughed.

His wife. Even after four years David still felt a sense of wonderment at the words—at the fact that he had finally done something normal. Two normal things, if you count fathering a child.

There had been other, smaller, things, of course. A certain degree of change was inevitable when one lived so closely with another person.

David still kept a room of his own, and likely always would, but he spent several hours in Calliope's bed most nights.

He doubted that he would ever be able to sleep beside her, but he knew that she liked him to stay at least until she fell asleep.

David had learned to do many small things that she liked and appreciated, and he knew she did the same.

They socialized and people came to their house for dinner and invited them to their houses in return. His wife made friends easily and liked to entertain them and David accommodated her whenever he could.

Astonishingly, his association with Gideon Banks, which he had always considered an annoying inconvenience but necessary to doing business with the syndicate, had reintroduced David to Elliot Jackson, the army sniper who had taught him how to play chess all those years ago.

David had been having port and cigars at Banks's house when Jackson—now a valet—had come into the dining room to give his employer a message.

David had been shocked to discover that the most accurate, lethal sniper he had ever met was now a domestic servant. Jackson had recognized David, too, although a person could never have guessed that based on his almost complete lack of reaction.

For six months, David had pondered the coincidence of running into the very man who'd taught him chess all those years ago, one of the few people, before Calliope, he'd enjoyed spending time with.

Finally, he decided to invite Jackson out for a pint. If the other man didn't wish to reestablish contact with David, he could always decline to meet him.

But when David sent his message, he discovered that Jackson had retired, even though he was not much older than David.

Evidently Banks had invested his valet's money so wisely that Jackson would never need to work another day in his life if he didn't want to.

In any event, Jackson had been eager to meet with David. And, for the first time in his life, David had somebody to talk to about things they had both done for Queen and country.

The evening had been a success and they continued to see each other every few weeks—even after Jackson tired of retirement and found a new valeting position—their friendship slowly but surely growing.

Suddenly, David had a friend. Well, other than Calliope who had the added benefit of being a friend *and* lover *and* wife.

Was he happy? That was a question he couldn't answer. But he did feel contentment, which was something he'd never had before.

It was that contentment which had made him turn down his government when it had called him back. Despite some rather ugly threats about what would happen if he stood by his refusal, nothing had ever come of it. David had not been surprised when they'd stopped applying pressure. After all, he was but one killer—and an aging one, at that—for a government that was always training, newer, younger, and better versions of him.

Calliope squeezed his arm and whispered, "Let's sneak out now that he's gone to sleep."

David had been too busy in his own mind and had missed Marcus falling asleep, something he found enjoyable and soothing.

He would come back again tomorrow night. And the night after. As often as he liked, in fact.

Cheered by that thought, he followed Calliope from the room.

"Are you going back to your chambers?" she asked when they paused at the foot of the stairs, David's room to the left, Calliope's to the right.

David set a hand on the curve of her lower back and guided her to the right. "No, we are going back to yours."

He felt her body melt against his and knew he had made the right choice.

"*Mmmm.* It is not the usual schedule. What is the occasion?"

"You need to be fucked."

Calliope gave one of her infectious gurgles of laughter, which had been David's intention. Just because he did not laugh often or easily did not mean he didn't enjoy hearing his wife.

"I thought that—according to *you*—I always needed to be fucked," she taunted as David opened the door to her room. It was the master bedchamber, which she had taken after they had married. She'd offered it to him first, but David liked his far smaller room with only a few pieces of furniture.

Calliope loved luxurious silks and velvets, thick carpets, and supple leathers so her rooms were a sensual bower. While

David enjoyed visiting, he could never live surrounded by such excess.

"I have a reason for breaking the schedule," he said, answering her question once he'd shut the door to her room and turned the lights up as bright as they would go.

"Oh? And what is that?"

"I have kept a calendar of your menses. Tonight, you need to be bred."

Calliope stopped in the middle of the enormous room and stared up at him, her lips parted. "Do you mean it?" she asked him softly, and then chortled and answered her own question. "Of course you do. You never say anything you do not mean." She slid her arms around his neck and stood on her toes to kiss him before saying, "I am so glad you finally agree we should have more children. It will all be fine. *I* will be fine."

He grunted at that. Her pregnancy had been difficult and she had been sick for months, losing a dangerous amount of weight, until her small body was worryingly fragile. And the labor itself—well, David did not like to think about how long and painful it had been, and how frail she had seemed afterward.

When she had suggested having another child a year after Marcus's birth, David had told her he wanted to wait. Every few months, she had asked him again.

While David still did not feel comfortable putting Calliope through such an ordeal again—the thought of her dying in childbed had superseded the other nightmares that woke him in the night, becoming his most hated dream—their son needed a sibling and Calliope wanted another child.

And David had learned in their years of marriage that he could not deny her anything she desired.

Well, except when it came to bed sport and sexual matters. Of late, he had discovered that strictly controlling her orgasms was as pleasurable as administering a thorough whipping.

"Strip," he ordered.

She smiled up at him before taking a step back and slowly removing her dressing gown and night rail.

His cock, already hard and leaking, throbbed at the sight of her shaved cunt. Her midwife had stripped her of all pubic hair for the birth of their son and David had been fascinated by the sight of his wife's bare sex and so she had continued the practice to please him.

David very much liked being able to see all of her. And something about her vulnerability made Calliope squirm and blush, which of course he liked even more.

"How do you want me?" she asked once she was naked.

David jerked his chin toward her dressing table, which had a huge mirror. "I want to watch while I impregnate you."

Her breath caught audibly at his explicit declaration and she hurried to the bench, kneeling on it to watch him undress.

David removed his clothing slowly, taking his time and making a show for her. It still perplexed him that she enjoyed looking at his scarred, battered body.

When he had carefully folded his drawers and laid them on the neat and tidy pile, he strode toward her.

Calliope scrambled off the bench and David seated himself. She knew exactly what to do and turned her back to him and straddled his thighs, so that her torso was caged by his.

David eagerly watched their reflected images as she spread her legs wide and positioned his erect cock at her entrance. He could see everything in the brightly lighted room, her slick pink sex, the tight opening of her cunt, and the way she clenched in anticipation of taking him.

"Mount me," he said, mesmerized by the sight of her small body stretching to accommodate him.

His cock looked obscene as he slowly sheathed himself inside her and she gave a soft grunt once he was hilted, wriggling her hips a little to take even more.

David flexed his shaft and she hissed in a breath as he pulsed inside her, the sight of their joined bodies so arousing that he could have stared all night.

But his greedy little lover had other ideas, and so he reached a hand around her body and used a finger to circle her engorged nub, caressing the tender flesh until the shy little bundle of nerves swelled beyond its protective hood.

Only when Callie was breathing heavily, her cunt swollen and slick with need, did he roll his pelvis, pumping his cock into her with slow, deliberate thrusts while continuing to caress, tease, and take her apart with his finger.

David ignored her amusing but futile efforts to get him to fuck her harder, faster, and deeper. She employed every weapon at her arsenal, from squeezing him with her pussy to shifting positions, to attempting to post him without his permission, which made him wrap an arm around her waist to hold her immobile.

"*David,*" she whined.

He ignored her, refusing to be rushed.

Despite her frustration, or perhaps because of it, his shaft was soon so wet that it looked as if one or both of them had already climaxed.

"Please, David," she said, the words almost a sob.

Well, since she asked so nicely…

David tightened his arm around her waist and pulled her down onto his cock while he pumped into her hard and fast. It took barely a dozen strokes before every muscle in her body stiffened. He pressed the pad of his thumb against her engorged bud and she moaned, her inner walls convulsing around his shaft.

"Yes," he murmured. "Come for me."

Her already snug sheath contracted at his order, squeezing him even more tightly.

David had learned early in his marriage that his wife liked to hear him talk in bed. She thrived on the vulgar commands and crude observations he made even though it often embarrassed her.

It had been difficult at first to give words to his basest thoughts while they had sex, but now, after four years, he enjoyed finding new ways to make her blush and squirm.

"Such a pretty pink slit," he praised, moving his finger away from her too-sensitive nub and caressing where they were joined. When her contractions ebbed to nothing, he met her heavy-lidded gaze in the looking glass and said, "Fuck yourself—slowly."

David reveled in the sight of her thigh muscles flexing as she lifted higher, exposing his ruddy glistening shaft before making him disappear again.

He made her post him until his heavy balls drew up to his body and then he reached around her again and with a few light flicks drove her toward her second climax.

When her knees turned to jelly, he slid his hands beneath her thighs and slowly stood, keeping her back snug to his front and his cock sheathed inside her as he carried her to the bed and set her down on her hands and knees.

David spread her cheeks and stared at her arse as he slowly pumped his hips. Even now, after four years and thousands of fucks, her tight little pucker clenched each and every time he exposed it.

A slight smile pulled at his lips. He would have liked nothing more than to pull out and take her arse, but that would not serve his purpose tonight.

So instead, he toyed with the tempting hole, teasing and probing and slicking it with their mingled juices while his other hand returned to her sex.

David ignored her soft whimpers of discomfort when he stroked the too-sensitive bundle of nerves. He had been far less strict with her since Marcus's birth, allowing her mewling and pleas to dissuade him from harder, crueler uses—like forcing multiple climaxes—but those days were over. Starting tonight.

He made her come twice more, edging himself dangerously close to climax both times.

"David *please*," she begged, when he began working her toward another orgasm.

He gave her buttock a stinging slap. "Because of that you will give me one more." David slammed into her hard enough to drive her to her elbows and then growled approvingly at the sudden shift in angle, which allowed him to sink even deeper.

Despite his best intentions, he knew he would not last too much longer. And so this time when she built toward her climax, David did not hold back; he fucked her harder and deeper. And when he felt her shatter, he gave in to his own need and sheathed himself to the hilt, joining her in release.

His body shook with the force of his orgasm and he filled her with jet after jet of hot spunk, her pussy milking him until his ballocks were empty and aching and he had nothing else to give.

Tonight, for the first time since Marcus's birth, Calliope would not cleanse herself afterward and they might very well make a child. While David had not forgotten about the dangers of childbirth, he knew this decision would make her very happy.

David sighed as a warm post-coital lassitude washed over him, sated not just in body, but also in mind. Ejaculating inside his wife was the second most pleasurable part of their physical couplings.

He rolled them both onto their sides, keeping them joined, and waited impatiently for the very *best* part of the night.

Calliope yawned and burrowed against him, her back pressed snugly to his front. When she sighed heavily, David worried that she might have drifted off and, for the first time since they had married, forgotten to—

"I love you, David," she said the words he'd come to look forward to in a voice that was more than half asleep.

Relief, and several other emotions he wisely left unscrutinized, surged through his body at her declaration.

David kissed the back of his wife's neck. "I know," he said, completing the ritual.

The End

Dearest Reader:

I hope you loved reading about David and Callie as much as I enjoyed writing about them!

This story just came out of the blue when I was in the middle of writing **AURELIA**. I was already behind schedule for that book and was NOT supposed to write anything else, but…

I told myself I would just jot down a few pages so I could pick up the book and write it later.

But once I started writing, I could not stop. I wrote both books at once, working on **AURELIA** during the day and my naughty villain story at night. I thought it would be a novella, but I should have known better.

I have wanted to write a sociopathic character for a while so I really had a fun time with David. He is one of those characters who wrote himself, I just sat back and watched my fingers tell his story.

Actually, Callie came out with very few changes, as well. Women of that time period who found themselves without a family or marketable skill had very few choices, and almost none of those choices were good. I think we modern readers can't really understand just how difficult it was to get a job if a person (man or woman) didn't have the right credentials.

Callie has been dealt a shitty hand, but she plays it without whining or living in a constant state of regret. Instead, her strength really shines through in the way she is always looking to the future. She's been down, but she has not given up on herself or her dream of a better life.

Her Villain

This series is my escape from reality, so I write whatever couple shows up next demanding to have their story told. There are many more books to come and lots of **VICTORIAN DECADENCE** percolating in my brain. Who will be next? I don't know. While I was editing **HER VILLAIN,** I started to write Mr. Nance's story (the wealthy banker from the dinner party) and I was having a lovely time before reality intruded and I realized I was—yet again—getting distracted and working on the wrong book.

Not only was there Nance wanting to be heard, but Elliot Jackson has been knocking around inside my head for years. I know exactly what he is going to do and it is shocking!

But that is a story for later…

Actually, if I am going to be completely honest, I worked on four books while editing **HER VILLAIN**. Fortunately, one of them was **IO: The Shrew**.

For a while I worried that I would not be able to deliver on **IO**, but I had one of the best weeks of writing in my entire life and—

But wait… that is a story I should save for the end of **IO: The Shrew**, right?

Yeah, that's right. Sorry to be getting ahead of myself.

Anyhow, I've just been having a blast writing, which is really nice after my bout with Covid earlier in the year.

I am on my second edit of **IO** right now and next I will move on to **A VERY BELLAMY CHRISTMAS**.

Once I started working on **AVBC**—which was supposed to be a holiday novella—I realized that it was definitely going to be a full novel. I seem to have trouble writing novellas, lol. I don't know why I even bother trying to write them.

The last two books in **THE ACADEMY OF LOVE** series—**A STORY OF LOVE** and **THE ETIQUETTE OF LOVE**—will be out in December 2024 and January 2025. Yes, they will be released only a month apart! Yay!

KATHRYN, book 6 in **THE BELLAMY SISTERS** will be out in May 2025.

I've just signed a contract for a seventh novel in the series, which will feature Dauntry Bellamy. Not sure about the pub date for that one, yet.

Oh, by the way, all the slang I used in this book—like *horny*, for example—really was in use during the late 1800s. I thought several of the words that popped into my brain sounded modern, but I looked them all up and discovered that a lot of the amusing terminology for sex and sexual organs have been around for a while. Evidently, people have always liked coming up with new and inventive ways to describe bodies and coitus.

As always, I want to shout out to those of you who wrote me lovely emails and made me want to keep on writing! Thank you, you really do help me out when I'm low on reserves.

I love getting emails and you can write to me at: minerva@minervaspencer.com.

If you enjoyed **HER VILLAIN** I'd love a review. I don't pay for reviews, nor do I give away hundreds of ARCs, so I rely on organic reviews from real readers who've spent their hard-earned money on my books. You can click HERE if you'd like to leave one.

Okay, that's all I've got for now.

Look for me in less than a month with **IO: The Shrew**.

Oh, and I'm putting my house on the market on June 1st, so keep your fingers crossed that it sells in the first month so I have more time to write books!

Take care and happy reading!

Xo

SM/Minerva

Who are Minerva Spencer & S.M. LaViolette?

Minerva is S.M.'s pen name (that's short for Shantal Marie) S.M. has been a criminal prosecutor, college history teacher, B&B operator, dock worker, ice cream manufacturer, reader for the blind, motel maid, and bounty hunter. Okay, so the part about being a bounty hunter is a lie. S.M. does, however, know how to hypnotize a Dungeness crab, sew her own Regency Era clothing, knit a frog hat, juggle, rebuild a 1959 American Rambler, and gain control of Asia (and hold on to it) in the game of RISK.

Read more about S.M. at: www.MinervaSpencer.com

Follow 'us' on Bookbub:

Minerva's BookBub

S.M.'s Bookbub

On Goodreads

Minerva's OUTCASTS SERIES

DANGEROUS

BARBAROUS

Her Villain

<u>SCANDALOUS</u>

THE REBELS OF THE *TON:*

<u>NOTORIOUS</u>

<u>OUTRAGEOUS</u>

<u>INFAMOUS</u>

<u>AUDACIOUS (NOVELLA)</u>

THE SEDUCERS:

<u>MELISSA AND THE VICAR</u>

<u>JOSS AND THE COUNTESS</u>

<u>HUGO AND THE MAIDEN</u>

VICTORIAN DECADENCE: (HISTORICAL EROTIC ROMANCE—SUPER STEAMY!)

<u>HIS HARLOT</u>

<u>HIS VALET</u>

<u>HIS COUNTESS</u>

<u>HER BEAST</u>

<u>THEIR MASTER</u>

<u>HER VILLAIN</u>

S.M. LaViolette

THE ACADEMY OF LOVE:

THE MUSIC OF LOVE

A FIGURE OF LOVE

A PORTRAIT OF LOVE

THE LANGUAGE OF LOVE

DANCING WITH LOVE

A STORY OF LOVE*

THE ETIQUETTE OF LOVE*

THE MASQUERADERS:

THE FOOTMAN

THE POSTILION

THE BASTARD

THE BELLAMY SISTERS

PHOEBE

HYACINTH

SELINA

A VERY BELLAMY CHRISTMAS*

Her Villain

THE HALE SAGA SERIES: AMERICANS IN LONDON

BALTHAZAR: THE SPARE

IO: THE SHREW*

THE WICKED WOMEN OF WHITECHAPEL:

THE BOXING BARONESS

THE DUELING DUCHESS

THE CUTTHROAT COUNTESS

THE BACHELORS OF BOND STREET:

A SECOND CHANCE FOR LOVE (A NOVELLA)

ANTHOLOGIES:

THE ARRANGEMENT